2.75

A

P.G. WODEHOUSE

CLASSIC

FISH
PREFERRED

SIMON AND SCHUSTER · NEW YORK

SBN 671-20308-8

MANUFACTURED IN THE UNITED STATES OF AMERICA

FISH
PREFERRED

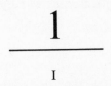

I

BLANDINGS CASTLE slept in the sunshine.

Dancing little ripples of heat mist played across its smooth lawns and stone-flagged terraces. The air was full of the lulling drone of insects. It was that gracious hour of a summer afternoon, midway between luncheon and tea, when nature seems to unbutton its waistcoat and put its feet up.

In the shade of a laurel bush outside the back premises of this stately home of England, Beach, butler to Clarence, ninth Earl of Emsworth, its proprietor, sat sipping the contents of a long glass and reading a weekly paper devoted to the doings of Society and the Stage. His attention had just been arrested by a photograph in an oval border on one of the inner pages; and for perhaps a minute he scrutinized this in a slow, thorough, pop-eyed way, absorbing its every detail. Then, with a fruity chuckle, he took a penknife from his pocket, cut out the photograph, and placed it in the recesses of his costume.

At this moment the laurel bush, which had hitherto not spoken, said, "Psst!"

The butler started violently. A spasm ran through his ample frame.

"Beach!" said the bush.

Something was now peering out of it. This might have been a wood nymph, but the butler rather thought not, and he was right. It was a tall young man with light hair. He recognized his employer's secretary, Mr. Hugo Carmody, and rose with pained reproach. His heart was still jumping, and he had bitten his tongue.

"Startle you, Beach?"

"Extremely, sir."

"I'm sorry. Excellent for the liver, though. Beach, do you want to earn a quid?"

The butler's austerity softened. The hard look died out of his eyes.

"Yes, sir."

"Can you get hold of Miss Millicent alone?"

"Certainly, sir."

"Then give her this note, and don't let anyone see you do it. Especially—and this is where I want you to follow me very closely, Beach—Lady Constance Keeble."

"I will attend to the matter immediately, sir."

He smiled a paternal smile. Hugo smiled back. A perfect understanding prevailed between these two. Beach understood that he ought not to be giving his employer's niece surreptitious notes; and Hugo understood that he ought not to be urging a good man to place such a weight upon his conscience.

"Perhaps you are not aware, sir," said the butler, having trousered the wages of sin, "that her ladyship went up to London on the three-thirty train?"

Hugo uttered an exclamation of chagrin.

"You mean that all this Red Indian stuff—creeping from bush to bush and not letting a single twig snap beneath my feet—has simply been a waste of time?" He emerged, dusting his clothes. "I wish I'd known that before," he said. "I've severely injured a good suit, and it's a very moot question whether I haven't got some kind of a beetle down my back. However, nobody ever took a toss through being careful."

"Very true, sir."

Relieved by the information that the X-ray eye of the aunt of the girl he loved was operating elsewhere, Mr. Carmody became conversational.

"Nice day, Beach."

"Yes, sir."

"You know, Beach, life's rummy. I mean to say, you can never tell what the future holds in store. Here I am at Blandings Castle, loving it. Sing of joy, sing of bliss, home was never like this.

8

And yet, when the project of my coming here was first placed on the agenda I don't mind telling you the heart was rather bowed down with weight of woe."

"Indeed, sir?"

"Yes. Noticeably bowed down. If you knew the circumstances you would understand why."

Beach did know the circumstances. There were few facts concerning the dwellers in Blandings Castle of which he remained in ignorance for long. He was aware that young Mr. Carmody had been until a few weeks back co-proprietor with Mr. Ronald Fish, Lord Emsworth's nephew, of a night club called the Hot Spot, situated just off Bond Street in the heart of London's pleasure-seeking area; that, despite this favoured position, it had proved a financial failure; that Mr. Ronald had gone off with his mother, Lady Julia Fish, to recuperate at Biarritz; and that Hugo, on the insistence of Ronnie that unless some niche was found for his boyhood friend he would not stir a step toward Biarritz or any other blighted place, had come to Blandings as Lord Emsworth's private secretary.

"No doubt you were reluctant to leave London, sir?"

"Exactly. But now, Beach, believe me or believe me not, as far as I am concerned, anyone who likes can have London. Mark you, I'm not saying that just one brief night in the Piccadilly neighbourhood would come amiss. But to dwell in give me Blandings Castle. What a spot, Beach!"

"Yes, sir."

"A Garden of Eden, shall I call it?"

"Certainly, sir, if you wish."

"And now that old Ronnie's coming here, joy, as you might say, will be unconfined."

"Is Mr. Ronald expected, sir?"

"Coming either to-morrow or the day after. I had a letter from him this morning. Which reminds me. He sends his regards to you and asks me to tell you to put your shirt on Baby Bones for the Medbury Selling Plate."

The butler pursed his lips dubiously.

"A long shot, sir. Not generally fancied."

"Rank outsider. Leave it alone is my verdict."

"And yet Mr. Ronald is usually very reliable. It is many years now since he first began to advise me in these matters, and I have done remarkably well by following him. Even as a lad at Eton he was always singularly fortunate in his information."

"Well, suit yourself," said Hugo indifferently. "What was that thing you were cutting out of the paper just now?"

"A photograph of Mr. Galahad, sir. I keep an album in which I paste items of interest relating to the Family."

"What that album needs is an eyewitness's description of Lady Constance Keeble falling out of a window and breaking her neck."

A nice sense of the proprieties prevented Beach from indorsing this view verbally, but he sighed a little wistfully. He had frequently felt much the same about the chatelaine of Blandings.

"If you would care to see the clipping, sir? There is a reference to Mr. Galahad's literary work."

Most of the photographs in the weekly paper over which Beach had been relaxing were of peeresses trying to look like chorus girls and chorus girls trying to look like peeresses; but this one showed the perky features of a dapper little gentleman in the late fifties. Beneath it, in large letters, was the single word—

GALLY

Under this ran a caption in smaller print:

The Hon. Galahad Threepwood, brother of the Earl of Emsworth. A little bird tells us that "Gally" is at Blandings Castle, Shropshire, the ancestral seat of the family, busily engaged in writing his Reminiscences. As every member of the Old Brigade will testify, they ought to be as warm as the weather, if not warmer.

Hugo scanned the exhibit thoughtfully and handed it back, to be placed in the archives.

"Yes," he observed, "I should say that about summed it up. That old bird must have been pretty hot stuff, I imagine, back in the days of Edward the Confessor."

"Mr. Galahad was somewhat wild as a young man," agreed the butler with a sort of feudal pride in his voice. It was the opinion of the Servants Hall that the Hon. Galahad shed lustre on Blandings Castle.

"Has it ever occurred to you, Beach, that that book of his is going to make no small stir when it comes out?"

"Frequently, sir."

"Well, I'm saving up for my copy. By the way, I knew there was something I wanted to ask you. Can you give me any information on the subject of a bloke named Baxter?"

"Mr. Baxter, sir? He used to be private secretary to his lordship."

"Yes, so I gathered. Lady Constance was speaking to me about him this morning. She happened upon me as I was taking the air in riding kit and didn't seem overpleased. 'You appear to enjoy a great deal of leisure, Mr. Carmody,' she said. 'Mr. Baxter,' she continued, giving me the meaning eye, 'never seemed to find time to go riding when he was Lord Emsworth's secretary. Mr. Baxter was always so hard at work. But then, Mr. Baxter,' she added, the old lamp becoming more meaning than ever, 'loved his work. Mr. Baxter took a real interest in his duties. Dear me! What a very conscientious man Mr. Baxter was, to be sure!' Or words to that effect. I may be wrong, but I classed it as a dirty dig. And what I want to know is, if Baxter was such a world beater why did they ever let him go?"

The butler gazed about him cautiously.

"I fancy, sir, there was some trouble."

"Pinched the spoons, eh? Always the way with these zealous workers."

"I never succeeded in learning the full details, sir, but there was something about some flower pots."

"He pinched the flower pots?"

"Threw them at his lordship, I was given to understand."

Hugo looked injured. He was a high-spirited young man who chafed at injustice.

"Well, I'm dashed if I see, then," he said, "where this Baxter can claim to rank so jolly high above me as a secretary. I may

11

be leisurely, I may forget to answer letters, I may occasionally on warm afternoons go in to some extent for the folding of the hands in sleep, but at least I don't throw flower pots at people. Not so much as a pen wiper have I ever bunged at Lord Emsworth. Well, I must be getting about my duties. That ride this morning and a slight slumber after lunch have set the schedule back a bit. You won't forget that note, will you?"

"No, sir."

Hugo reflected.

"On second thoughts," he said, "perhaps you'd better hand it back to me. Safer not to have too much written matter circulating about the place. Just tell Miss Millicent that she will find me in the rose garden at six sharp."

"In the rose garden . . ."

"At six sharp."

"Very good, sir. I will see that she receives the information."

II

For two hours after this absolutely nothing happened in the grounds of Blandings Castle. At the end of that period there sounded through the mellow, drowsy stillness a drowsy, mellow chiming. It was the clock over the stables striking five. Simultaneously a small but noteworthy procession filed out of the house and made its way across the sun-bathed lawn to where the big cedar cast a grateful shade. It was headed by James, a footman, bearing a laden tray. Following him came Thomas, another footman, with a gate-leg table. The rear was brought up by Beach, who carried nothing but merely lent a tone.

The instinct that warns all good Englishmen when tea is ready immediately began to perform its silent duty. Even as Thomas set gate-leg table to earth there appeared, as if answering a cue, an elderly gentleman in stained tweeds and a hat he should have been ashamed of: Clarence, ninth Earl of Emsworth, in person. He was a long, lean, stringy man of about sixty, slightly speckled at the moment with mud, for he had spent most of the afternoon pottering round pigsties. He surveyed the preparations for the meal with vague amiability through rimless pince-nez.

"Tea?"

"Yes, your lordship."

"Oh?" said Lord Emsworth. "Ah? Tea, eh? Tea? Yes. Tea. Quite so. To be sure, tea. Capital."

One gathered from his remarks that he realized that the tea hour had arrived and was glad of it. He proceeded to impart his discovery to his niece, Millicent, who, lured by that same silent call, had just appeared at his side.

"Tea, Millicent."

"Yes."

"Er—tea," said Lord Emsworth, driving home his point.

Millicent sat down and busied herself with the pot. She was a tall, fair girl with soft blue eyes and a face like the Soul's Awakening. Her whole appearance radiated wholesome innocence. Not even an expert could have told that she had just received a whispered message from a bribed butler and was proposing at six sharp to go and meet a quite ineligible young man among the rose bushes.

"Been down seeing the Empress, Uncle Clarence?"

"Eh? Oh, yes. Yes, my dear. I have been with her all the afternoon."

Lord Emsworth's mild eyes beamed. They always did when that noble animal, Empress of Blandings, was mentioned. The ninth Earl was a man of few and simple ambitions. He had never desired to mould the destinies of the State, to frame its laws and make speeches in the House of Lords that would bring all the peers and bishops to their feet, whooping and waving their hats. All he yearned to do, by way of insuring admittance to England's Hall of Fame, was to tend his prize sow, Empress of Blandings, so sedulously that for the second time in two consecutive years she would win the silver medal in the Fat Pigs class at the Shropshire Agricultural Show. And every day, it seemed to him, the glittering prize was coming more and more within his grasp.

Earlier in the summer there had been one breathless, sickening moment of suspense, and disaster had seemed to loom. This was when his neighbour, Sir Gregory Parsloe-Parsloe of Matchingham Hall, had basely lured away his pig man, the superbly gifted George Cyril Wellbeloved, by the promise of higher wages. For a while Lord Emsworth had feared lest the Empress, mourning for her old friend and valet, might refuse food and fall from her high standard of obesity. But his apprehensions had proved groundless. The Empress had taken to Pirbright, George Cyril's successor, from the first, and was tucking away her meals with all the old abandon. The Right triumphs in this world far more often than we realize.

"What do you do to her?" asked Millicent curiously. "Read her bedtime stories?"

Lord Emsworth pursed his lips. He had a reverent mind and disliked jesting on serious subjects.

"Whatever I do, my dear, it seems to effect its purpose. She is in wonderful shape."

"I didn't know she had a shape. She hadn't when I last saw her."

This time Lord Emsworth smiled indulgently. Gibes at the Empress's rotundity had no sting for him. He did not desire for her that schoolgirl slimness which is so fashionable nowadays.

"She has never fed more heartily," he said. "It is a treat to watch her."

"I'm so glad. Mr. Carmody," said Millicent, stooping to tickle a spaniel which had wandered up to take pot luck, "told me he had never seen a finer animal in his life."

"I like that young man," said Lord Emsworth emphatically. "He is sound on pigs. He has his head screwed on the right way."

"Yes, he's an improvement on Baxter, isn't he?"

"Baxter!" His lordship choked over his cup.

"You didn't like Baxter much, did you, Uncle Clarence?"

"Hadn't a peaceful moment while he was in the place. Dreadful feller! Always fussing. Always wanting me to do things. Always coming round corners with his infernal spectacles gleaming and making me sign papers when I wanted to be out in the garden. Besides, he was off his head. Thank goodness I've seen the last of Baxter."

14

"But have you?"

"What do you mean?"

"If you ask me," said Millicent, "Aunt Constance hasn't given up the idea of getting him back."

Lord Emsworth started with such violence that his pince-nez fell off. She had touched on his favourite nightmare. Sometimes he would wake trembling in the night, fancying that his late secretary had returned to the castle. And though on these occasions he always dropped off to sleep again with a happy smile of relief he had never ceased to be haunted by the fear that his sister Constance, in her infernal managing way, was scheming to restore the fellow to office.

"Good God! Has she said anything to you?"

"No. But I have a feeling. I know she doesn't like Mr. Carmody."

Lord Emsworth exploded.

"Perfect nonsense! Utter, absolute, dashed nonsense. What on earth does she find to object to in young Carmody? Most capable, intelligent boy. Leaves me alone. Doesn't fuss me. I wish to heaven she would—"

He broke off, and stared blankly at a handsome woman of middle age who had come out of the house and was crossing the lawn.

"Why, here she is!" said Millicent, equally and just as disagreeably surprised. "I thought you had gone up to London, Aunt Constance."

Lady Constance Keeble had arrived at the table. Declining with a distrait shake of the head her niece's offer of the seat of honour by the teapot, she sank into a chair. She was a woman of still remarkable beauty, with features cast in a commanding mould, and fine eyes. These eyes were at the moment dull and brooding.

"I missed my train," she explained. "However, I can do all I have to do in London to-morrow. I shall go up by the eleven-fifteen. In a way, it will be more convenient, for Ronald will be able to motor me back. I will look in at Norfolk Street and pick him up there before he starts."

"What made you miss your train?"

"Yes," said Lord Emsworth complainingly. "You started in good time."

The brooding look in his sister's eyes deepened.

"I met Sir Gregory Parsloe." Lord Emsworth stiffened at the name. "He kept me talking. He is extremely worried." Lord Emsworth looked pleased. "He tells me he used to know Galahad very well a number of years ago, and he is very much alarmed about this book of his."

"And I bet he isn't the only one," murmured Millicent.

She was right. Once a man of the Hon. Galahad Threepwood's antecedents starts taking pen in hand and being reminded of amusing incidents that happened to my dear old friend So-and-So you never know where he will stop; and all over England, among the more elderly of the nobility and gentry, something like a panic had been raging ever since the news of his literary activities had got about. From Sir Gregory Parsloe-Parsloe of Matchingham Hall to gray-headed pillars of society in distant Cumberland and Kent, whole droves of respectable men who in their younger days had been rash enough to chum with the Hon. Galahad were recalling past follies committed in his company and speculating agitatedly as to how good the old pest's memory was.

For Galahad in his day had been a notable lad about town. A *beau sabreur* of Romano's. A Pink 'Un. A Pelican. A crony of Hughie Drummond and Fatty Coleman; a brother in arms of the Shifter, the Pitcher, Peter Blobbs, and the rest of an interesting but not straitlaced circle. Bookmakers had called him by his pet name; barmaids had simpered beneath his gallant chaff. He had heard the chimes at midnight. And when he looked in at the old Gardenia commissionaires had fought for the privilege of throwing him out. A man, in a word, who should never have been taught to write and who, if unhappily gifted with that ability, should have been restrained by Act of Parliament from writing reminiscences.

So thought Lady Constance, his sister. So thought Sir Gregory Parsloe-Parsloe, his neighbour. And so thought the pillars of Society in distant Cumberland and Kent. Widely as they differed on many points, they were unanimous on this.

16

"He wanted me to try to find out if Galahad was putting anything about him into it."

"Better ask him now," said Millicent. "He's just come out of the house and seems to be heading in this direction."

Lady Constance turned sharply; and, following her niece's pointing finger, winced. The mere sight of her deplorable brother was generally enough to make her wince. When he began to talk and she had to listen the wince became a shudder. His conversations had the effect of making her feel as if she had suddenly swallowed something acid.

"It always makes me laugh," said Millicent, "when I think what a frightfully bad shot Uncle Gally's godfathers and godmothers made when they christened him."

She regarded her approaching relative with that tolerant—indeed, admiring—affection which the young of her sex, even when they have Madonna-like faces, are only too prone to lavish on such of their seniors as have had interesting pasts.

"Doesn't he look marvellous?" she said. "It really is an extraordinary thing that anyone who has had as good a time as he has can be so amazingly healthy. Everywhere you look you see men leading model lives and pegging out in their prime, while good old Uncle Gally, who apparently never went to bed till he was fifty, is still breezing along as fit and rosy as ever."

"All our family have had excellent constitutions," said Lord Emsworth.

"And I'll bet Uncle Gally needed every ounce of his," said Millicent.

The Author, ambling briskly across the lawn, had now joined the little group at the tea table. As his photograph had indicated, he was a short, trim, dapper little man of the type one associates automatically in one's mind with checked suits, tight trousers, white bowler hats, pink carnations, and race glasses bumping against the left hip. Though bareheaded at the moment and in his shirt sleeves and displaying on the tip of his nose the ink spot of the literary life, he still seemed out of place away from a paddock or an American bar. His bright eyes, puckered at the

17

corners, peered before him as though watching horses rounding into the straight. His neatly shod foot had about it a suggestion of pawing in search of a brass rail. A jaunty little gentleman, and, as Millicent had said, quite astonishingly fit and rosy. A thoroughly misspent life had left the Hon. Galahad Threepwood, contrary to the most elementary justice, in what appeared to be perfect, even exuberantly perfect, physical condition. How a man who ought to have had the liver of the century could look and behave as he did was a constant mystery to his associates. His eyes were not dimmed, nor his natural force abated; and when, skipping blithely across the turf, he tripped over the spaniel, so graceful was the agility with which he recovered his balance that he did not spill a drop of the whisky-and-soda in his hand. He continued to bear the glass aloft like some brave banner beneath which he had often fought and won. Instead of the blot on a proud family he might have been a teetotal acrobat.

Having disentangled himself from the spaniel and soothed the animal's wounded feelings by permitting it to sniff the whisky-and-soda, the Hon. Galahad produced a black-rimmed monocle and, screwing it into his eye, surveyed the table with a frown of distaste.

"Tea?"

Millicent reached for a cup.

"Cream and sugar, Uncle Gally?"

He stopped her with a gesture of shocked loathing.

"You know I never drink tea. Too much respect for my inside. Don't tell me you are ruining your inside with that poison."

"Sorry, Uncle Gally. I like it."

"You be careful," urged the Hon. Galahad, who was fond of his niece and did not like to see her falling into bad habits. "You be very careful how you fool about with that stuff. Did I ever tell you about poor Buffy Struggles back in 'ninety-three? Some misguided person lured poor old Buffy into one of those temperance lectures illustrated with coloured slides, and he called on me next day ashen, poor old chap—ashen. 'Gally,' he said. 'What would you say the procedure was when a fellow wants to buy tea? How would a fellow set about it?' 'Tea?' I said. 'What do you want tea

18

for?' 'To drink,' said Buffy. 'Pull yourself together, dear boy,' I said.'You're talking wildly. You can't drink tea. Have a brandy-and-soda.' 'No more alcohol for me,' said Buffy. 'Look what it does to the common earthworm.' 'But you're not a common earthworm.' I said, putting my finger on the flaw in his argument right away. 'I dashed soon shall be if I go on drinking alcohol,' said Buffy. Well, I begged him with tears in my eyes not to do anything rash, but I couldn't move him. He ordered in ten pounds of the muck and was dead inside the year."

"Good heavens! Really?"

The Hon. Galahad nodded impressively.

"Dead as a doornail. Got run over by a hansom cab, poor dear old chap, as he was crossing Piccadilly. You'll find the story in my book."

"How's the book coming along?"

"Magnificently, my dear. Splendidly. I had no notion writing was so easy. The stuff just pours out. Clarence, I wanted to ask you about a date. What year was it there was that terrible row between young Gregory Parsloe and Lord Burper, when Parsloe stole the old chap's false teeth and pawned them at a shop in the Edgeware Road? '96? I should have said later than that—'97 or '98. Perhaps you're right, though. I'll pencil in '96 tentatively."

Lady Constance uttered a sharp cry. The sunlight had now gone quite definitely out of her life. She felt, as she so often felt in her brother Galahad's society, as if foxes were gnawing her vitals. Not even the thought that she could now give Sir Gregory Parsloe-Parsloe the inside information for which he had asked was able to comfort her.

"Galahad! You are not proposing to print libellous stories like that about our nearest neighbour?"

"Certainly I am." The Hon Galahad snorted militantly. "And as for libel, let him bring an action if he wants to. I'll fight him to the House of Lords. It's the best documented story in my book. Well, if you insist it was '96, Clarence—I'll tell you what," said the Hon. Galahad, inspired, "I'll say 'toward the end of the nineties.' After all, the exact date isn't so important. It's the facts that matter." And, leaping lightly over the spaniel, he flitted away across the lawn.

Lady Constance sat rigid in her chair. Her fine eyes were now protruding slightly, and her face was drawn. This, and not the Mona Lisa's, you would have said, looking at her, was the head on which all the sorrows of the world had fallen.

"Clarence!"

"My dear?"

"What are you going to do about this?"

"Do?"

"Can't you see that something must be done? Do you realize that if this awful book of Galahad's is published it will alienate half our friends? They will think we are to blame. They will say we ought to have stopped him somehow. Imagine Sir Gregory's feelings when he reads that appalling story!"

Lord Emsworth's amiable face darkened.

"I am not worrying about Parsloe's feelings. Besides, he did steal Burper's false teeth. I remember him showing them to me. He had them packed up in cotton wool in a small cigar box."

The gesture known as wringing the hands is one that is seldom seen in real life, but Lady Constance Keeble at this point did something with hers which might by a liberal interpretation have been described as wringing.

"Oh, If Mr. Baxter were only here!" she moaned.

Lord Emsworth started with such violence that his pince-nez fell off and he dropped a slice of seed cake.

"What on earth do you want that awful feller here for?"

"He would find a way out of this dreadful business. He was always so efficient."

"Baxter's off his head."

Lady Constance uttered a sharp exclamation.

"Clarence, you really can be the most irritating person in the world. You get an idea and you cling to it in spite of whatever anybody says. Mr. Baxter was the most wonderfully capable man I ever met."

"Yes, capable of anything," retorted Lord Emsworth with spirit. "Threw flower pots at me in the middle of the night. I woke

20

up in the small hours and found flower pots streaming in at my bedroom window and looked out and there was this feller Baxter standing on the terrace in lemon-coloured pajamas, hurling the dashed things as if he thought he was a machine gun or something. I suppose he's in an asylum by this time."

Lady Constance had turned a bright scarlet. Even in their nursery days she had never felt quite so hostile toward the head of the family as now

"You know perfectly well that there was a quite simple explanation. My diamond necklace had been stolen, and Mr. Baxter thought the thief had hidden it in one of the flower pots. He went to look for it and got locked out and tried to attract attention by—"

"Well, I prefer to think the man was crazy, and that's the line that Galahad takes in his book."

"His—! Galahad is not putting that story in his book?"

"Of course he's putting it in his book. Do you think he's going to waste excellent material like that? And, as I say, the line Galahad takes—and he's a clear-thinking, level-headed man—is that Baxter was a raving, roaring lunatic. Well, I'm going to have another look at the Empress."

He pottered off pigward.

III

For some moments after he had gone there was silence at the tea table. Millicent lay back in her chair, Lady Constance sat stiffly upright in hers. A little breeze that brought with it a scent of wallflowers began whispering the first tidings that the cool of evening was on its way.

"Why are you so anxious to get Mr. Baxter back, Aunt Constance?" asked Millicent.

Lady Constance's rigidity had relaxed. She was looking her calm, masterful self again. She had the air of a woman who has just solved a difficult problem.

"I think his presence here essential," she said.

"Uncle Clarence doesn't seem to agree with you."

21

"Your Uncle Clarence has always been completely blind to his best interests. He ought never to have dismissed the only secretary he has ever had who was capable of looking after his affairs."

"Isn't Mr. Carmody any good?"

"No. He is not. And I shall never feel easy in my mind until Mr. Baxter is back in his old place."

"What's wrong with Mr. Carmody?"

"He is grossly inefficient. And," said Lady Constance, unmasking her batteries, "I consider that he spends far too much of his time mooning around you, my dear. He appears to imagine that he is at Blandings Castle simply to dance attendance on you."

The charge struck Millicent as unjust. She thought of pointing out that she and Hugo only met occasionally and then on the sly, but it occurred to her that the plea might be injudicious. She bent over the spaniel. A keen observer might have noted a defensiveness in her manner. She looked like a girl preparing to cope with an aunt.

"Do you find him an entertaining companion?"

Millicent yawned.

"Mr. Carmody? No, not particularly."

"A dull young man, I should have thought."

"Deadly."

"Vapid."

"Vap to a degree."

"And yet you went riding with him last Tuesday."

"Anything's better than riding alone."

"You play tennis with him, too."

"Well, tennis is a game I defy you to play by yourself."

Lady Constance's lips tightened.

"I wish Ronald had never persuaded your uncle to employ him. Clarence should have seen by the mere look of him that he was impossible." She paused. "It will be nice having Ronald here," she said.

"Yes."

"You must try to see something of him. If," said Lady Constance, in the manner which her intimates found rather less pleasant than some of her other manners, "Mr. Carmody can spare you for a moment from time to time."

She eyed her niece narrowly. But Millicent was a match for any number of narrow glances, and had been from her sixteenth birthday. She was also a girl who believed that the best form of defence is attack.

"Do you think I'm in love with Mr. Carmody, Aunt Constance?"

Lady Constance was not a woman who relished the direct methods of the younger generation. She coloured.

"Such a thought never entered my head."

"That's fine. I was afraid it had."

"A sensible girl like you would naturally see the utter impossibility of marriage with a man in his position. He has no money and very little prospects. And, of course, your uncle holds your own money in trust for you and would never dream of releasing it if you wished to make an unsuitable marriage."

"So it does seem lucky I'm not in love with him, doesn't it?"

"Extremely fortunate."

Lady Constance paused for a moment, then introduced a topic on which she had frequently touched before. Millicent had seen it coming by the look in her eyes.

"Why you won't marry Ronald I can't think. It would be so suitable in every way. You have been fond of one another since you were children."

"Oh, I like old Ronnie a lot."

"It has been a great disappointment to your Aunt Julia."

"She must cheer up. She'll get him off all right if she sticks at it."

Lady Constance bridled.

"It is not a question of . . . If you will forgive my saying so, my dear, I think you have allowed yourself to fall into a way of taking Ronald far too much for granted. I am afraid you have the impression that he will always be there, ready and waiting for you when you at last decide to make up your mind. I don't think you realize what a very attractive young man he is."

"The longer I wait, the more fascinating it will give him time to become."

At a moment less tense Lady Constance would have taken time off to rebuke this flippancy; but she felt it would be unwise to depart from her main theme.

"He is just the sort of young man that girls are drawn to. In fact, I have been meaning to tell you. I had a letter from your Aunt Julia saying that during her stay at Biarritz they met a most charming American girl, a Miss Schoonmaker, whose father, it seems, used to be a friend of your Uncle Galahad. She appeared to be quite taken with Ronald, and he with her. He travelled back to Paris with her and left her there."

"How fickle men are!" sighed Millicent.

"She had some shopping to do," said Lady Constance sharply. "By this time she is probably in London. Julia invited her to stay at Blandings, and she accepted. She may be here any day now. And I do think, my dear," proceeded Lady Constance earnestly, "that before she arrives you ought to consider very carefully what your feelings toward Ronald really are."

"You mean, if I don't watch my step this Miss Doopenhacker may steal my Ronnie away from me?"

It was not quite how Lady Constance would have put it herself, but it conveyed her meaning.

"Exactly."

Millicent laughed. It was plain that her flesh declined to creep at the prospect.

"Good luck to her," she said. "She can count on a fish slice from me, and I'll be a bridesmaid, too, if wanted. Can't you understand, Aunt Constance, that I haven't the slightest desire to marry Ronnie? We're great pals and all that, but he's not my style. Too short, for one thing."

"Short?"

"I'm inches taller than he is. When we went up the aisle I should look like someone taking her little brother for a walk."

Lady Constance would undoubtedly have commented on this remark, but before she could do so the procession reappeared, playing an unexpected return date. Footman James bore a dish

24

of fruit; Footman Thomas a salver with a cream jug on it. Beach, as before, confined himself to a straight ornamental rôle.

"Oo!" said Millicent welcomingly. And the spaniel, who liked anything involving cream, gave a silent nod of approval.

"Well," said Lady Constance, as the procession withdrew, giving up the lost cause, "if you won't marry Ronald, I suppose you won't."

"That's about it," agreed Millicent, pouring cream.

"At any rate, I am relieved to hear that there is no nonsense going on between you and this Mr. Carmody. That I could not have endured."

"He's only moderately popular with you, isn't he?"

"I dislike him extremely."

"I wonder why. I should have thought he was fairly all right, as young men go. Uncle Clarence likes him. So does Uncle Gally."

Lady Constance had a high, arched nose, admirably adapted for sniffing. She used it now to the limits of its power.

"Mr. Carmody," she said, "is just the sort of young man your Uncle Galahad would like. No doubt he reminds him of the horrible men he used to go about London with in his young days."

"Mr. Carmody isn't a bit like that."

"Indeed?" Lady Constance sniffed again. "Well, I dislike mentioning it to you, Millicent, for I am old-fashioned enough to think that young girls should be shielded from a knowledge of the world, but I happen to know that Mr. Carmody is not at all a nice young man. I have it on the most excellent authority that he is entangled with some impossible chorus girl."

It is not easy to sit suddenly bolt upright in a deep garden chair, but Millicent managed the feat.

"What!"

"Lady Allardyce told me so."

"And how does she know?"

"Her son Vernon told her. A girl of the name of Brown. Vernon Allardyce says that he used to see her repeatedly, lunching and dining and dancing with Mr. Carmody."

There was a long silence.

"Nice boy, Vernon," said Millicent.

25

"He tells his mother everything."

"That's what I meant. I think it's so sweet of him." Millicent rose. "Well, I'm going to take a short stroll."

She wandered off toward the rose garden.

IV

A young man who has arranged to meet the girl he loves in the rose garden at six sharp naturally goes there at five-twenty-five, so as not to be late. Hugo Carmody had done this, with the result that by three minutes to six he was feeling as if he had been marooned among roses since the beginning of the summer.

If anybody had told Hugo Carmody six months before that halfway through the following July he would be lurking in trysting places like this, his whole being alert for the coming of a girl, he would have scoffed at the idea. He would have laughed lightly. Not that he had not been fond of girls. He had always liked girls. But they had been, as it were, the mere playthings, so to speak, of a financial giant's idle hour. Six months ago he had been the keen, iron-souled man of business, all his energies and thoughts devoted to the management of the Hot Spot.

But now he stood shuffling his feet and starting hopefully at every sound, while the leaden moments passed sluggishly on their way. Then his vigil was enlivened by a wasp, which stung him on the back of the hand. He was leaping to and fro, licking his wounds, when he perceived the girl of his dreams coming down the path.

"Ah!" cried Hugo.

He ceased to leap and, rushing forward, would have clasped her in a fond embrace. Many people advocate the old-fashioned blue-bag for wasp stings, but Hugo preferred this treatment.

To his astonishment she drew back. And she was not a girl who usually drew back on these occasions.

"What's the matter?" he asked, pained. It seemed to him that a spanner had been bunged into a holy moment.

"Nothing."

26

Hugo was concerned. He did not like the way she was looking at him. Her soft blue eyes appeared to have been turned into stone.

"I say," he said, "I've just been stung by a beastly great wasp."

"Good!" said Millicent. The way she was talking seemed to him worse than the way she was looking.

Hugo's concern increased.

"I say, what's up?"

The granite eye took on an added hardness.

"You want to know what's up?"

"Yes—what's up?"

"I'll tell you what's up."

"Well, what's up?" asked Hugo.

He waited for enlightenment, but she had fallen into a chilling silence.

"You know," said Hugo, breaking it, "I'm getting pretty fed up with all this secrecy and general snakiness. Seeing you for an occasional odd five minutes a day and having to put on false whiskers and hide in bushes to manage that. I know the Keeble looks on me as a sort of cross between a leper and a nosegay of deadly nightshade, but I'm strong with the old boy. I talk pig to him. You might almost say I play on him as on a stringed instrument. So what's wrong with going to him and telling him in a frank and manly way that we love each other and are going to get married?"

The marble of Millicent's face was disturbed by one of those quick, sharp, short, bitter smiles that do nobody any good.

"Why should we lie to Uncle Clarence?"

"Eh?"

"I say why should we tell him something that isn't true?"

"I don't get your drift."

"I will continue snowing," said Millicent coldly. "I am not quite sure if I am ever going to speak to you again in this world or the next. Much will depend on how good you are as an explainer. I have it on the most excellent authority that you are entangled with a chorus girl. How about it?"

27

Hugo reeled. But then St. Anthony himself would have reeled if a charge like that had suddenly been hurled at him. The best of men require time to overhaul their consciences on such occasions. A moment, and he was himself again.

"It's a lie!"

"Name of Brown."

"Not a word of truth in it. I haven't set eyes on Sue Brown since I first met you."

"No. You've been down here all the time."

"And when I *was* setting eyes on her—why, dash it, my attitude from start to finish was one of blameless, innocent, one hundred per cent brotherliness. A wholesome friendship. Brotherly. Nothing more. I liked dancing and she liked dancing and our steps fitted. So occasionally we would go out together and tread the measure. That's all there was to it. Pure brotherliness. Nothing more. I looked on myself as a sort of brother."

"Brother, eh?"

"Absolutely a brother. Don't," urged Hugo earnestly, "go running away, my dear old thing, with any sort of silly notion that Sue Brown was something in the nature of a vamp. She's one of the nicest girls you would ever want to meet."

"Nice, is she?"

"A sweet girl. A girl in a million. A real good sort. A sound egg."

"Pretty, I suppose?"

The native good sense of the Carmodys asserted itself at the eleventh hour.

"Not pretty," said Hugo decidedly. "Not pretty, no. Not at all pretty. Far from pretty. Totally lacking in sex appeal, poor girl. But nice. A good sort. No nonsense about her. Sisterly."

Millicent pondered.

"H'm," she said.

Nature paused, listening. Birds checked their song, insects their droning. It was as if it had got about that this young man's fate hung in the balance and the returns would be in shortly.

"Well, all right," she said at length. "I suppose I'll have to believe you."

"'At's the way to talk!"

"But just you bear this in mind, my lad. Any funny business from now on . . ."

"As if . . . !"

"One more attack of that brotherly urge . . ."

"As though . . . ,"

"All right, then."

Hugo inhaled vigorously. He felt like a man who has just dodged a wounded tigress.

"*Banzai!*" he said. "Sweethearts still!"

V

Blandings Castle dozed in the twilight. Its various inmates were variously occupied. Clarence, ninth Earl of Emsworth, after many a longing, lingering look behind, had dragged himslef away from the Empress's boudoir and was reading his well-thumbed copy of *British Pigs.* The Hon. Galahad, having fixed up the Parsloe-Burper passage, was skimming through his day's output with an artist's complacent feeling that this was the stuff to give 'em. Butler Beach was pasting the Hon. Galahad's photograph into his album. Millicent, in her bedroom, was looking a little thoughtfully into her mirror. Hugo, in the billiard room, was practising pensive cannons and thinking loving thoughts of his lady, coupled with an occasional reflection that a short, swift binge in London would be a great wheeze if he could wangle it.

And in her boudoir on the second floor Lady Constance Keeble had taken pen in hand and was poising it over a sheet of notepaper.

"Dear Mr. Baxter," she wrote.

2

THE BRILLIANT sunshine which so enhanced the attractions of life
at Blandings Castle had brought less pleasure to those of England's workers whose duties compelled them to remain in London. In his offices on top of the Regal Theatre in Shaftesbury
Avenue, Mr. Mortimer Mason, the stout senior partner in the
firm of Mason and Saxby, Theatrical Enterprises, Ltd., was of
opinion that what the country really needed was one of those
wedge-shaped depressions off the Coast of Iceland. Apart from
making him feel like a gaffed salmon, Flaming July was ruining
business. Only last night, to cut down expenses, he had had to
dismiss some of the chorus from the show downstairs, and he hated
dismissing the chorus girls. He was a kind-hearted man and, having
been in the profession himself in his time, knew what it meant to
get one's notice in the middle of the summer.

There was a tap on the door. The human watchdog who guarded
the outer offices entered.

"Well?" said Mortimer Mason wearily.

"Can you see Miss Brown, sir?"

"Which Miss Brown? Sue?"

"Yes, sir."

"Of course." In spite of the heat Mr. Mason brightened. "Is
she outside?"

"Yes, sir."

"Then pour her in."

Mortimer Mason had always felt a fatherly fondness for this
girl, Sue Brown. He liked her for her own sake, for her unvary-
ing cheerfulness and the honest way she worked. But what en-
deared her more particularly to him was the fact that she was

Dolly Henderson's daughter. London was full of elderly gentlemen who became pleasantly maudlin when they thought of Dolly
Henderson and the dear old days when the heart was young and
they had had waists. He heaved himself from his chair; then fell
back again, filled with a sense of intolerable injury.

"My God!" he cried. "Don't look so cool."

The rebuke was not undeserved. On an afternoon when the
asphalt is bubbling in the roadways and theatrical managers
melting where they sit, no girl has a right to resemble a dewy rose
plucked from some old-world garden. And that, Mr. Mason considered, was just what this girl was deliberately resembling. She
was a tiny thing, mostly large eyes and a wide happy smile. She had
a dancer's figure, and in every movement of her there was Youth.

"Sorry, Pa." She laughed, and Mr. Mason moaned faintly. Her
laugh had reminded him, for his was a nature not without its poetical side, of ice tinkling in a jug of beer. "Try not looking at
me."

"Well, Sue, what's on your mind? Come to tell me you're going to be married?"

"Not at the moment, I'm afraid."

"Hasn't that young man of yours got back from Biarritz yet?"

"He arrived this morning. I had a note during the matinée. I
suppose he's outside now, waiting for me. Want to have a look
at him?"

"Does it mean walking downstairs?" asked Mr. Mason guardedly.

"No. He'll be in his car. You can see him from the window."

Mr. Mason was equal to getting to the window. He peered down
at the rakish sports model two-seater in the little street below.
Its occupant was lying on his spine, smoking a cigarette in a long
holder and looking austerely at certain children of the neighbourhood whom he seemed to suspect of being about to scratch his
paint.

"They're making fiancés very small this season," said Mr. Mason, concluding his inspection.

"He is small, isn't he? He's sensitive about it, poor darling. Still,
I'm small, too, so that's all right."

31

"Fond of him?"

"Frightfully."

"Who is he, anyway? Yes, I know his name's Fish, and it doesn't mean a thing to me. Any money?"

"I believe he's got quite a lot, only his uncle keeps it all. Lord Emsworth. He's Ronnie's trustee or something."

"Emsworth? I knew his brother years ago." Mr. Mason chuckled reminiscently. "Old Gally! What a lad! I've got a scheme I'd like to interest old Gally in. I wonder where he is now."

"The *Prattler* this week said he was down at Blandings Castle. That's Lord Emsworth's place in Shropshire. Ronnie's going down there this evening."

"Deserting you so soon?" Mortimer Mason shook his head. "I don't like this."

Sue laughed.

"Well, I don't," said Mr. Mason. "You be careful. These lads will all bear watching."

"Don't worry, Pa. He means to do right by our Nell."

"Well, don't say I didn't warn you. So old Gally is at Blandings, is he? I must remember that. I'd like to get in touch with him. And now, what was it you wanted to see me about?"

Sue became grave.

"I've come to ask you a favour."

"Go ahead. You know me."

"It's about those girls you're getting rid of."

Mr. Mason's genial face took on a managerial look.

"Got to get rid of them."

"I know. But one of them's Sally Field."

"Meaning what?"

"Well, Sally's awfully hard up, Pa. And what I came to ask," said Sue breathlessly, "was, will you keep her on and let me go instead?"

Utter amazement caused Mortimer Mason momentarily to forget the heat. He sat up, gaping.

"Do what?"

"Let me go instead."

"Let you go instead?"

"Yes."

"You're crazy."

"No, I'm not. Come on, Pa. Be a dear."

"Is she a great friend of yours?"

"Not particularly. I'm sorry for her."

"I won't do it."

"You must. She's down to her last bean."

"But I need you in the show."

"What nonsense! As if I made the slightest difference."

"You do. You've got—I don't know—" Mr. Mason twiddled his fingers—"something. Your mother used to have it. Did you know I was the second juvenile in the first company she was ever in?"

"Yes, you told me. And haven't you got on! There's enough of you now to make two second juveniles. Well, you will do it, won't you?"

Mr. Mason reflected.

"I suppose I'll have to, if you insist," he said at length. "If I don't you'll just hand your notice in anyway. I know you. You're a sportsman, Sue. Your mother was just the same. But are you sure you'll manage all right? I shan't be casting the new show till the end of August, but I may be able to fix you up somewhere if I look round."

"I don't see how you could look any rounder if you tried, you poor darling. Do you realize, Pa, that if you got up early every morning and did half an hour's Swedish exercises—"

"If you don't want to be murdered, stop!"

"It would do you all the good in the world, you know. Well, it's awfully sweet of you to bother about me, Pa, but you musn't. You've got enough to worry you already. I shall be all right. Good-bye. You've been an angel about Sally. It'll save her life."

"If she's that cross-eyed girl at the end of the second row who's always out of step I'm not sure I want to save her life."

"Well, you're going to do it, anyway. Good-bye."

"Don't run away."

"I must. Ronnie's waiting. He's going to take me to tea somewhere. Up the river, I hope. Think how nice it will be there, under the trees, with the water rippling—"

"The only thing that stops me hitting you with this ruler," said Mr. Mason, "is the thought that I shall soon be getting out of this Turkish bath myself. I've a show opening at the Blackpool next week. Think how nice and cool it will be on the sands there, with the waves splashing—"

"—And you with your little spade and bucket, paddling! Oh, Pa, do send me a photograph. Well, I can't stand here all day chatting over your vacation plans. My poor darling Ronnie must be getting slowly fried."

II

The process of getting slowly fried, especially when you are chafing for a sight of the girl you love after six weeks of exile from her society, is never an agreeable one. After enduring it for some time the pink-faced young man with the long cigarette holder had left his seat in the car and had gone for shade and comparative coolness to the shelter of the stage entrance, where he now stood reading the notices on the call board. He read them moodily. The thought that, after having been away from Sue for all these weeks, he was now compelled to leave her again and go to Blandings Castle was weighing on Ronald Overbury Fish's mind sorely.

Mac, the guardian of the stage door, leaned out of his hutch. The matinée over, he had begun to experience that solemn joy which comes to camels approaching an oasis and stage-door men who will soon be at liberty to pop round the corner. He endeavoured to communicate his happiness to Ronnie.

"Won't be long now, Mr. Fish."

"Eh?"

"Won't be long now, sir."

"Ah," said Ronnie.

Mac was concerned at his companion's gloom. He liked smiling faces about him. Reflecting, he fancied he could diagnose its cause.

"I was sorry to hear about that, Mr. Fish."

"Eh?"

"I say I was sorry to hear about that, sir."

"About what?"

"About the Hot Spot, sir. That night club of yours. Busting up that way. Going West so prompt."

Ronnie Fish winced. He presumed the man meant well, but there are certain subjects one does not want mentioned. When you have contrived with infinite pains to wheedle a portion of your capital out of a reluctant trustee and have gone and started a night club with it and have seen that night club flash into the receiver's hands like some frail eggshell engulfed by a whirlpool, silence is best.

"Ah," he said briefly, to indicate this.

Mac had many admiriable qualities, but not tact. He was the sort of man who would have tried to cheer Napoleon up by talking about the winter sports at Moscow.

"When I heard that you and Mr. Carmody was starting one of those places I said to the fireman, 'I give it two months,' I said. And it was six weeks, wasn't it, sir?"

"Seven."

"Six or seven. Immaterial which. Point is I'm usually pretty right. I said to the fireman, 'It takes brains to run a night club,' I said. 'Brains and a certain what-shall-I-say.' Won me half a crown, that did."

He searched in his mind for other topics to interest and amuse.

"Seen Mr. Carmody lately, sir?"

"No. I've been in Biarritz. He's down in Shropshire. He's got a job as secretary to an uncle of mine."

"And I shouldn't wonder," said Mac cordially, "if he wouldn't make a mess of *that*."

He began to feel that the conversation was now going with a swing.

"Used to see a lot of Mr. Carmody round here at one time."

The advance guard of the company appeared, in the shape of a flock of musicians. They passed out of the stage door, first a couple of thirsty-looking flutes, then a group of violins, finally an oboe by himself with a scowl on his face. Oboes are always savage in captivity.

"Yes, sir. Came here a lot, Mr. Carmody did. Asking for Miss Brown. Great friends those two was."

"Oh?" said Ronnie thickly.

"Used to make me laugh to see them together."

Ronnie appeared to swallow something large and jagged.

"Why?"

"Well, him so tall and her so small. But there," said Mac philosophically, "they say it's opposites that get on best. I know I weigh seventeen stone and my missus looks like a ninepenny rabbit, and yet we're as happy as can be."

Ronnie's interest in the poundage of the stage-door keeper's domestic circle was slight.

"Ah," he said.

Mac, having got onto the subject of Sue Brown, stayed there.

"You see the flowers arrived all right, sir."

"Eh?"

"The flowers you sent Miss Brown, sir," said Mac, indicating with a stubby thumb a bouquet on the shelf behind him. "I haven't given her them yet. Thought she'd rather have them after the performance."

It was a handsome bouquet, but Ronnie Fish stared at it with a sort of dumb horror. His pink face had grown pinker, and his eyes were glassy.

"Give me those flowers, Mac," he said in a strangled voice.

"Right, sir. Here you are, sir. Now you look just like a bridegroom, sir," said the stage-door keeper, chuckling the sort of chuckle that goes with seventeen stone and a fat head.

This thought had struck Ronnie, also. It was driven home a moment later by the displeasing behaviour of two of the chorus girls who came flitting past. Both looked at him in a way painful to a sensitive young man, and one of them giggled. Ronnie turned to the door.

"When Miss Brown comes, tell her I'm waiting outside in my car."

"Right, sir. You'll be in again, I suppose, sir?"

"No." The sombre expression deepened on Ronnie's face. "I've got to go down to Shropshire this evening."

"Be away long?"

"Yes. Quite a time."

"Sorry to hear that, sir. Well, good-bye, sir. Thank you, sir."

Ronnie, clutching the bouquet, walked with leaden steps to the two-seater. There was a card attached to the flowers. He read it, frowned darkly and threw the bouquet into the car.

Girls were passing now in shoals. They meant nothing to Ronnie Fish. He eyed them sourly, marvelling why the papers talked about "beauty choruses." And then, at last, there appeared one at the sight of whom his heart, parting from its moorings, began to behave like a jumping bean. It had reached his mouth when she ran up with both hands extended.

"Ronnie, you precious angel lambkin!"

"Sue!"

To a young man in love, however great the burden of sorrows beneath which he may be groaning, the spectacle of the only girl in the world, smiling up at him, seldom fails to bring a temporary balm. For the moment Ronnie's gloom ceased to be. He forgot that he had recently lost several hundred pounds in a disastrous commercial venture. He forgot that he was going off that evening to live in exile. He even forgot that this girl had just been sent a handsome bouquet by a ghastly bargee named P. Frobisher Pilbeam, belonging to the Junior Constitutional Club. These thoughts would return, but for the time being the one that occupied his mind to the exclusion of all others was the thought that after six long weeks of separation he was once more looking upon Sue Brown.

"I'm so sorry I kept you waiting, precious. I had to see Mr. Mason."

Ronnie started.

"What about?"

A student of the motion pictures, he knew what theatrical managers were.

"Just business."

"Did he ask you to lunch or anything?"

"No. He just fired me."

"Fired you!"

37

"Yes, I've lost my job," said Sue happily.

Ronnie quivered.

"I'll go and break his neck."

"No, you won't. It isn't his fault. It's the weather. They have to cut down expenses when there's a heat wave. It's all the fault of people like you for going abroad instead of staying in London and coming to the theatre." She saw the flowers and uttered a delightful squeal. "For me?"

A moment before, Ronnie had been all chivalrous concern—a knight prepared to battle to the death for his lady love. He now froze.

"Apparently," he said coldly.

"How do you mean, apparently?"

"I mean they are."

"You pet!"

"Leap in."

Ronnie's gloom was now dense and foglike once more. He gestured fiercely at the clustering children and trod on the self-starter. The car moved smoothly round the corner into Shaftesbury Avenue.

Opposite the Monico there was a traffic block, and he unloaded his soul.

"In re those blooms."

"They're lovely."

"Yes, but I didn't send them."

"You brought them. Much nicer."

"What I'm driving at," said Ronnie heavily, "is that they aren't from me at all. They're from a blighter named P. Frobisher Pilbeam."

Sue's smile had faded. She knew her Ronald's jealousy so well. It was the one thing about him which she could have wished changed.

"Oh?" she said dismally.

The crust of calm detachment from all human emotion, built up by years of Eton and Cambridge, cracked abruptly, and there peeped forth a primitive Ronald Overbury Fish.

"Who is this Pilbeam?" he demanded. "Pretty much the Boy Friend, I take it, what?"

"I've never even met him!"

"But he sends you flowers."

"I know he does," wailed Sue, mourning for a golden afternoon now probably spoiled beyond repair. "He keeps sending me his beastly flowers and writing me his beastly letters."

Ronnie gritted his teeth.

"And I tell you I've never set eyes on him in my life."

"You don't know who he is?"

"One of the girls told me that he used to edit that paper, *Society Spice*. I don't know what he does now."

"When he isn't sending you flowers, you mean?"

"I can't help him sending me flowers."

"I don't suppose you want to."

Sue's eyes flickered. Realizing, however, that her Ronnie in certain moods resembled a child of six, she made a pathetic attempt to lighten the atmosphere.

"It's not my fault if I get persecuted with loathsome addresses, is it? I suppose, when you go to the movies, you blame Lillian Gish for being pursued by the heavy."

Ronnie was not to be diverted.

"Sometimes I ask myself," he said darkly, "if you really care a hang for me."

"Oh, Ronnie!"

"Yes, I do—repeatedly. I look at you and I look at myself and that's what I ask myself. What on earth is there about me to make a girl like you fond of a fellow? I'm a failure. Can't even run a night club. No brains. No looks."

"You've got a lovely complexion."

"Too pink. Much too pink. And I'm so damned short."

"You're not a bit too short."

"I am. My Uncle Gally once told me I looked like the protoplasm of a minor jockey."

"He ought to have been ashamed of himself."

"Why the dickens," said Ronnie, laying bare his secret dreams,

"I couldn't have been born a decent height, like Hugo . . ." He paused. His hand shook on the steering wheel. "That reminds me. That fellow Mac at the stage door was saying that you and Hugo used to be as thick as thieves. Always together, he said."

Sue sighed. Things were being difficult to-day.

"That was before I met you," she explained patiently, "I used to like dancing with him. He's a beautiful dancer. You surely don't suppose for a minute that I could ever be in love with Hugo."

"I don't see why not."

"Hugo!" Sue laughed. There was something about Hugo Carmody that always made her want to laugh.

"Well, I don't see why not. He's better looking than I am. Taller. Not so pink. Plays the saxophone."

"Will you stop being silly about Hugo!"

"Well, I fear that bird. He's my best pal, and I know his work. He's practically handsome. And lissom, to boot." A hideous thought smote Ronnie like a blow. "Did he ever—" he choked— "did he ever hold your hand?"

"Which hand?"

"Either hand."

"How can you suggest such a thing!" cried Sue, shocked.

"Well, will you swear there's nothing between him and you?"

"Of course there isn't."

"And nothing between this fellow Pilbeam and you?"

"Of course not."

"Ah!" said Ronnie. "Then I can go ahead as planned."

His was a mercurial temperament, and it had lifted him in an instant from the depths to the heights. The cloud had passed from his face, the look of Byronic despair from his eyes. He beamed.

"Do you know why I'm going down to Blandings to-night?" he asked.

"No. I only wish you weren't."

"Well, I'll tell you. I've got to get round my uncle."

"Do what?"

"Make myself solid with my Uncle Clarence. If you've ever had anything to do with trustees you'll know that the one thing they bar like poison is parting with money. And I've simply got

40

to have another chunk of my capital, and a good big one, too. Without money, how on earth can I marry you? Let me get hold of funds, and we'll dash off to the registrar's the moment you say the word. So now you understand why I've got to get to Blandings at the earliest possible moment and stay there till further notice."

"Yes. I see. And you're a darling. Tell me about Blandings, Ronnie."

"How do you mean?"

"Well, what sort of a place is it? I want to imagine you there while you're away."

Ronnie pondered. He was not at his best as a word painter.

"Oh, you know the kind of thing. Parks and gardens and terraces and immemorial elms and all that. All the usual stuff."

"Any girls there?"

"My Cousin Millicent. She's my Uncle Lancelot's daughter. He's dead. The family want Millicent and me to get married."

"To each other, you mean? What a perfectly horrible idea."

"Oh, it's all right. We're both against the scheme."

"Well, that's some comfort. What other girls will there be at Blandings?"

"Only one that I know of. My mother met a female called Schoonmaker at Biarritz. American. Pots of money, I believe. One of those beastly tall girls. Looked like something left over from Dana Gibson. I couldn't stand her myself, but mother was all for her, and I didn't at all like the way she seemed to be trying to shove her off onto me. You know— 'Why don't you ring up Myra Schoonmaker, Ronnie? I'm sure she would like to go to the Casino to-night. And then you could dance afterward.' Sinister, it seemed to me."

"And she's going to Blandings? H'm!"

"There's nothing to 'h'm' about."

"I'm not so sure. Oh, well, I suppose your family are quite right. I suppose you ought really to marry some nice girl in your own set."

Ronnie uttered a wordless cry and in his emotion allowed the mudguard of the two-seater to glide so closely past an Austin

41

Seven that Sue gave a frightened squeak and the Austin Seven went on its way thinking black thoughts.

"Do be careful, Ronnie, you old chump!"

"Well, what do you want to go saying things like that for? I get enough of that from the family without having *you* start."

"Poor old Ronnie! I'm sorry. Still, you must admit that they'd be quite within their rights, objecting to me. I'm not so hot, you know. Only a chorus girl. Just one of the ensemble!"

Ronnie said something between his teeth that sounded like "Juk!" What he meant was, be her station never so humble, a pure, sweet girl is a fitting mate for the highest in the land.

"And my mother was a music-hall singer."

"A what?"

"A music-hall singer. What they used to call a 'serio.' You know —pink tights and rather risky songs."

This time Ronnie did not say, "Juk!" He merely swallowed painfully. The information had come as a shock to him. Somehow or other he had never thought of Sue as having encumbrances in the shape of relatives; and he could not hide from himself the fact that a pink-tighted serio might stir the Family up quite a little. He pictured something with peroxide hair who would call his Uncle Clarence "dearie."

"English, do you mean? On the halls here in London?"

"Yes. Her stage name was Dolly Henderson."

"Never heard of her."

"I dare say not. But she was the rage of London twenty years ago."

"I always thought you were American," said Ronnie, aggrieved. "I distinctly recollect Hugo, when he introduced us, telling me that you had just come over from New York."

"So I had. Father took me to America soon after Mother died."

"Oh, your mother is—er—no longer with us?"

"No."

"Too bad," said Ronnie, brightening.

"My father's name was Cotterleigh. He was in the Irish Guards."

"What!"

Ronnie's ecstatic cry seriously inconvenienced a traffic police-man in the exercise of his duties.

"But this is fine! This is the goods! It doesn't matter to me, of course, one way or the other. I'd love you just the same if your father had sold jellied eels. But think what an enormous differ-ence this will make to my blasted family!"

"I doubt it."

"But it will. We must get him over at once and spring him on them. Or is he in London?"

Sue's brown eyes clouded.

"He's dead."

"Eh? Oh! Sorry!" said Ronnie.

He was dashed for a moment.

"Well, at least let me tell the family about him," he urged, re-covering. "Let me dangle him before their eyes a bit,"

"If you like. But they'll still object to me because I'm in the chorus."

Ronnie scowled. He thought of his mother, he thought of his Aunt Constance, and reason told him that her words were true.

"Dash all this rot people talk about chorus girls!" he said. "They seem to think that just because a girl works in the chorus she must be a sort of animated champagne vat—"

"Ugh!"

"—spending her life dancing on supper tables with tight stock-brokers—"

"And not a bad way of passing an evening," said Sue medita-tively. "I must try it some time."

"—with the result that when it's question of her marrying any-body, fellow's people look down their noses and kick like mules. It's happened in our family before. My Uncle Gally was in love with some girl on the stage back in the dark ages, and they formed a wedge and bust the thing up and shipped him off to South Africa or somewhere to forget her. And look at him! Drew three sober breaths in the year nineteen hundred and then decided that was enough. I expect I shall be the same. If I don't take to drink, cooped up at Blandings a hundred miles away from you,

I shall be vastly surprised. It's all a lot of silly nonsense. I haven't any patience with it. I've a jolly good mind to go to Uncle Clarence to-night and simply tell him that I'm in love with you and intend to marry you and that if the family don't like it they can lump it."

"I wouldn't."

Ronnie simmered down.

"Perhaps you're right."

"I'm sure I am. If he hears about me he certainly won't give you your money; whereas, if he doesn't, he may. What sort of a man is he?"

"Uncle Clarence? Oh, a mild, dreamy old boy. Mad about gardening and all that. At the moment I hear he's wrapped up in his pig."

"That sounds cosy."

"I'd feel a lot easier in my mind, I can tell you, going down there to tackle him, if I were a pig. I'd expect a much warmer welcome."

"You were rather a pig just now, weren't you?"

Ronnie quivered. Remorse gnawed the throbbing heart beneath his beautifully cut waistcoat.

"I'm sorry. I'm frightfully sorry. The fact is, I'm so crazy about you I get jealous of everybody you meet. Do you know, Sue, if you ever let me down, I'd—I don't know what I'd do. Er—Sue!"

"Hullo?"

"Swear something."

"What?"

"Swear that while I'm at Blandings you won't go out with a soul. Not even to dance."

"Not even to dance?"

"No."

"All right."

"Especially this man Pilbeam."

"I thought you were going to say Hugo."

"I'm not worrying about Hugo. He's safe at Blandings."

"Hugo at Blandings?"

"Yes. He's secretarying for my Uncle Clarence. I made my mother get him the job when the Hot Spot conked."

"So you'll have him *and* Millicent *and* Miss Schoonmaker there to keep you company! How nice for you."

"Millicent!"

"It's all very well to say 'Millicent!' like that. If you ask me, I think she's a menace. She sounds coy and droopy. I can see her taking you for walks by moonlight under those immemorial elms and looking up at you with big dreamy eyes."

"Looking down at me, you mean. She's about a foot taller than I am. And, anyway, if you imagine there's a girl on earth who could extract so much as a kindly glance from me when I've got you to think about you're very much mistaken. I give you my honest word . . ."

He became lyrical. Sue, leaning back, listened contentedly. The cloud had been a threatening cloud, blackening the skies for a while, but it had passed. The afternoon was being golden, after all.

III

"By the way," said Ronnie, the flood of eloquence subsiding. "A thought occurs. Have you any notion where we're headed for?"

"Heaven!"

"I mean at the moment."

"I supposed you were taking me to tea somewhere."

"But where? We've got right out of the tea zone. What with one thing and another I've just been driving at random—to and fro, as it were—and we seem to have worked round to somewhere in the Swiss Cottage neighbourhood. We'd better switch back and set a course for the Carlton or some place. How do you feel about the Carlton?"

"All right."

"Or the Ritz?"

"Whichever you like."

"Or—gosh!"

"What's the matter?"

"Sue! I've got an idea."

"Beginner's luck."

"Why not go to Norfolk Street?"

"To your home?"

"Yes. There's nobody there, and our butler is a staunch bird—he'll get us tea and say nothing."

"I'd like to meet a staunch butler."

"Then shall we?"

"I'd love it. You can show me all your little treasures and belongings and the photographs of you as a small boy."

Ronnie shook his head. It irked him to discourage her pretty enthusiasm, but a man cannot afford to take risks.

"Not those. No love could stand up against the sight of me in a sailor suit at the age of ten. I don't mind," he said, making a concession, "letting you see the one of me and Hugo, taken just before the Public Schools Rackets Competition, my last year at school. We were the Eton pair."

"Did you win?"

"No. At a critical moment in the semifinal that ass Hugo foozled a shot a one-armed cripple ought to have taken with his eyes shut. It dished us."

"Awful!" said Sue. "Well, if I ever had any impulse to love Hugo that's killed it." She looked about her. "I don't know this aristocratic neighbourhood at all. How far is it to Norfolk Street?"

"Next turning."

"You're sure there's nobody in the house? None of the dear old family?"

"Not a soul."

He was right. Lady Constance Keeble was not actually in the house. At the moment when he spoke she had just closed the front door behind her. After waiting half an hour in the hope of her nephew's return she had left a note for him on the hall table and was going to Claridge's to get a cup of tea.

It was not until he had drawn up immediately opposite the house that Ronnie perceived what stood upon the steps. Having done so, he blanched visibly.

"Oh, my sainted aunt!" he said.

And seldom can the familiar phrase have been used with more appropriateness.

The sainted aunt was inspecting the two-seater and its contents

46

with a frozen stare. Her eyebrows were two marks of interrogation. As she had told Millicent, she was old-fashioned, and when she saw her flesh and blood snuggled up to girls of attractive appearance in two-seaters she suspected the worst.

"Good-afternoon, Ronald."

"Er—hullo, Aunt Constance."

"Will you introduce me?"

There is no doubt that peril sharpens the intellect. His masters at school and his tutors at the university, having had to do with Ronald Overbury Fish almost entirely at times when his soul was at rest, had classed him among the less keen-witted of their charges. Had they seen him now in this crisis they would have pointed at him with pride. And, being the sportsmen and gentlemen that they were, they would have hastened to acknowledge that they had grossly underestimated his ingenuity and initiative.

For, after turning a rather pretty geranium tint and running a finger round the inside of his collar for an instant, as if he found it too tight, Ronnie Fish spoke the only two words in the language which could have averted disaster.

"Miss Schoonmaker," he said huskily.

Sue, at his side, gave a little gasp. These were unsuspected depths.

"Miss Schoonmaker!"

Lady Constance's resemblance to Apollyon straddling right across the way had vanished abruptly. Remorse came upon her that she should have wronged her blameless nephew with unfounded suspicion.

"Miss Schoonmaker, my aunt, Lady Constance Keeble," said Ronnie, going from strength to strength and speaking now quite easily and articulately.

Sue was not the girl to sit dumbly by and fail a partner in his hour of need. She smiled brightly.

"How do you do, Lady Constance?" she said. She smiled again, if possible even more brightly than before. "I feel I know you already. Lady Julia told me so much about you at Biarritz."

A momentary qualm lest, in the endeavour to achieve an easy cordiality, she had made her manner a shade too patronizing

47

melted in the sunshine of the older woman's smile. Lady Constance had become charming, almost effusive. She had always hoped that Ronald and Millicent would make a match of it; but, failing that, this rich Miss Schoonmaker was certainly the next best thing. And driving chummily about London together like this must surely, she thought, mean something, even in these days when chummy driving is so prevalent between the sexes. At any rate, she hoped so.

"So here you are in London!"

"Yes."

"You did not stay long in Paris."

"No."

"When can you come down to Blandings?"

"Oh, very soon, I hope."

"I am going there this evening. I only ran up for the day. I want you to drive me back, Ronald."

Ronnie nodded silently. The crisis passed, a weakness had come upon him. He preferred not to speak, if speech could be avoided.

"Do try to come soon. The gardens are looking delightful. My brother will be so glad to see you. I was just on my way to Claridge's for a cup of tea. Won't you come too?"

"I'd love to," said Sue, "but I really must be getting on. Ronnie was taking me shopping."

"I thought you stayed in Paris to do your shopping."

"Not all of it."

"Well, I shall hope to see you soon."

"Oh, yes."

"At Blandings."

"Thank you so much. Ronnie, I think we ought to be getting along."

"Yes." Ronnie's mind was blurred, but he was clear on that point. "Yes, getting along. Pushing off."

"Well, I'm so delighted to have seen you. My sister told me so much about you in her letters. After you have put your luggage on the car, Ronald, will you come and pick me up at Claridge's?"

48

"Right ho."

"I would like to make an early start, if possible."

"Right ho."

"Well, good-bye for the present, then."

"Right ho."

"Goodbye, Lady Constance."

"Goodbye."

The two-seater moved off, and Ronnie, taking his right hand from the wheel as it turned the corner, groped for a handkerchief, found it, and passed it over his throbbing brow.

"So that was Aunt Constance!" said Sue.

Ronnie breathed deeply.

"Nice meeting one of whom I have heard so much."

Ronnie replaced his hand on the wheel and twiddled it feebly to avoid a dog. Reaction had made him limp.

Sue was gazing at him almost reverently.

"What genius, Ronnie! What ready wit! What presence of mind! If I hadn't heard it with my own ears I wouldn't have believed it. Why didn't you ever tell me you were one of those swift thinkers?"

"I didn't know it myself."

"Of course, I'm afraid it has complicated things a little."

"Eh?" Ronnie started. This aspect of the matter had not struck him. "How do you mean?"

"When I was a child they taught me a poem—"

Ronnie raised a suffering face to hers.

"Don't let's talk about your childhood now, old thing," he pleaded. "Feeling rather shaken. Any other time—"

"It's all right. I'm not wandering from the subject. I can only remember two lines of the poem. They were, 'Oh, what a tangled web we weave when first we practise to deceive.' You do see the web is a bit tangled, don't you, Ronnie, darling?"

"Eh? Why? Everything looks pretty smooth to me. Aunt Constance swallowed you without a yip."

"And when the real Miss Schoonmaker arrives at Blandings with her jewels and her twenty-four trunks?" said Sue gently.

The two-seater swerved madly across Grosvenor Street.

49

"Gosh!" said Ronnie.

Sue's eyes were sparkling.

"There's only one thing to do," she said. "Now you're in you'll have to go in deeper. You'll have to put her off."

"How?"

"Send her a wire saying she mustn't come to Blandings because scarlet fever or something has broken out."

"I couldn't."

"You must. Sign it in Lady Constance's name."

"But suppose—"

"Well, suppose they do find out? You won't be in any worse hole than you will be if she comes sailing up to the front door all ready to stay a couple of weeks. And she will unless you wire."

"That's true."

"What it means," said Sue, "is that instead of having plenty of time to get that money out of Lord Emsworth you'll have to work quick." She touched his arm. "Here's a post office," she said. "Go in and send that wire before you weaken."

Ronnie stopped the car.

"You will have to do the most rapid bit of trustee touching in the history of the world, I should think," said Sue reflectively. "Do you think you can manage it?"

"I'll have a jolly good prod."

"Remember what it means."

"I'll do that all right. The only trouble is that in the matter of biting Uncle Clarence's ear I've nothing to rely on but my natural charm. And as far as I've been able to make out," said Ronnie, "he hasn't noticed yet that I have any."

He strode into the post office, thinking deeply.

3

I

It was the opinion of the poet Calverley, expressed in his immortal "Ode to Tobacco," that there is no heaviness of the soul which will not vanish beneath the influence of a quiet smoke. Ronnie Fish would have disputed this theory. It was the third morning of his sojourn at Blandings Castle; and, taking with him a tennis ball which he proposed to bounce before him in order to assist thought, he had wandered out into the grounds, smoking hard. And tobacco, though Turkish and costly, was not lightening his despondency at all. It seemed to Ronnie that the present was bleak and the future gray. Roaming through the sunflooded park, he bounced his tennis ball and groaned in spirit.

On the credit side of the ledger one single item could be inscribed. Hugo was at the castle. He had the consolation, therefore, of knowing that that tall and lissom young man was not in London, exercising his fatal fascination on Sue. But when you had said this you had said everything. After all, even eliminating Hugo, there still remained in the metropolis a vast population of adult males, all either acquainted with Sue or trying to make her acquaintance. The poison sac Pilbeam, for instance. By now it might well be that that bacillus had succeeded in obtaining an introduction to her. A devastating thought.

And even supposing he hadn't, even supposing that Sue, as she had promised, was virtuously handing the mitten to all the young thugs who surged around her with invitations to lunch and supper; where did that get a chap? What, in other words, of the future?

In coming to Blandings Castle Ronnie was only too well aware he had embarked on an expedition the success or failure of which would determine whether his life through the years was to be roses, roses all the way or a dreary desert. And so far, in his efforts to win the favour and esteem of his Uncle Clarence, he seemed to have made no progress whatsoever. On the occasions when he had found himself in Lord Emsworth's society the latter had looked at him sometimes as if he did not know he was there, more often as if he wished he wasn't. It was only too plain that the collapse of the Hot Spot had left his stock in bad shape. There had been a general sagging of the market. Fish preferred, taking the most sanguine estimate, could scarcely be quoted at more than about thirty to thirty-five.

Plunged in thought and trying without any success to conjure up a picture of a benevolent uncle patting him on the head with one hand while writing checks with the other, he had wandered some distance from the house and was passing a small spinney when he observed in a little dell to his left a peculiar object.

It was a large yellow caravan. And what, he asked himself, was a caravan doing in the grounds of Blandings Castle?

To aid him in grappling with the problem he flung the tennis ball at it. Upon which the door opened and a spectacled head appeared.

"Hullo!" said the head.

"Hullo!" said Ronnie.

"Hullo!"

"Hullo!"

The thing threatened to become a hunting chorus. At this moment, however, the sun went behind a cloud, and Ronnie was enabled to recognize the head's proprietor. Until now the light, shining on the other's glasses, had dazzled him.

"Baxter!" he exclaimed.

The last person he would have expected to meet in the park of Blandings. He had heard all about that row a couple of years ago. He knew that if his own stock with Lord Emsworth was low that of the Efficient Baxter was down in the cellar with no takers. Yet here the fellow was, shoving his head out of caravans as if nothing had happened.

"Ah, Fish!"

Rupert Baxter descended the steps, a swarthy-complexioned young man with a supercilious expression which had always been displeasing to Ronnie.

"What are you doing here?" asked Ronnie.

"I happened to be taking a caravan holiday in the neighbourhood. And, finding myself at Market Blandings last night, I thought I would pay a visit to the place where I had spent so many happy days."

"I see."

"Perhaps you could tell me where I could find Lady Constance?"

"I haven't seen her since breakfast. She's probably about somewhere."

"I will go and inquire. If you meet her perhaps you would not mind mentioning that I am here."

The Efficient Baxter strode off, purposeful as ever; and Ronnie, having speculated for a moment as to how his Uncle Clarence would comport himself if he came suddenly round a corner and ran into this bit of the dead past, and having registered an idle hope that, when this happened, he might be present with a camera, inserted another cigarette in its holder and passed on his way.

II

Five minutes later Lord Emsworth, leaning pensively out of the library window and sniffing the morning air, received an unpleasant shock. He could have sworn he had seen his late secretary, Rupert Baxter, cross the gravel and go in at the front door.

"Bless my soul!" said Lord Emsworth.

The only explanation that occurred to him was that Baxter, having met with some fatal accident, had come back to haunt the place. To suppose the fellow could be here in person was absurd. When you shoot a secretary out for throwing flower pots at you in the small hours he does not return to pay social calls. A frown furrowed his lordship's brow. The spectre of one of his ancestors he could have put up with, but the idea of a Blandings

53

Castle haunted by Baxter he did not relish at all. He decided to visit his sister Constance in her boudoir and see what she had to say about it.

"Constance, my dear."

Lady Constance looked up from the letter she was writing. She clicked her tongue, for it annoyed her to be interrupted at her correspondence.

"Well, Clarence?"

"I say, Constance, a most extraordinary thing happened just now. I was looking out of the library window and—you remember Baxter?"

"Of course I remember Mr. Baxter."

"Well, his ghost has just walked across the gravel."

"What *are* you talking about, Clarence?"

"I'm telling you. I was looking out of the library window and I suddenly saw—"

"Mr. Baxter," announced Beach, flinging open the door.

"Mr. Baxter!"

"Good-morning, Lady Constance."

Rupert Baxter advanced with joyous camaraderie glinting from both lenses. Then he perceived his former employer, and his exuberance diminished. "Er—good-morning, Lord Emsworth," he said, flashing his spectacles austerely upon him.

There was a pause. Lord Emsworth adjusted his pince-nez and regarded the visitor dumbly. Of the relief which was presumably flooding his soul at the discovery that Rupert Baxter was still on this side of the veil he gave no outward sign.

Baxter was the first to break an uncomfortable silence.

"I happened to be taking a caravan holiday in this neighbourhood, Lady Constance, and finding myself near Market Blandings last night I thought I would . . ."

"Why, of course! We should never have forgiven you if you had not come to see us. Should we, Clarence?"

"Eh?"

"I said, should we?"

"Should we what?" said Lord Emsworth, who was still adjusting his mind.

54

Lady Constance's lips tightened, and a moment passed during which it seemed always a fifty-fifty chance that a handsome silver ink pot would fly through the air in the direction of her brother's head. But she was a strong woman. She fought down the impulse.

"Did you say you were travelling in a caravan, Mr. Baxter?"

"In a caravan. I left it in the park."

"Well, of course you must come and stay with us. The castle," she continued, raising her voice a little, to compete with a sort of wordless bubbling which had begun to proceed from her brother's lips, "is almost empty just now. We shall not be having our first big house party till the middle of next month. You must make quite a long visit. I will send somebody over to fetch your things."

"It is exceedingly kind of you."

"It will be delightful having you here again. Won't it, Clarence?"

"Eh?"

"I said, won't it?"

"Won't it what?"

Lady Constance's hand trembled above the ink pot like a hovering butterfly. She withdrew it.

"Will it not be delightful," she said, catching her brother's eye and holding it like a female Ancient Mariner, "having Mr. Baxter back at the castle again?"

"I'm going down to see my pig," said Lord Emsworth.

A silence followed his departure, such as would have fallen had a coffin just been carried out. Then Lady Constance shook off gloom.

"Oh, Mr. Baxter, I'm so glad you were able to come. And how clever of you to come in a caravan. It prevented your arrival seeming prearranged."

"I thought of that."

"You think of everything."

Rupert Baxter stepped to the door, opened it, satisfied himself that no listeners lurked in the passage, and returned to his seat.

"Are you in any trouble, Lady Constance? Your letter seemed so very urgent."

55

"I am in dreadful trouble, Mr. Baxter."

If Rupert Baxter had been a different type of man and Lady Constance Keeble had been a different type of woman he would probably at this point have patted her hand. As it was he merely hitched his chair an inch closer to hers.

"If there is anything I can do?"

"There is nobody except you who can do anything. But I hardly like to ask you."

"Ask me whatever you please. And if it is in my power . . ."

"Oh, it is."

Rupert Baxter gave his chair another hitch.

"Tell me."

Lady Constance hesitated.

"It seems such an impossible thing to ask of anyone."

"Please!"

"Well—you know my brother?"

Baxter seemed puzzled. Then an explanation of the peculiar question presented itself.

"Oh, you mean Mr. . . ?"

"Yes, yes, yes. Of course I wasn't referring to Lord Emsworth. My brother Galahad."

"I have met him. Oddly enough, though he visited the castle twice during the period when I was Lord Emsworth's secretary, I was away both times on my holiday. Is he here now?"

"Yes. Finishing his Reminiscences."

"I saw in some paper that he was writing the history of his life."

"And if you know what a life his has been you will understand why I am distracted."

"Certainly I have heard stories," said Baxter guardedly.

Lady Constance performed that movement with her hands which came so close to wringing.

"The book is full from beginning to end of libellous anecdotes, Mr. Baxter. About all our best friends. If it is published we shall not have a friend left. Galahad seems to have known everybody in England when they were young and foolish and to remember everything particularly foolish and disgraceful that they did. So—"

"So you want me to get hold of the manuscript and destroy it?"

Lady Constance stared, stunned by this penetration. She told herself that she might have known that she would not have to make long explanations to Rupert Baxter. His mind was like a searchlight, darting hither and thither, lighting up whatever it touched.

"Yes," she gasped. She hurried on. "It does seem, I know, an extraordinary thing to—"

"Not at all."

"—but Lord Emsworth refuses to do anything."

"I see."

"You know how he is in the face of any emergency."

"Yes, I do, indeed."

"So supine. So helpless. So vague and altogether incompetent."

"Precisely."

"Mr. Baxter, you are my only hope."

Baxter removed his spectacles, polished them, and put them back again.

"I shall be delighted, Lady Constance, to do anything to help you that lies in my power. And to obtain possession of this manuscript should be an easy task. But is there only one copy of it in existence?"

"Yes, yes, yes. I am sure of that. Galahad told me that he was waiting till it was finished before sending it to the typist."

"Then you need have no further anxiety."

It was a moment when Lady Constance Keeble would have given much for eloquence. She sought for words that should adequately express her feelings, but could find none.

"Oh, Mr. Baxter!" she said.

Ronnie Fish's aimlessly wandering feet had taken him westward. It was not long, accordingly, before there came to his nostrils a familiar and penetrating odour, and he found that he was within a short distance of the detached residence employed by Empress of Blandings as a combined bedroom and restaurant. A few steps and he was enabled to observe that celebrated animal in person. With her head tucked well down and her tail wiggling with pure *joie de vivre*, the Empress was hoisting in a spot of lunch.

Everybody likes to see somebody eating. Ronnie leaned over the rail, absorbed. He poised the tennis ball and with an absent-minded flick of the wrist bounced it on the silver medallist's back. Finding the pleasant, ponging sound which resulted soothing to harassed nerves, he did it again. The Empress made excellent bouncing. She was not one of your razor-backs. She presented a wide and resistant surface. For some minutes, therefore, the pair carried on according to plan—she eating, he bouncing, until presently Ronnie was thrilled to discover that this outdoor sport of his was assisting thought. Gradually—mistily at first, then assuming shape—a plan of action was beginning to emerge from the murk of his mind.

How would this be, for instance?

If there was one thing calculated to appeal to his Uncle Clarence, to induce in his Uncle Clarence a really melting mood, it was the announcement that somebody desired to return to the land. He loved to hear of people returning to the land. How, then, would this be? Go to the old boy, state that one had seen the light and was in complete agreement with him that England's future depended on checking the drift to the towns, and then ask for a good fat slice of capital with which to start a farm.

The project of starting a farm was one which was bound to— Half a minute. Another idea on the way. Yes, here it came, and it was a pippin. Not merely just an ordinary farm, but a pig farm! Wouldn't Uncle Clarence leap in the air and shower gold on anybody who wanted to live in the country and breed pigs? You bet your Sunday cuffs he would. And, once the money was safely deposited to the account of Ronald Overbury Fish in Cox's Bank, then ho! for the registrar's hand in hand with Sue.

There was a musical *plonk* as Ronnie bounced the ball for the last time on the Empress's complacent back. Then, no longer with dragging steps but treading on air, he wandered away to sketch out the last details of the scheme before going indoors and springing it.

III

Too often it happens that, when you get these brain waves, you take another look at them after a short interval and suddenly detect some fatal flaw. No such disappointment came to mar the happiness of Ronnie Fish.

"I say, Uncle Clarence," he said, prancing into the library some half hour later.

Lord Emsworth was deep in the current issue of a weekly paper of porcine interest. It seemed to Ronnie, as he looked up, that his eye was not any too chummy. This, however, did not disturb him. That eye, he was confident, would melt anon. If, at the moment, Lord Emsworth could hardly have sat for his portrait in the rôle of a benevolent uncle, there would, Ronnie felt, be a swift change of demeanour in the very near future.

"I say, Uncle Clarence, you know that capital of mine."

"That what?"

"My capital. My money. The money you're trustee of. And a jolly good trustee," said Ronnie handsomely. "Well, I've been thinking things over, and I want you, if you will, to disgorge a segment of it for a sort of venture I've got in mind."

He had not expected the eye to melt yet, and it did not. Seen through the glass of his uncle's pince-nez it looked like an oyster in an aquarium.

"You wish to start another night club?"

Lord Emsworth's voice was cold, and Ronnie hastened to disabuse him of the idea.

"No, no. Nothing like that. Night clubs are a mug's game. I ought never to have touched them. As a matter of fact, Uncle Clarence, London as a whole seems to me a bit of a washout these days. I'm all for the country. What I feel is that the drift to the towns should be checked. What England wants is more blokes going back to the land. That's the way it looks to me."

Ronnie Fish began to experience the first definite twinges of uneasiness. This was the point at which he had been confident that the melting process would set in. Yet, watching the eye, he

59

was dismayed to find it as oysterlike as ever. He felt like an actor who has been counting on a round of applause and goes off after his big speech without a hand. The idea occurred to him that his uncle might possibly have grown a little hard of hearing.

"To the land," he repeated, raising his voice. "More blokes going back to the land. so I want a dollop of capital to start a farm."

He braced himself to the supreme revelation.

"I want to breed pigs," he said reverently.

Something was wrong. There was no blinking the fact any longer. So far from leaping in the air and showering gold his uncle merely stared at him in an increasingly unpleasant manner. Lord Emsworth had removed his pince-nez and was wiping them; and Ronnie thought that his eye looked rather less agreeable in the nude than it had done through glass.

"Pigs!" he cried, fighting against a growing alarm.

"Pigs?"

"Pigs."

"You wish to breed pigs?"

"That's right," bellowed Ronnie. "Pigs!" and from somewhere in his system he contrived to dig up and fasten on his face an ingratiating smile.

Lord Emsworth replaced his pince-nez.

"And I suppose," he said throatily, quivering from his head to his roomy shoes, "that when you've got 'em you'll spend the whole day bouncing tennis balls on their backs?"

Ronnie gulped. The shock had been severe. The ingratiating smile lingered on his lips, as if fastened there with pins, but his eyes were round and horrified.

"Eh!" he said feebly.

Lord Emsworth rose. So long as he insisted on wearing an old shooting jacket with holes in the elbows and letting his tie slip down and show the head of a brass stud, he could never hope to be completely satisfactory as a figure of outraged majesty; but he achieved as imposing an effect as his upholstery would permit. He drew himself up to his full height, which was considerable, and from this eminence glared balefully down on his nephew.

"I saw you! I was on my way to the piggery and I saw you bouncing your infernal tennis balls on my pig's back. Tennis balls!" Fire seemed to stream from the pince-nez. "Are you aware that Empress of Blandings is an excessively nervous, highly strung animal, only too ready on the lightest provocation to refuse her meals? You might have undone the work of months with your idiotic tennis ball."

"I'm sorry."

"What's the good of being sorry?"

"I never thought—"

"You never do. That's what's the trouble with you. Pig farm!" said Lord Emsworth vehemently, his voice soaring into the upper register. "You couldn't manage a pig farm. You aren't fit to manage a pig farm. You aren't worthy to manage a pig farm. If I had to select somebody out of the whole world to manage a pig farm I would choose you last."

Ronnie Fish groped his way to the table and supported himself on it. He had a sensation of dizziness. On one point he was reasonably clear, viz.: that his Uncle Clarence did not consider him ideally fitted to manage a pig farm, but apart from that his mind was in a whirl. He felt as if he had stepped on something and it had gone off with a bang.

"Here! What *is* all this?"

It was the Hon. Galahad who had spoken, and he had spoken peevishly. Working in the small library with the door ajar, he had found the babble of voices interfering with literary composition and, justifiably annoyed, had come to investigate.

"Can't you do your reciting some time when I'm not working, Clarence?" he said. "What's all the trouble about?"

Lord Emsworth was still full of his grievance.

"He bounced tennis balls on my pig!"

The Hon. Galahad was not impressed. He did not register horror.

"Do you mean to tell me," he said sternly, "that all this fuss, ruining my morning's work, was simply about that blasted pig of yours?"

"I refuse to allow you to call the Empress a blasted pig! Good heavens!" cried Lord Emsworth passionately. "Can none of my family appreciate the fact that she is the most remarkable animal in Great Britain? No pig in the whole annals of the Shrop-shire Agricultural Show has ever won the silver medal two years in succession. And that, if only people will leave her alone and refrain from incessantly pelting her with tennis balls, is what the Empress is quite certain to do. It is an unheard of feat."

The Hon. Galahad frowned. He shook his head reprovingly. It was all very well, he felt, a stable being optimistic about its nomi-nee, but he was a man who could face facts. In a long and check-ered life he had seen so many good things unstuck. Besides, he had his superstitions, and one of them was that counting your chickens in advance brought bad luck.

"Don't be too cocksure, my boy," he said gravely. "I looked in at the Emsworth Arms the other day for a glass of beer, and there was a fellow in there offering three to one on an animal called Pride of Matchingham. Offering it freely. Tall, red-haired fellow with a squint. Slightly bottled."

Lord Emsworth forgot Ronnie, forgot tennis balls, forgot in the shock of this announcement everything except that deeper wrong which so long had been poisoning his peace.

"Pride of Matchingham belongs to Sir Gregroy Parsloe," he said, "and I have no doubt that the man offering such ridiculous odds was his pig man. Well beloved. As you know, the fellow used to be in my employment, but Parsloe lured him away from me by the promise of higher wages." Lord Emsworth's expres-sion had now become positively ferocious. The thought of George Cyril Wellbeloved, that perjured pig man, always made the iron enter into his soul. "It was a most abominable and unneighbourly thing to do."

The Hon. Galahad whistled.

"So that's it, is it? Parsloe's pig man going about offering three to one—against the form book, I take it?"

"Most decidedly. Pride of Matchingham was awarded second prize last year, but it is a quite inferior animal to the Empress."

"Then you look after that pig of yours, Clarence." The Hon. Galahad spoke earnestly. "I see what this means. Parsloe's up to his old games and intends to queer the Empress somehow."

"Queer her?"

"Nobble her; or, if he can't do that, steal her."

"You don't mean that?"

"I do mean it. The man's as slippery as a greased eel. He would nobble his grandmother if it suited his book. Let me tell you I've known young Parsloe for thirty years, and solemnly state that if his grandmother was entered in a competition for fat pigs and his commitments made it desirable for him to get her out of the way, he would dope her bran mash and acorns without a moment's hesitation."

"God bless my soul!" said Lord Emsworth, deeply impressed.

"Let me tell you a little story about young Parsloe. One or two of us used to meet at the Black Footman in Gossiter Street in the old days—they've pulled it down now—and match our dogs against rats in the room behind the bar. Well, I put my Towser, an admirable beast, up against young Parsloe's Banjo on one occasion for a hundred pounds a side. And when the night came and he was shown the rats I'm dashed if he didn't just give a long yawn and roll over and go to sleep. I whistled him—called him—Towser, Towser!—No good—fast asleep. And my firm belief has always been that young Parsloe took him aside just before the contest was to start and gave him about six pounds of steak and onions. Couldn't prove anything, of course, but I sniffed the dog's breath, and it was like opening the kitchen door of a Soho chophouse on a summer night. That's the sort of man young Parsloe is."

"Galahad!"

"Fact. You'll find the story in my book."

Lord Emsworth was tottering to the door.

"God bless my soul! I never realized . . . I must see Pirbright at once. I didn't suspect . . . It never occurred . . ."

The door closed behind him. The Hon. Galahad, preparing to return to his labours, was arrested by the voice of his nephew Ronald.

"Uncle Gally!"

The young man's pink face had flamed to bright crimson. His eyes gleamed strangely.

"Well?"

"You don't really think Sir Gregory will try to steal the Empress?"

"I certainly do. Known him for thirty years, I tell you."

"But how could he?"

"Go to her sty at night, of course, and take her away."

"And hide her somewhere?"

"Yes."

"But an animal of that size. Rather like looking in at the Zoo and pocketing one of the elephants, what?"

"Don't talk like an idiot. She's got a ring through her nose, hasn't she?"

"You mean, Sir Gregory would catch hold of the ring and she would breeze along quite calmly?"

"Certainly. Puffy Benger and I stole old Wivenhoe's pig the night of the Bachelors Ball at Hammers Easton in the year '95. We put it in Plug Basham's bedroom. There was no difficulty about the thing whatsoever. A little child could have led it."

He withdrew into the small library, and Ronnie slid limply into the chair which Lord Emsworth had risen from so majestically. He felt the need of sitting. The inspiration which had just come to him had had a stunning effect. The brillance of it almost frightened him. That idea about starting a pig farm had shown that this was one of his bright mornings, but he had never foreseen that he would be as bright as this.

"Golly!" said Ronnie.

Could he . . . ?

Well, why not?

Suppose . . .

No, the thing was impossible.

Was it? Why? Why was it impossible? Suppose he had a stab at it. Suppose, following his Uncle Galahad's expert hints, he were to creep out to-night, abstract the Empress from her home, hide her somewhere for a day or two, and then spectacularly restore her to her bereaved owner? What would be the result? Would Uncle Clarence sob on his neck or would he not? Would he feel that no reward was too good for his benefactor or wouldn't he?

64

Most decidedly he would. Fish Preferred would soar immediately. That little matter of the advance of capital would solve itself. Money would stream automatically from the Emsworth coffers.

But could it be done? Ronnie forced himself to examine the scheme dispassionately, with a mind alert for snags.

He could detect none. A suitable hiding place occurred to him immediately—that disused gamekeeper's cottage in the west wood. Nobody ever went there. It would be good as a Safe Deposit.

Risk of detection? Why should there be any risk of detection? Who would think of connecting Ronald Fish with the affair?

Feeding the animal? . . .

Ronnie's face clouded. Yes, here at last was the snag. This did present difficulties. He was vague as to what pigs ate, but he knew that they needed a lot of whatever it was. It would be no use restoring to Lord Emsworth a skeleton Empress. The cuisine must be maintained at its existing level or the thing might just as well be left undone.

For the first time he began to doubt the quality of his recent inspiration. Scanning the desk with knitted brows, he took from the book rest the volume entitled *Pigs, and How to Make Them Pay*. A glance at page 61 and his misgivings were confirmed.

"'myes," said Ronnie, having skimmed through all the stuff about barley meal and maize meal and linseed meal and potatoes and separated milk or buttermilk. This, he now saw clearly, was no one-man job. It called not only for a dashing principal but a zealous assistant.

And what assistant?

Hugo?

No. In many respects the ideal accomplice for an undertaking of this nature, Hugo Carmody had certain defects that automatically disqualified him. To enroll Hugo as his lieutenant would mean revealing to him the motives that lay at the back of the venture. And if Hugo knew that he, Ronnie, was endeavouring to collect funds in order to get married the thing would be all over Shropshire in a couple of days. Short of putting it on the front page of the *Daily Mail* or having it broadcast over the wireless,

65

the surest way of obtaining publicity for anything you wanted kept dark was to confide it to Hugo Carmody. A splendid chap, but the real, genuine human colander. No, not Hugo.

Then who . . . ?

Ah!

Ronnie Fish sprang from his chair, threw his head back, and uttered a yodel of joy so loud and penetrating that the door of the small library flew open as if he had touched a spring.

A tousled literary man emerged.

"Stop the damned noise! How the devil can I write with a row like that going on?"

"Sorry, Uncle. I was just thinking of something."

"Well, think of something else. How do you spell 'intoxicated'?"

"One 'x.' "

"Thanks," said the Hon. Galahad, and vanished again.

IV

In his pantry, in shirt-sleeved ease, Beach, the butler, sat taking the well-earned rest of a man whose silver is all done and who has no further duties to perform till lunch time. A bullfinch sang gaily in a cage on the window sill, but it did not disturb him, for he was absorbed in the Racing Intelligence page of the *Morning Post*.

Suddenly he rose, palpitating. A sharp rap had sounded on the door, and he was a man who reacted nervously to sudden noises. There entered his employer's nephew, Mr. Ronald Fish.

"Hullo, Beach."

"Sir?"

"Busy?"

"No, sir."

"Just thought I'd look in."

"Yes, sir."

"For a chat."

"Very good, sir."

Although the butler spoke with his usual smooth courtesy he was far from feeling easy in his mind. He did not like Ronnie's looks. It seemed to him that his young visitor was feverish. The limbs twitched, the eyes gleamed, the blood pressure appeared heightened, and there was a supernormal pinkness in the epidermis of the cheek.

"Long time since we had a cosy talk, Beach."

"Yes, sir."

"When I was a kid I used to be in and out of this pantry of yours all day long."

"Yes, sir."

A mood of extreme sentimentality now appeared to grip the young man. He sighed like a centenarian recalling far-off, happy things.

"Those were the days, Beach."

"Yes, sir."

"No problems then. No worries. And even if I had worries I could always bring them to you, couldn't I?"

"Yes, sir."

"Remember the time I hid in here when my uncle Gally was after me with a whangee for putting tin-tacks on his chair?"

"Yes, sir."

"It was a close call, but you saved me. You were staunch and true. A man in a million. I've always thought that if there were more people like you in the world it would be a better place."

"I do my best to give satisfaction, sir."

"And how you succeed! I shall never forget your kindness in those dear old days, Beach."

"Extremely good of you to say so, sir."

"Later, as the years went by, I did my best to repay you by sharing with you such snips as came my way. Remember the time I gave you Blackbird for the Manchester November Handicap?"

"Yes, sir."

"You collected a packet."

"It did prove a remarkably sound investment, sir."

"Yes. And so it went on. I look back through the years, and

67

I seem to see you and me standing side by side, each helping each, each doing the square thing by the other. You certainly always did the square thing by me."

"I trust I shall always continue to do so, sir."

"I know you will, Beach. It isn't in you to do otherwise. And that," said Ronnie, beaming on him lovingly, "is why I feel so sure that, when I have stolen my uncle's pig, you will be there helping to feed it till I give it back."

The butler blinked. He was plainly endeavouring to conquer time for a look of utter astonishment to cover its full acreage. Such a look had spread to perhaps two thirds of its surface when Ronnie went on.

"You see, Beach, strictly between ourselves, I have made up my mind to sneak the Empress away and keep her hidden in that gamekeeper's cottage in the west wood, and then, when Uncle Clarence is sending out SOS's and offering large rewards, I shall find it there and return it, thus winning his undying gratitude and putting him in the right frame of mind to yield up a bit of my money that I want to get out of him. You get the idea?"

The butler blinked. He was plainly endeavouring to conquer a suspicion that his mind was darkening. Ronnie nodded kindly at him as he fought for speech.

"It's the scheme of a lifetime, you were going to say? You're quite right. It is. But it's one of these schemes that call for a sympathetic fellow worker. You see, pigs like the Empress, Beach, require large quantities of food at frequent intervals. I can't possibly handle the entire commissariat department myself. That's where you're going to help me, like the splendid fellow you are and always have been."

The butler had now begun to gargle slightly. He cast a look of agonized entreaty at the bullfinch, but the bird had no comfort to offer. It continued to chirp reflectively to itself, like a man trying to remember a tune in his bath.

"An enormous quantity of food they need," proceeded Ronnie. "You'd be surprised. Here it is in this book I took from my uncle's desk. At least six pounds of meal a day, not to mention milk or buttermilk and bran made sloppy with swill."

Speech at last returned to the butler. It took the form at first of a faint sound like the cry of a frightened infant. Then words came.

"But, Mr. Ronald . . . !"

Ronnie stared at him incredulously. He seemed to be wrestling with an unbelieveable suspicion.

"Don't tell me you're thinking of throwing me down, Beach? You? My friend since I was so high?" He laughed. He could see now how ridiculous the idea was. "Of course you aren't! You couldn't. Apart from wanting to do me a good turn you've gathered by this time with that quick intelligence of yours that there's money in the thing. Ten quid down, Beach, the moment you give the nod. And nobody knows better than yourself that ten quid, invested on Baby Bones for the Medbury Selling Plate at the current odds, means considerably more than a hundred in your sock on settling day."

"But, sir—it's impossible. I couldn't dream . . . If ever it was found out . . . Really, I don't think you ought to ask me, Mr. Ronald."

"Beach!"

"Yes, but really, sir . . ."

Ronnie fixed him with a compelling eye.

"Think well, Beach. Who gave you Creole Queen for the Lincolnshire?"

"But, Mr. Ronald . . ."

"Who gave you Mazawattee for the Jubilee Stakes, Beach? What a beauty!"

A tense silence fell upon the pantry. Even the bullfinch was hushed.

"And it may interest you to know," said Ronnie, "that just before I left London I heard of something really hot for the Goodwood Cup."

A low gasp escaped Beach. All butlers are sportsmen, and Beach had been a butler for eighteen years. Mere gratitude for past favours might not have been enough in itself to turn the scale, but this was different. On the subject of form for the Goodwood Cup he had been quite unable to reach a satisfying decision. It had baffled him. For days he had been groping in the darkness.

"Jujube, sir?" he whispered.

"Not Jujube."

"Ginger George?"

"Not Ginger George. It's no use your trying to guess, for you'll never do it. Only two touts and the stable cat know this one. But you shall know it, Beach, the minute I give that pig back and claim my reward. And that pig needs to be fed. Beach, how about it?"

For a long minute the butler stared before him, silent. Then, as if he felt that some simple, symbolic act of the sort was what this moment demanded, he went to the bullfinch's cage and put a green baize cloth over it.

"Tell me just what it is you wish me to do, Mr. Ronald," he said.

V

The dawn of another day crept upon Blandings Castle. Hour by hour the light grew stronger till, piercing the curtains of Ronnie's bedroom, it woke him from a disturbed slumber. He turned sleepily on the pillow. He was dimly conscious of having had the most extraordinary dream, all about stealing pigs. In this dream . . .

He sat up with a jerk. Like cold water dashed in his face had come the realization that it had been no dream.

"Gosh!" said Ronnie, blinking.

Few things have such a tonic effect on a young man accustomed to be a little heavy on waking in the morning as the discovery that he has stolen a prize pig overnight. Usually, at this hour, Ronnie was more or less of an inanimate mass till kindly hands brought him his early cup of tea; but to-day he thrilled all down his pajama-clad form with a novel alertness. Not since he had left school had he sprung out of bed, but he did so now. Bed, generally so attractive to him, had lost its fascination. He wanted to be up and about.

He had bathed, shaved, and was slipping into his trousers when his toilet was interrupted by the arrival of his old friend Hugo

Carmody. On Hugo's face there was an expression which it was impossible to misread. It indicated as plainly as a label that he had come bearing news, and Ronnie, guessing the nature of this news, braced himself to be suitably startled.

"Ronnie!"

"Well?"

"Heard what's happened?"

"What?"

"You know that pig of your uncle's?"

"What about it?"

"It's gone."

"Gone!"

"Gone!" said Hugo, rolling the word round his tongue. "I met the old boy half a minute ago, and he told me. It seems he went down to the pig bin for a before-breakfast look at the animal and it wasn't there."

"Wasn't there?"

"Wasn't there."

"How do you mean, wasn't there?"

"Well, it wasn't. Wasn't there at all. It had gone."

"Gone?"

"Gone! Its room was empty and its bed had not been slept in."

"Well, I'm dashed!" said Ronnie.

He was feeling pleased with himself. He felt he had played his part well. Just the right incredulous amazement, changing just soon enough into stunned belief.

"You don't seem very surprised," said Hugo.

Ronnie was stung. The charge was monstrous.

"Yes, I do," he cried. "I seem frightfully surprised. I *am* surprised. Why shouldn't I be surprised?"

"All right. Just as you say. Spring about a bit more, though, another time when I bring you these sensational items. Well, I'll tell you one thing," said Hugo with satisfaction. "Out of evil cometh good. It's an ill wind that has no turning. For me this startling occurrence has been a life saver. I've got thirty-six hours' leave out of it. The old boy is sending me up to London to get a detective."

71

"A what?"

"A detective."

"A detective!"

Ronnie was conscious of a marked spasm of uneasiness. He had not bargained for detectives.

"From a place called the Argus Enquiry Agency."

Ronnie's uneasiness increased. This thing was not going to be so simple after all. He had never actually met a detective, but he had read a lot about them. They nosed about and found clues. For all he knew he might have left a hundred clues.

"Naturally I shall have to stay the night in town. And, much as I like this place," said Hugo, "there's no denying that a night in town won't hurt. I've got fidgety feet, and a spot of dancing will do me all the good in the world. Bring back the roses to my cheeks."

"Yours, eh?"

"All mine. I suggested it."

"You did, did you?" said Ronnie.

He directed at his companion a swift glance of a kind that no one should have directed at an old friend.

"Oh?" he said morosely. "Well, buzz off. I want to dress."

VI

A morning spent in solitary wrestling with a guilty conscience had left Ronnie Fish thoroughly unstrung. By the time the clock over the stable struck the hour of one his mental condition had begun to resemble that of the late Eugene Aram. He paced the lower terrace with bent head, starting occasionally at the sudden chirp of a bird, and longed for Sue. Five minutes of Sue, he felt, would make him a new man.

It was perfectly foul, mused Ronnie, This being separated from the girl he loved. There was something about Sue—he couldn't describe it, but something that always seemed to act on a fellow's whole system like a powerful pick-me-up. She was the human equivalent of those pink drinks you went and got—or, rather, which you used to go and get before a good woman's love had made you give up all that sort of thing—at that chemist's at the top of the Haymarket after a wild night on the moors. It must have been with a girl like Sue in mind, he felt, that the poet had written those lines "When something something something brow, a ministering angel thou"!

At this point in his meditations, a voice from immediately behind him spoke his name.

"I say, Ronnie."

It was only his cousin Millicent. He became calmer. For an instant, so deep always is a criminal's need for a confidant, he had a sort of idea of sharing his hideous secret with this girl, between whom and himself there had long existed a pleasant friendship. Then he abandoned the notion. His secret was not one that could be lightly shared. Momentary relief of mind was not worth purchasing at the cost of endless anxiety.

"Ronnie, have you seen Mr. Carmody anywhere?"

"Hugo? He went up to London on the ten-thirty."

"Went up to London? What for?"

"He's gone to a place called the Argus Enquiry Agency to get a detective."

"What, to investigate this business of the Empress?"

"Yes."

Millicent laughed. The idea tickled her.

"I'd like to be there to see old man Argus's face when he finds that all he's wanted for is to track down missing pigs. I should think he would beat Hugo over the head with a bloodstain."

Her laughter trailed away. There had come into her face the look of one suddenly visited by a displeasing thought.

"Ronnie!" she said.

"Hullo?"

"Do you know what?"

"What?"

"This looks fishy to me."

"How do you mean?"

"Well, I don't know how it strikes you, but this Argus Enquiry Agency is presumably on the 'phone. Why didn't Uncle Clarence just ring them up and ask them to send down a man?"

"Probably didn't think of it."

"Who's idea was it, anyway, getting down a man?"

"Hugo's."

"He suggested that he should run up to town?"

"Yes."

"I thought as much," said Millicent darkly.

"What do you mean?"

Millicent's eyes narrowed. She kicked moodily at a passing worm.

"I don't like it," she said. "It's fishy. Too much zeal. It looks very much to me as if our Mr. Carmody had a special reason for wanting to get up to London for the night. And I think I know what the reason was. Did you ever hear of a girl named Sue Brown?"

The start which Ronnie gave eclipsed in magnitude all the other starts he had given that morning. And they had been many and severe.

"It isn't true!"

"What isn't true?"

"That there's anything whatever between Hugo and Sue Brown."

"Oh? Well, I had it from an authoritative source."

It was not the worm's lucky morning. It had now reached Ronnie, and he kicked at it, too. The worm had the illusion that it had begun to rain shoes.

"I've got to go in and make a 'phone call," said Millicent abruptly.

Ronnie scarcely noticed her departure. He had supposed himself to have been doing some pretty tense thinking all the morning, but compared with its activity now his brain hitherto had been stagnant.

It couldn't be true, he told himself. Sue had said definitely that it wasn't, and she couldn't have been lying to him. Girls like Sue didn't lie. And yet . . .

The sound of the luncheon gong floated over the garden.

Well, one thing was certain. It was simply impossible to remain here at Blandings Castle, getting his mind poisoned with doubts and speculations which for the life of him he could not keep out of it. If he took the two-seater and drove off in it the moment this infernal meal was over he could be in London before eight. He could call at Sue's flat; receive her assurance once more that Hugo Carmody, tall and lissom though he might be, expert on the saxophone though he admittedly was, meant nothing to her; take her out to dinner and, while dining, ease his mind of that which weighed upon it. Then, fortified with comfort and advice, he could pop into the car and be back at the castle by lunch time on the following day.

It wasn't, of course, that he didn't trust her implicitly. Nevertheless . . .

Ronnie went in to lunch.

4

IF YOU go up Beeston Street in the southwestern postal division
of London and follow the pavement on the right-hand side, you
come to a blind alley called Hayling Court. If you enter the first
building on the left of this blind alley and mount a flight of stairs
you find yourself facing a door, on the ground glass of which is
the legend:

ARGUS
ENQUIRY
AGENCY
LTD.

and below it, to one side, the smaller legend

P. FROBISHER PILBEAM, MGR.

And if, at about the hour when Ronnie Fish had stepped into
his two-seater in the garage of Blandings Castle, you had opened
this door and gone in and succeeded in convincing the gentlemanly office boy that yours was a bona fide visit, having nothing
to do with the sale of life insurance, proprietary medicines, or
handsomely bound sets of Dumas, you would have been admitted to the august presence of the manager himself. P. Frosbisher
Pilbeam was seated at his desk, reading a telegram which had
arrived during his absence at lunch.

This is peculiarly an age of young men starting out in busness
for themselves; of rare, unfettered spirits chafing at the bonds

of employment and refusing to spend their lives working forty-eight weeks in the year for a salary. Quite early in his career Pilbeam had seen where the big money lay and decided to go after it.

As editor of that celebrated weekly scandal sheet, *Society Spice*, Percy Pilbeam had had exceptional opportunities of discovering in good time the true bent of his genius; with the result that, after three years of nosing out people's discreditable secrets on behalf of the Mammoth Publishing Company, his employers, he had come to the conclusion that a man of his gifts would be doing far better for himself nosing out such secrets on his own behalf. Considerably to the indignation of Lord Tilbury, the Mammoth's guiding spirit, he had borrowed some capital, handed in his portfolio, and was now in an extremely agreeable financial position.

The telegram over which he sat brooding with wrinkled forehead was just the sort of telegram an inquiry agent ought to have been delighted to receive, being thoroughly cryptic and consequently a pleasing challenge to his astuteness as a detective: but Percy Pilbeam, in his ten minutes' acquaintance with it, had come to dislike it heartily. He preferred his telegrams easier.

It ran as follows:

Be sure send best man investigate big robbery.

It was unsigned.

What made the thing particularly annoying was that it was so tantalizing. A big robbery probably meant jewels, with a correspondingly big fee attached to their recovery. But you cannot scour England at random asking people if they have had a big robbery in their neighbourhood.

Reluctantly he gave the problem up and, producing a pocket mirror, began with the aid of a pen nib to curl his small and revolting moustache. His thoughts had drifted now to Sue. They were not altogether sunny thoughts, for the difficulty of making

Sue's acquaintance was beginning to irk Percy Pilbeam. He had written her notes. He had sent her flowers. And nothing had happened. She ignored the notes, and what she did with the flowers he did not know. She certainly never thanked him for them.

Brooding upon these matters, he was interrupted by the opening of the door. The gentlemanly office boy entered. Pilbeam looked up, annoyed.

"How many times have I told you not to come in here without knocking?" he asked sternly.

The office boy reflected.

"Seven," he replied.

"What would you have done if I had been in conference with an important client?"

"Gone out again," said the office boy. Working in a Private Enquiry Agency, you drop into the knack of solving problems.

"Well, go out now."

"Very good, sir. I merely wished to say that while you were absent at lunch a gentleman called."

"Eh? Who was he?"

The office boy, who liked atmosphere and hoped some day to be promoted to the company of Mr. Murphy and Mr. Jones, the two active assistants who had their lair on the ground floor, thought for a moment of saying that, beyond the obvious facts that the caller was a Freemason, left-handed, a vegetarian and a traveller in the East, he had made no deductions from his appearance. He perceived, however, that his employer was not in the vein for that sort of thing.

"A Mr. Carmody, sir. Mr. Hugo Carmody."

"Ah!" Pilbeam displayed interest. "Did he say he would call again?"

"He mentioned the possibility, sir."

"Well, if he does, inform Mr. Murphy and tell him to be ready when I ring."

The office boy retired, and Pilbeam returned to his thoughts of Sue. He was quite certain now that he did not like her attitude.

Her attitude wounded him. Another thing he deplored was the reluctance of stagedoor keepers to reveal the private addresses of the personnel of the company. Really, there seemed to be no way of getting to know the girl at all.

Eight respectful knocks sounded on the door. The office boy, though occasionally forgetful, was conscientious. He had restored the average.

"Well?"

"Mr. Carmody to see you, sir."

Pilbeam once more relegated Sue to the hinterland of his mind. Business was business.

"Show him in."

"This way, sir," said the office boy with a graceful courtliness which, even taking into account the fact that he suffered from adenoids, had an old-world flavour, and Hugo sauntered across the threshold.

Hugo felt, and was looking, quietly happy. He seemed to bring the sunshine with him. Nobody could have been more wholeheartedly attached than he to Blandings Castle and the society of his Millicent, but he was finding London, revisited, singularly attractive.

"And this, if I mistake not, Watson, is our client now," said Hugo genially.

Such was his feeling of universal benevolence that he embraced with his goodwill even the repellent-looking young man who had risen from the desk. Percy Pilbeam's eyes were too small and too close together, and he marcelled his hair in a manner distressing to right-thinking people, but to-day he had to be lumped in with the rest of the species as a man and a brother, so Hugo bestowed a dazzling smile upon him. He still thought Pilbeam should not have been wearing pimples with a red tie. One or the other if he liked, but not both. Nevertheless, he smiled upon him.

"Fine day," he said.

"Quite," said Pilbeam.

"Very jolly, the smell of the asphalt and carbonic gas."

"Quite."

"Some people might call London a shade on the stuffy side on an afternoon like this, but not Hugo Carmody."

"No?"

"No. H. Carmody finds it just what the doctor ordered." He sat down. "Well, sleuth," he said, "to business. I called before lunch but you were out."

"Yes."

"But here I am again. And I suppose you want to know what I've come about?"

"When you're ready to get round to it," said Pilbeam patiently.

Hugo stretched his long legs comfortably.

"Well, I know you detective blokes always want a fellow to begin at the beginning and omit no detail, for there is no saying how important some seemingly trivial fact may be. Omitting birth and early education, then, I am at the moment private secretary to Lord Emsworth at Blandings Castle in Shropshire. And," said Hugo, "I maintain, a jolly good secretary. Others may think differently, but that is my view."

"Blandings Castle?"

A thought had struck the proprietor of the Argus Enquiry Agency. He fumbled in his desk and produced the mysterious telegram. Yes, as he had fancied, it had been handed in at a place called Market Blandings.

"Do you know anything about this?" he asked, pushing it across the desk.

Hugo glanced at the document.

"The old boy must have sent that after I left," he said. "The absence of signature is, no doubt, due to mental stress. Lord Emsworth is greatly perturbed. A-twitter. Shaken to the core, you might say."

"About this robbery?"

"Exactly. It has got right in amongst him."

Pilbeam reached for pen and paper. There was a stern, set, bloodhound sort of look in his eyes.

"Kindly give me the details."

Hugo pondered for a moment.

"It was a dark and stormy night—No, I'm a liar. The moon was riding serenely in the sky—"

"This big robbery—tell me about it."

Hugo raised his eyebrows.

"Big?"

"The telegram says 'big.'"

"These telegraph operators will try to make sense. You can't stop them editing. The word should be 'pig.' Lord Emsworth's pig has been stolen!"

"Pig!" cried Percy Pilbeam.

Hugo looked at him a little anxiously.

"You know what a pig is, surely? If not, I'm afraid there is a good deal of tedious spade work ahead of us."

The roseate dreams which the proprietor of the Argus had had of missing jewels broke like bubbles. He was deeply affronted. A man of few ideals, the one deep love of his life was for the inquiry agency which he had created and nursed to prosperity through all the dangers and vicissitudes which beset inquiry agencies in their infancy. And the thought of being expected to apply its complex machinery to a search for lost pigs cut him, as Millicent had predicted, to the quick.

"Does Lord Emsworth seriously suppose that I have time to waste looking for stolen pigs?" he demanded shrilly. "I never heard such nonsense in my life."

"Almost the exact words which all the other Hawkshaws used. Finding you not at home," explained Hugo, "I spent the morning going round to other agencies. I think I visited six in all, and every one of them took the attitude you do."

"I am not surprised."

"Nevertheless, it seemed to me that they, like you, lacked vision. This pig, you see, is a prize pig. Don't picture to yourself something with a kink in its tail sporting idly in the mud. Imagine, rather, a favourite daughter kidnapped from her ancestral home. This is heavy stuff, I assure you. Restore the animal in time for the Agricultural Show and you may ask of Lord Emsworth what you will, even unto half his kingdom."

Percy Pilbeam rose. He had heard enough.

"I will not trouble Lord Emsworth. The Argus Enquiry Agency—"

"—does not detect pigs? I feared as much. Well, well, so be it. And now," said Hugo affably, "may I take advantage of the beautiful friendship which has sprung up between us to use your telephone?"

Without waiting for permission—for which, indeed, he would have had to wait some time—he drew the instrument to him and gave a number. He then began to chat again.

"You seem a knowledgeable sort of bloke," he said. "Perhaps you can tell me where the village swains go these days when they want to dance upon the green? I have been absent for some little time from the centre of the vortex, and I have become as a child in these matters. What is the best that London has to offer to a young man with his blood up and the vine leaves more or less in his hair?"

Pilbeam was a man of business. He had no wish to converse with this client who had disappointed him and wounded his finest feelings, but it so happened that he had recently bought shares in a rising restaurant.

"Mario's," he replied promptly. "It's the only place."

Hugo sighed. Once he had dreamed that the answer to a question like that would have been "The Hot Spot." But where was the Hot Spot now? Gone like the flowers that wither in the first frost. The lion and the lizard kept the courts where Jamshyd gloried and—after hours, unfortunately, which had started all the trouble—drank deep. Ah, well, life was pretty complex.

A voice from the other end of the wire broke in on his reverie. He recognized it as that of the porter of the block of flats where Sue had her tiny abode.

"Hullo? Bashford? Mr. Carmody speaking. Will you make a long arm and haul Miss Brown to the instrument. Eh? Miss Sue Brown, of course. No other Browns are any use to me whatsoever. Right ho, I'll wait."

The astute detective never permits himself to exhibit emotion.

Pilbeam turned his start of surprise into a grave, distrait nod, as if he were thinking out deep problems. He took up his pen and drew three crosses and a squibble on the blotting paper. He was glad that no gentlemanly instinct had urged him to leave his visitor alone to do his telephoning.

"Mario's, eh?" said Hugo. "What's the band like?"

"It's Leopold's."

"Good enough for me," said Hugo with enthusiasm. He hummed a bar or two and slid his feet dreamily about the carpet. "I'm shockingly out of practice, dash it. Well, that's that. Touching this other matter, you're sure you won't come to Blandings?"

"Quite."

"Nice place. Gravel soil, spreading views, well laid out pleasure ground, company's own water. I would strongly advise you to bring your magnifying glass and spend the summer. However, if you really feel—Sue! Hullo-ullo-ullo! This is Hugo. Yes, just up in town for the night on a mission of extraordinary secrecy and delicacy which I am not empowered to reveal. Speaking from the Argus Enquiry Agency, by courtesy of proprietor. I was wondering if you would care to come out and help me restore my lost youth, starting at about eight-thirty. Eh?"

A silence had fallen at the other end of the wire. What was happening was that in the hall of the block of flats Sue's conscience was fighting a grim battle against heavy odds. Ranged in opposition to it were her loneliness, her love of dancing, and her desire once more to see Hugo, who, though he was not a man one could take seriously, always cheered her up and made her laugh. And she had been needing a laugh for days.

Hugo thought he had been cut off.

"Hullo-ullo-ullo-ullo-ullo-ullo!" he barked peevishly.

"Don't yodel like that," said Sue. "You've nearly made me deaf."

"Sorry, dear heart. I thought the machine had conked. Well, how do you react? Is it a bet?"

"I do want to see you again," said Sue hesitatingly.

"You shall. In person. Clean shirt, white waistcoat, the Carmody studs, and everything."

"Well . . ."

A psychically gifted bystander, standing in the hall of the block of flats, would have heard at this moment a faint moan. It was Sue's conscience collapsing beneath an unexpected flank attack. She had just remembered that if she went to dine with Hugo she would learn all the latest news about Ronnie. It put the whole thing in an entirely different light. Surely Ronnie himself could have no objection to the proposed feast if he knew that all she was going for was to talk about him? She might dance a little, of course, but purely by the way. Her real motive in accepting the invitation, she now realized quite clearly, was to hear all about Ronnie.

"All right," she said. "Where?"

"Mario's. They tell me it's the posh spot these days."

"Mario's?"

"Yes. M for manage, A for Asthma, R for rheumatism . . . Oh, you've got it? All right, then. At eight-thirty."

Hugo put the receiver back. Once more he allowed his dazzling smile to play upon the Argus's proprietor.

"Much obliged for use of instrument," he said. "Thank you."

"Thank *you*," said Pilbeam.

"Well, I'll be pushing along. Ring us up if you change your mind. Market Blandings 32X. If you don't take on the job no one will. I suppose there are other sleuths in London besides the bevy I've interviewed to-day, but I'm not going to see them. I consider that I have done my bit and am through." He looked about him. "Make a good thing out of this business?" he asked, for he was curious on these points and was never restrained by delicacy from seeking information.

"Quite."

"What does the work consist of? I've often wondered. Measuring footprints and putting the tips of your fingers together and all that, I suppose?"

"We are frequently asked to follow people and report on their movements."

Hugo laughed amusedly.

"Well, don't go following me and reporting on my movements. Much trouble might ensue. Bung-oh."

"Good-bye," said Percy Pilbeam.

He pressed a bell on the desk and moved to the door to show his visitor out.

II

Leopold's justly famous band, its cheeks puffed out and its eyeballs rolling, was playing a popular melody with lots of stomp in it, and for the first time since she had accepted Hugo's invitation to the dance Sue, gliding round the floor, was conscious of a spiritual calm. Her conscience, quieted by the moaning of the saxophones, seemed to have retired from business. It realized, no doubt, the futility of trying to pretend that there was anything wrong in a girl enjoying this delightful exercise.

How absurd, she felt, Ronnie's objections were. It was, considered Sue, becoming analytical, as if she were to make a tremendous fuss because he played tennis and golf with girls. Dancing was just a game like those two pastimes, and it so happened that you had to have a man with you or you couldn't play it. To get all jealous and throaty just because one went out dancing was simply ridiculous.

On the other hand, placid though her conscience now was, she had to admit that it was a relief to feel that he would never know of this little outing.

Men were such children when they were in love. Sue found herself sighing over the opposite sex's eccentricities. If they were only sensible, how simple life would be. It amazed her that Ronnie could ever have any possible doubt, however she might spend her leisure hours, that her heart belonged to him alone. She marvelled that he should suppose for a moment that even if she danced all night and every night with every other man in the world it would make any difference to her feelings toward him.

All the same, holding the peculiar views he did, he must undoubtedly be humoured.

"You won't breathe a word to Ronnie about our coming here, will you, Hugo?" she said, repeating an injunction which had been her opening speech on arriving at the restaurant.

"Not a syllable."

"I can trust you?"

"Implicitly. Telegraphic address, Discretion, Market Blandings."

"Ronnie's funny, you see."

"One long scream."

"I mean, he wouldn't understand."

"No. Great surprise it was to me," said Hugo, doing complicated things with his feet, "to hear that you and the old leper had decided to team up. You could have knocked me down with a feather. Odd he never confided in his boyhood friend."

"Well, it wouldn't do for it to get about."

"Are you suggesting that Hugo Carmody is a babbler?"

"You do like gossiping. You know you do."

"I know nothing of the sort," said Hugo with dignity. "If I were asked to give my opinion I should say that I was essentially a strong silent man."

He made a complete circle of the floor in that capacity. His taciturnity surprised Sue.

"What's the matter?" she asked.

"Dudgeon," said Hugo.

"What?"

"I'm sulking. That remark of yours rankles. That totally unfounded accusation that I cannot keep a secret. It may interest you to know that I, too, am secretly engaged and have never so much as mentioned it to a soul."

"Hugo!"

"Yes. Betrothed. And so at long last came a day when love wound his silken fetters about Hugo Carmody."

"Who's the unfortunate girl?"

"There is no unfortunate girl. The lucky girl—Was that your foot?"

"Yes."

"Sorry. I haven't got the hang of these new steps yet. The lucky girl, I was saying, is Miss Millicent Threepwood."

As if stunned by the momentousness of the announcement the band stopped playing; and, chancing to be immediately opposite their table, the man who never revealed secrets led his partner to her chair. She was gazing at him ecstatically.

"You don't mean that?"

"I do mean that. What did you think I meant?"

"I never heard anything so wonderful in my life!"

"Good news?"

"I'm simply delighted."

"I'm pleased, too," said Hugo.

"I've been trying not to admit it to myself, but I was very scared about Millicent. Ronnie told me the family wanted him and her to marry, and you never know what may happen when families throw their weight about. And now it's all right!"

"Quite all right."

The music had started again, but Sue remained in her seat.

"Not?" said Hugo, astonished.

"Not just yet. I want to talk. You don't realize what this means to me. Besides, your dancing's gone off, Hugo. You're not the man you were."

"I need practice." He lighted a cigarette and tapped a philosophical vein of thought, eying the gyrating couples meditatively. "It's the way they're always introducing new steps that bothers the man who has been living out in the woods. I have become a rusty rustic."

"I didn't mean you were bad. Only you used to be such a marvel. Dancing with you was like floating on a pink cloud above an ocean of bliss."

"A very accurate description, I should imagine," agreed Hugo. "But don't blame me. Blame these Amalgamated Professors of the Dance, or whatever they call themselves—the birds who get together every couple of weeks or so to decide how they can make things more difficult. Amazing thing that they won't leave well alone."

"You must have change."

"I disagree with you," said Hugo. "No other walk in life is afflicted by a gang of thugs who are perpetually altering the rules of the game. When you learn to play golf the professional doesn't tell you to bring the club up slowly and keep the head steady and roll the forearms and bend the left knee and raise the left heel and keep your eye on the ball and not sway back, and a few more things, and then, after you've sweated yourself to the bone learning all that, suddenly add, 'Of course you understand that this is merely intended to see you through till about three weeks from next Thursday. After that the Supreme Grand Council of Consolidated Divot Shifters will scrap these methods and invent an entirely new set!'"

"Is this more dudgeon?"

"No. Not dudgeon."

"It sounds like dudgeon. I believe your little feelings are hurt because I said your dancing wasn't as good as it used to be."

"Not at all. We welcome criticism."

"Well, get your mind off it and tell me all about you and Millicent and . . ."

"When I was about five," resumed Hugo, removing his cigarette from the holder and inserting another, "I attended my first dancing school. I'm a bit shaky on some of the incidents of the days when I was trailing clouds of glory, but I do remember that dancing school. At great trouble and expense I was taught to throw up a rubber ball with my left hand and catch it with my right, keeping the small of the back rigid and generally behaving in a graceful and attractive manner. It doesn't sound a likely sort of thing to learn at a dancing school, but I swear to you that that's what the curriculum was. Now, the point I am making—"

"Did you fall in love with Millicent right away, or was it gradual?"

"The point I am making is this. I became very good at throwing and catching that rubber ball. I dislike boasting, but I stood out conspicuously among a pretty hot bunch. People would nudge each other and say, 'Who is he?' behind their hands. I don't suppose, when I was feeling right, I missed the rubber ball more than once in twenty goes. But what good does it do me now? Absolutely none. Long before I got a chance of exhibiting my accomplishment in public and having beautiful women fawn on me for my skill, the Society of Amalgamated Professors of the Dance decided that the Rubber-Ball Glide, or whatever it was called, was out of date."

"Is she very pretty?"

"And what I say is that all this chopping and changing handicaps a chap. I am perfectly prepared at this moment to step out on that floor and heave a rubber ball about, but it simply isn't being done nowadays. People wouldn't understand what I was driving at. In other words, all the time and money and trouble that I spent on mastering the Rubber-Ball Shimmy is a dead loss. I tell you, if the Amalgamated Professors want to make people cynics, they're going the right way to work."

"I wish you would tell me all about Millicent."

"In a moment. Dancing, they taught me at school, dates back to the early Egyptians, who ascribed the invention to the god Thoth. The Phrygian Corybantes danced in honour of somebody whose name I've forgotten, and every time the festival of Rhea Silvia came round the ancient Roman hoofers were there with their hair in a braid. But what was good enough for the god Thoth isn't good enough for these blighted Amalgamated Professors! Oh, no! And it's been the same all through the ages. I don't suppose there has been a moment in history when some poor, well-meaning devil, with ambition at one end of him and two left feet at the other, wasn't getting it in the neck."

"And all this," said Sue, "because you trod on my foot for just one half second."

"Hugo Carmody dislikes to tread on women's feet, even for half a second. He has his pride. Ever hear of Father Mariana?"

"No."

"Mariana, George. Born twelve hundred and something. Educated privately and at Leipsig University. Hobbies, fishing, illuminating vellum, and mangling the wurzel. You must have heard of old Pop Mariana?"

"I haven't and I don't want to. I want to hear about Millicent."

"It was the opinion of Father Mariana that dancing was a deadly sin. He was particularly down, I may mention, on the saraband. He said the saraband did more harm than the plague. I know just how he felt. I'll bet he had worked like a dog at twenty-five pazazas the complete course of twelve lessons, guaranteed to teach the fandango: and, just when his instructor had finally told him that he was fit to do it at the next Saturday Night Social, along came the Amalgamated Brothers with their new-fangled saraband, and where was Pop? Leaning against the wall with the other foot-and-mouth diseasers, trying to pretend dancing bored him. Did I hear you say you wanted a few facts about Millicent?"

"You did."

"Sweetest girl on earth."

"Really?"

"Absolutely. It's well known. All over Shropshire."

"And she really loves you?"

"Between you and me," said Hugo confidentially, "I don't wonder you speak in that amazed tone. If you saw her you'd be still more surprised. I am a man who thinks before he speaks. I weigh my words. And I tell you solemnly that that girl is too good for me."

"But you're a sweet darling precious pet."

"I know I'm a sweet darling precious pet. Nevertheless, I still maintain that she is too good for me. She is the nearest thing to an angel that ever came glimmering through the laurels in the quiet evenfall in the garden by the turrets of the old manorial hall."

"Hugo! I'd no idea you were so poetical."

"Enough to make a chap poetical, loving a girl like that."

"And you really do love her?"

Hugo took a feverish gulp of champagne and rolled his eyeballs as if he had been a member of Leopold's justly famous band.

"Madly. Devotedly. And when I think how I have deceived her my soul sickens."

"Have you deceived her?"

"Not yet. But I'm going to in about five minutes. I put in a 'phone call to Blandings just now, and when I get through I shall tell her I'm speaking from my hotel bedroom, where I am on the point of going to bed. You see," said Hugo confidentially, "Millicent, though practically perfect in every other respect, is one of those girls who might misunderstand this little night out of mine did it but come to her ears. Speaking of which, you ought to see them. Like alabaster shells."

"I know what you mean. Ronnie's like that."

Hugo stared.

"Ronnie?"

"Yes."

"You mean to sit there and tell me that Ronnie's ears are like alabaster shells?"

"No, I meant that he would be furious if he knew that I had come out dancing. And, oh, I do love dancing so," sighed Sue.

"He must never know!"

"No. That's why I asked you just now not to tell him."

"I won't. Secrecy and silence. Thank goodness, there's nobody who could tell Millicent even if they wanted to. Ah! this must be the bringer of glad tidings, come to say my call is through. All set?" he asked the page boy who had threaded his way through the crowd to their table.

"Yes, sir."

Hugo rose.

"Amuse yourself somehow till I return."

"I shan't be dull," said Sue.

She watched him disappear, then leaned back in her seat, watching the dancers. Her eyes were bright, and Hugo's news had brought a flush to her cheeks. Percy Pilbeam, who had been hovering in the background, hoping for such an opportunity ever since his arrival at the restaurant, thought he had never seen her looking prettier. He edged between the tables and took Hugo's vacated chair. There are men who, approaching a member of the other sex, wait for permission before sitting down, and men who sit down without permission. Pilbeam was one of the latter.

"Good-evening," he said.

She turned and was aware of a nasty-looking little man at her elbow. He seemed to have materialized from nowhere.

"May I introduce myself, Miss Brown?" said this blot. "My name is Pilbeam."

At the same moment there appeared in the doorway and stood there raking the restaurant with burning eyes the flannel-suited figure of Ronald Overbury Fish.

III

Ronnie Fish's estimate of the time necessary for reaching London from Blandings Castle in a sports-model two-seater had been thrown out of gear by two mishaps. Halfway down the drive the car had developed some mysterious engine trouble, which had necessitated taking it back to the stables and having it overhauled by Lord Emsworth's chauffeur. It was not until nearly an hour later that he had been able to resume his journey, and a blow-out near Oxford had delayed him still further. He arrived at Sue's flat just as Sue and Hugo were entering Mario's.

Ringing Sue's front-door bell produced no result. Ronnie regretted that in the stress of all the other matters that occupied his mind he had forgotten to send her a telegram. He was about to creep away and have a bite of dinner at the Drones Club—a prospect which pleased him not at all, for the Drones at dinner time was always full of hearty eggs who talked much too loud for a worried man's nerves and might even go so far as to throw bread at him, when, descending the stairs into the hall, he came upon Bashford, the porter.

Bashford, who knew Ronnie well said, "'Ullo, Mr. Fish," and Ronnie said, "Hullo, Bashford," and Bashford said the weather seemed to keep up, and Ronnie said, Yes, that's right, it did, and it was at this point that the porter uttered these memorable and, as events proved, epoch-making words:

"If you're looking for Miss Brown, Mr. Fish, I've an idea she's gone to a place called Mario's."

He poured further details into Ronnie's throbbing ear. Mr. Carmody had rung up on the 'phone, might have been ar-parse four, and he, Bashford, not listening but happening to hear, had thought he had caught something said about this place Mario's.

"Mario's?" said Ronnie. "Thanks, Bashford. Mario's, eh? Right!"

The porter, for Eton and Cambridge train their sons well, found nothing in the way Mr. Fish spoke to cause a thrill. Totally unaware that he had been conversing with Othello's younger brother he went back to his den in the basement and sat down with a good appetite to steak and chips. And Ronnie, quivering from head to foot, started the car and drove off.

Jealousy, said Shakespeare, and he was about right, is a green-eyed monster which doth mock the meat he feeds on. By the time Ronald Overbury Fish pushed through the swinging door that guards the revelry at Mario's from the gaze of the passer-by, he was, like the Othello he so much resembled, perplexed in the extreme. He felt hot all over, then cold all over, then hot again, and the waiter who stopped him on the threshold of the dining room to inform him that evening dress was indispensable on the dancing floor and that flannel suits must go up to the balcony, was running a risk which would have caused his insurance company to purse it's lips and shake its head.

Fortunately for him Ronnie did not hear. He was scanning the crowd before him in an effort to find Sue.

"Plenty of room in the balcony, sir," urged the waiter, continuing to play with fire.

This time Ronnie did become dimly aware that somebody was addressing him, and he was about to turn and give the man one look when halfway down a grove of black coats and gaily coloured frocks he suddenly saw what he was searching for. The next moment he was pushing a path through the throng, treading on the toes of brave men and causing fair women to murmur bitterly that this sort of thing ought to be prevented by the management.

Five yards from Sue's table Ronnie Fish would have said that his cup was full and could not possibly be made any fuller. But when he had covered another two and pushed aside a fat man who was standing in the fairway he realized his mistake. It was not Hugo who was Sue's companion, but a reptilian-looking squirt with narrow eyes and his hair done in ridges. And as he saw him something seemed to go off in Ronnie's brain like a released spring.

A waiter, pausing with a tray of glasses, pointed out to him that on the dancing floor evening dress was indispensable.

Gentlemen in flannel suits, he added, could be accommodated in the balcony.

"Plenty of room in the balcony, sir," said the waiter.

Ronnie reached the table. Pilbeam at the moment was saying that he had wanted for a long time to meet Sue. He hoped she had got his flowers all right.

It was perhaps a natural desire to look at anything but this odious and thrusting individual who had forced his society upon her that caused Sue to raise her eyes.

Raising them, she met Ronnie's. And as she saw him her conscience, which she had supposed lulled for the night, sprang to life more vociferous than ever. It had but been crouching, the better to spring.

"Ronnie!"

She started up. Pilbeam also rose. The waiter with the glasses pressed the edge of his tray against Ronnie's elbow in a firm but respectful manner and told him that on the dancing floor evening dress was indispensable. Gentlemen in flannel suits, however, would find ample accommodation in the balcony.

Ronnie did not speak. And it would have been better if Sue had not done so. For at this crisis some subconscious instinct, of the kind which is always waiting to undo us at critical moments, suggested to her dazed mind that when two men who do not know each other are standing side by side in a restaurant one ought to introduce them.

"Mr. Fish, Mr. Pilbeam," murmured Sue.

Only the ringing of the bell that heralds the first sound of a heavy-weight championship fight could have produced more instant and violent results. Through Ronnie's flannel-clad body a sort of galvanic shock seemed to pass. Pilbeam! He had come expecting Hugo, and Hugo would have been bad enough. But Pilbeam! The man she had said she didn't even know. The man she hadn't met. The man whose gifts of flowers she had professed

94

to resent. In person! In the flesh! Hobnobbing with her in a restaurant! By God, he meant to say! By George! Good Gosh!

His fists clenched. Eton was forgotten, Cambridge not even a memory. He inhaled so sharply that a man at the next table who was eating a mousse of chicken stabbed himself in the chin with his fork. He turned on Pilbeam with a hungry look. And at this moment the waiter, raising his voice a little, for he was beginning to think that Ronnie's hearing was slightly affected, mentioned as an interesting piece of information that the management of Mario's preferred to reserve the dancing floor exclusively for clients in evening dress. But there was a bright side. Gentlemen in flannel suits could be accommodated in the balcony.

It was the waiter who saved Percy Pilbeam. Just as a mosquito may divert for an instant a hunter who is about to spring at and bite in the neck a tiger of the jungle, so did this importunate waiter divert Ronnie Fish. What it was all about he was too overwrought to ascertain, but he knew that the man was annoying him, pestering him, trying to chat with him when he had business elsewhere. With all the force of a generous nature sorely tried, he plugged the waiter in the stomach with his elbow. There was a crash which even Leopold's band could not drown. The man who had stabbed himself with the fork had his meal still further spoiled by the fact that it suddenly began to rain glass. And, as regards the other occupants of the restaurant, the word "sensation" about sums the situation up.

Ronnie and the management of Mario's now formed two sharply contrasted schools of thought. To Ronnie the only thing that seemed to matter was this Pilbeam—this creeping, slinking, cuckoo-in-the-nest Pilbeam, the Lothario who had lowered all speed records in underhand villainy by breaking up his home before he had got one. He concentrated all his faculties to the task of getting round the table, to the other side of which the object of his dislike had prudently withdrawn, and showing him in no uncertain manner where he got off.

To the management, on the other hand, the vital issue was all this broken glassware. The waiter had risen from the floor, but the glasses was still there, and scarcely one of them was in a condition ever to be used again for the refreshment of Mario's customers. The head waiter, swooping down on the fray like some god in the Iliad descending from a cloud, was endeavouring to place this point of view before Ronnie. Assisting him with word and gesture were two inferior waiters—Waiter A and Waiter B.

Ronnie was in no mood for abstract debate. He hit the head waiter in the abdomen, Waiter A in the ribs, and was just about to dispose of Waiter B when his activities were hampered by the sudden arrival of reenforcements. From all parts of the room other waiters had assembled—to name but a few, Waiters C, D, E, F, G, and H—and he found himself hard pressed. It seemed to him that he had dropped into a Waiters' Convention. As far as the eye could reach the arena was crammed with waiters, and more coming. Pilbeam had disappeared altogether, and so busy was Ronnie now that he did not even miss him. He had reached that condition of mind which the old Vikings used to call "berserk" and which among modern Malays is termed "running amok."

Ronnie Fish, in the course of his life, had had many ambitions. As a child he had yearned some day to become an engine driver. At school it had seemed to him that the most attractive career the world had to offer was that of the professional cricketer. Later he had hoped to run a prosperous night club. But now, in his twenty-sixth year, all these desires were cast aside and forgotten. The only thing in life that seemed really worth while was to massacre waiters; and to this task he addressed himself with all the energy and strength at his disposal.

Matters now began to move briskly. Waiter C, who rashly clutched the sleeve of Ronnie's coat, reeled back with a hand pressed to his right eye. Waiter D, a married man, contented himself with standing on the outskirts and talking Italian. But Waiter E, made of sterner stuff, hit Ronnie rather hard with a dish containing *omelette aux champignons;* and it was as the latter reeled beneath this buffet that there suddenly appeared in the forefront of the battle a figure wearing a gay uniform and almost completely concealed behind a vast moustache, waxed at the ends. It was the commissionaire from the street door; and anybody who has ever

96

been bounced from a restaurant knows that commissionaires are heavy metal.

This one, whose name was McTeague, and who had spent many lively years in the army before retiring to take up his present duties, had a grim face made of some hard kind of wood, and the muscles of a village blacksmith. A man of action rather than words, he clove his way through the press in silence. Only when he reached the centre of the maelstrom did he speak. This was when Ronnie, leaping onto a chair the better to perform the operation, hit him on the nose. On receipt of this blow he uttered the brief monosyllable "Ho!" and then, without more delay, scooped Ronnie into an embrace of steel and bore him toward the door, through which was now moving a long, large, leisurely policeman.

IV

It was some few minutes later that Hugo Carmody, emerging from the telephone booth on the lower floor where the cocktail bar is, sauntered back into the dancing room and was interested to find waiters massaging bruised limbs, other waiters replacing fallen tables, and Leopold's band playing in a sort of hushed undertone like a band that has seen strange things.

"Hullo!" said Hugo. "Anything up?"

He eyed Sue inquiringly. She looked to him like a girl who has had some sort of a shock. Not, or his eyes deceived him, at all her old bright self.

"What's up?" he asked.

"Take me home, Hugo!"

Hugo stared.

"Home? Already? With the night yet young?"

"Oh, Hugo! Take me home, quick."

"Just as you say," assented Hugo agreeably. He was now pretty certain that something was up. "One second to settle the bill, and then homeward ho. And on the way you shall tell me about it. For I jolly well know," said Hugo, who prided himself on his keenness of observation, "that something is—or has been—up."

5

The Law of Great Britain is a remorseless machine which, once set in motion, ignores first causes and takes into account only results. It will not accept shattered dreams as an excuse for shattering glassware; nor will you get far by pleading a broken heart in extenuation of your behaviour in breaking waiters. Haled on the morrow before the awful majesty of Justice at Bosher Street Police Court and charged with disorderly conduct in a public place—to wit, Mario's Restaurant—and resisting an officer—to wit, P. C. Murgatroyd—in the execution of his duties, Ronald Fish made no impassioned speeches. He did not raise clenched fists aloft and call upon Heaven to witness that he was a good man wronged. Experience, dearly bought in the days of his residence at the university, had taught him that when the Law gripped you with its talons the only thing to do was to give a false name, say nothing, and hope for the best.

Shortly before noon, accordingly, on the day following the painful scene just described, Edwin Jones, of 7 Nasturtium Villas, Cricklewood, poorer by the sum of five pounds, was being conveyed in a swift taxicab to his friend Hugo Carmody's hotel, there to piece together his broken life and try to make a new start.

On the part of the man Jones himself during the ride there was a disposition toward silence. He gazed before him bleakly and gnawed his lower lip. Hugo Carmody, on the other hand, was inclined to be rather jubilant. It seemed to Hugo that, after a rocky start, things had panned out pretty well.

"A nice smooth job," he said approvingly. "I was scanning the beak's face closely during the summing up, and I couldn't help fearing for a moment that it was going to be a case of fourteen days without the option. As it is, here you are, a free man, and no chance of your name being in the paper. A moral victory, I call it."

Ronnie released his lower lip in order to bare his teeth in a bitter sneer.

"I wouldn't care if my name were in every paper in London."

"Oh, come, old loofah! The honoured name of Fish?"

"What do I care about anything now?"

Hugo was concerned. This morbid strain, he felt, was unworthy of a Nasturtium Villas Jones.

"Aren't you rather tending to make a bit too much heavy weather over this?"

"Heavy weather!"

"I think you are. After all, when you come right down to it, what has happened? You find poor little Sue—"

"Don't call her 'poor little Sue!'"

"You find the party of the second part," amended Hugo, "at a dance place. Well, why not? What, if you follow me, of it? Where's the harm in her going out to dance?"

"With a man she swore she didn't know!"

"Well, at the time when you asked her probably she didn't know him. Things move quickly in a great city. I wish I had a quid for every girl I've been out dancing with whom I hadn't known from Eve a couple of days before."

"She promised me she wouldn't go out with a soul."

"Ah, but with a merry twinkle in her eye, no doubt? I mean to say, you can't expect a girl nowadays to treat a promise like that seriously. I mean, dash it, be reasonable!"

"And with that little worm of all people!"

Hugo cleared his throat. He was conscious of a slight embarrassment. He had not wished to touch on this aspect of the affair, but Ronnie's last words gave a Carmody and a gentleman no choice.

"As a matter of fact, Ronnie, old man," he said, "you are wrong in supposing that she went to Mario's with the above Pilbeam. She went with me. Blameless Hugo, what. I mean, more like a brother than anything."

Ronnie declined to be comforted.

"I don't believe you."

"My dear chap!"

"I suppose you think you're damned clever, trying to smooth things over. She was at Mario's with Pilbeam."

"I took her there."

"You may have taken her, but she was dining with Pilbeam."

"Nothing of the kind."

"Do you think I can't believe my own eyes? It's no use your saying anything, Hugo, I'm through with her. She's let me down. Less than a week I've been away," said Ronnie, his voice trembling, "and she lets me down. Well, it serves me right for being such a fool as to think she ever cared a curse for me."

He relapsed into silence. And Hugo, after turning over in his mind a few specimen remarks, decided not to make them. The cab drew up before the hotel, and Ronnie, getting out, uttered a wordless exclamation.

"No, let me," said Hugo considerately. A bit rough on a man, he felt, after coughing up five quid to the hellhounds of the law, to be expected to pay the cab. He produced money and turned to the driver. It was some moments before he turned back again, for the driver, by the rules of the taxi chauffeurs' union, kept his petty cash tucked into his underclothing. When he did so he was considerably astonished to find that Ronnie, while his back was turned, had in some unaccountable manner become Sue. The changeling was staring unhappily at him from the exact spot where he had left his old friend.

"Hullo!" he said.

"Ronnie's gone," said Sue.

"Gone?"

"Yes. He walked off as quick as he could round the corner when he saw me. He—" Sue's voice broke—"he didn't say a word."

"How did you get here?" asked Hugo. There were other matters, of course, to be discussed later, but he felt he must get this point cleared up first.

"I thought you would bring him back to your hotel, and I thought that if I could see him I could—say something."

Hugo was alarmed. He was now practically certain that this

girl was going to cry, and if there was one thing he disliked it was being with crying girls in a public spot. He would not readily forget the time when a female named Yvonne Something had given way to a sudden twinge of neuralgia in his company not far from Piccadilly Circus and an old lady had stopped and said that it was brutes like him who caused all the misery in the world.

"Come inside," he urged quickly. "Come and have a cocktail or a cup of tea or a bun or something. I say," he said, as he led the way into the hotel lobby and found two seats in a distant corner, "I'm frightfully sorry about all this. I can't help feeling it's my fault."

"Oh, no."

"If I hadn't asked you to dinner—"

"It isn't that that's the trouble. Ronnie might have been a little cross for a minute or two if he had found you and me together, but he would soon have got over it. It was finding me with that horrid little man Pilbeam. You see, I told him—and it was quite true—that I didn't know him."

"Yes, so he was saying to me in the cab."

"Did he—what did he say?"

"Well, he plainly resented the Pilbeam, I'm afraid. His manner, when touching on the Pilbeam, was austere. I tried to drive into his head that that was just an accidental meeting and that you had come to Mario's with me, but he would have none of it. I fear, old thing, there's nothing to be done but leave the whole binge to Time, the Great Healer."

A page boy was making a tour of the lobby. He seemed to be seeking a Mr. Gargery.

"If only I could get hold of him and make him listen. I haven't been given a chance to explain."

"You think you could explain, even if given a chance?"

"I could try. Surely he couldn't help seeing that I really loved him if we had a real talk?"

"And the trouble is you're here and he'll be back at Blandings in a few hours. Difficult," said Hugo, shaking his head. "Complex."

"Mr. Carmody," chanted the page boy, coming nearer. "Mr. Carmody."

101

"Hi!" cried Hugo.

"Mr. Carmody? Wanted on the telephone, sir."

Hugo's face became devout and saintlike.

"Awfully sorry to leave you for an instant," he said, "but do you mind if I rush? It must be Millicent. She's the only person who knows I'm here."

He sped away, and Sue, watching him, found herself choking with sudden tears. It seemed to emphasize her forlornness so, this untimely evidence of another love story that had not gone awry. She seemed to be listening to that telephone conversation, hearing Hugo's delighted yelps as the voice of the girl he loved floated to him over the wire.

She pulled herself together. Beastly of her to be jealous of Hugo just because he was happy. . . .

Sue sat up abruptly. She had had an idea.

It was a breath-taking idea, but simple. It called for courage, for audacity, for a reckless disregard of consequences, but nevertheless it was simple.

"Hugo," she cried, as that lucky young man returned and dropped into the chair at her side. "Hugo, listen!"

"I say," said Hugo.

"I've suddenly thought—"

"I say," said Hugo.

"Do listen!"

"I say," said Hugo, "that was Millicent on the 'phone."

"Was it? How nice. Listen, Hugo."

"Speaking from Blandings."

"Yes. But—"

"And she has broken off the engagement!"

"What!"

"Broken off the bally engagement," repeated Hugo. He signalled urgently to a passing waiter. "Get me a brandy-and-soda, will you?" he said. His face was pale and set. "A stiffish brandy-and-soda, please."

"Brandy-and-soda, sir?"

"Yes," said Hugo. "Stiffish."

102

6

SUE STARED at him, bewildered.

"Broken off the engagement?"

"Broken off the engagement."

In moments of stress the foolish question is always the one that comes uppermost in the mind.

"Are you sure?"

Hugo emitted a sound which resembled the bursting of a paper bag. He would have said himself, if asked, that he was laughing mirthlessly.

"Sure? Not much doubt about it."

"But why?"

"She knows all."

"All what?"

"Everything, you poor fish," said Hugo, forgetting in a strong man's agony the polish of the Carmodys. "She's found out that I took you to dinner last night."

"What!"

"She has."

"But how?"

The paper bag exploded again. A look of intense bitterness came into Hugo's face.

"If ever I meet that slimy, slinking, marcelle-waved by-product Pilbeam again," he said, "let him commend his soul to God! If he has time," he added.

He took the brandy-and-soda from the waiter and eyed Sue dully.

"Anything on similar lines for you?"

"No, thanks."

"Just as you like. It's not easy for a man in my position to realize," said Hugo drinking deeply, "that refusing a brandy-and-soda is possible. I shouldn't have said, offhand, that it could be done."

Sue was a warm-hearted girl. In the tragedy of this announcement she had almost forgotten that she had troubles herself.

"Tell me all about it, Hugo."

He put down the empty glass.

"I came up from Blandings yesterday," he said, "to interview the Argus Enquiry Agency on the subject of sending a man down to investigate the theft of Lord Emsworth's pig."

Sue would have liked to hear more about this pig, but she knew that this was no time for questions.

"I went to the Argus and saw this wen Pilbeam, who runs it."

Again Sue would have liked to speak. Once more she refrained. She felt as if she were at a sick-bed, hearing a dying man's last words. On such occasions one does not interrupt.

"Meanwhile," proceeded Hugo tonelessly, "Millicent, suspecting—and I am surprised at her having a mind like that; I always looked on her as a pure, white soul—suspecting that I might be up to something in London, got the Argus on the long-distance telephone and told them to follow my movements and report to her. And, apparently, just before she called me up, she had been talking to them on the wire and getting their statement. All this she revealed to me in short, burning sentences, and then she said that if I thought we were still engaged I could have three more guesses. But, to save me trouble, she would tell me the right answer—viz.: No wedding bells for me. And to think," said Hugo, picking up the glass and putting it down again, after inspection, with a hurt and disappointed look, "that I actually rallied this growth Pilbeam on the subject of following people and reporting on their movements. Yes, I assure you. Rallied him blithely. Just as I was leaving his office we kidded merrily back and forth. And then I went out into the world, happy and carefree, little knowing that my every step was dogged by a blasted bloodhound. Well, all I can say is that, if Ronnie wants this Pilbeam's gore, and I gather that he does, he will jolly well have to wait till I've helped myself."

Sue, womanlike, blamed the woman.

104

"I don't think Millicent can be a very nice girl," she said primly.

"An angel," said Hugo. "Always was. Celebrated for it. I don't blame her."

"I do."

"I don't."

"I do."

"Well, have it your own way," said Hugo handsomely. He beckoned to the waiter. "Another of the same, please."

"This settles it," said Sue.

Her eyes were sparkling. Her chin had a resolute tilt.

"Settles what?"

"While you were at the telephone, I had an idea."

"I have had ideas in my time," said Hugo. "Many of them. At the moment I have but one. To get within arm's length of the yam Pilbeam and twist his greasy neck till it comes apart in my hands. 'What do you do here?' I said. 'Measure footprints?' 'We follow people and report on their movements,' said he. 'Ha-ha!' I laughed carelessly. 'Ha-ha!' laughed he. General mirth and jollity. And all the while—"

"Hugo, will you listen?"

"And this is the bitter thought that now strikes me. What chance have I of scooping out the man's inside with my bare hands? I've got to go back to Blandings on the two-fifteen or I lose my job. Leaving him unscathed in his bally lair, chuckling over my downfall and following some other poor devil's movements."

"Hugo!"

The broken man passed a weary hand over his forehead.

"You spoke?"

"I've been speaking for the last ten minutes, only you won't listen."

"Say on," said Hugo listlessly, starting on the second restorative.

"Have you ever heard of a Miss Schoonmaker?"

"I seem to know the name. Who is she?"

"Me."

Hugo lowered his glass, pained.

"Don't talk drip to a broken-hearted man," he begged. "What do you mean?"

105

"When Ronnie was driving me in his car we met Lady Constance Keeble."

"A blister," said Hugo. "Always was. Generally admitted all over Shropshire."

"She thought I was this Miss Schoonmaker."

"Why?"

"Because Ronnie said I was."

Hugo sighed hopelessly.

"Complex. Complex. My God. How complex!"

"It was quite simple and natural. Ronnie had just been telling me about this girl—how he had met her at Biarritz and that she was coming to Blandings, and so on, and when he saw Lady Constance looking at me with frightful suspicion it suddenly occurred to him to say that I was her."

"That you were Lady Constance?"

"No, idiot. Miss Schoonmaker. And now I'm going to wire her—Lady Constance, not Miss Schoonmaker, in case you were going to ask—saying that I'm coming to Blandings right away."

"Pretending to be this Miss Schoonmaker?"

"Yes."

Hugo shook his head.

"Imposs."

"Why?"

"Absolutely out of the q."

"Why? Lady Constance is expecting me. Do be sensible."

"I'm being sensible all right. But somebody is gibbering and, naming no names, it's you. Don't you realize that, just as you reach the front door, this Miss Schoonmaker will arrive in person, dishing the whole thing?"

"No, she won't"

"Why won't she?"

"Because Ronnie sent her a telegram, in Lady Constance's name, saying that there's scarlet fever or something at Blandings and she wasn't to come."

Hugo's air of the superior critic fell from him like a garment. He sat up in his chair. So moved was he that he spilled his brandy-

and-soda and did not give it so much as a look of regret. He let it soak into the carpet unheeded.

"Sue!"

"Once I'm at Blandings I shall be able to see Ronnie and make him be sensible."

"That's right."

"And then you'll be able to tell Millicent that there couldn't have been much harm in my being out with you last night because I'm engaged to Ronnie."

"That's right, too."

"Can you see any flaws?"

"Not a flaw."

"I suppose, as a matter of fact, you'll give the whole thing away in the first five minutes by calling me Sue."

Hugo waved an arm buoyantly.

"Don't give the possibility another thought," he said. "If I do I'll cover it up adroitly by saying I mean 'Schoo.' Short for Schoonmaker. And now go and send her another telegram. Keep on sending telegrams. Leave nothing to chance. Send a dozen and pitch it strong. Say that Blandings Castle is ravaged with disease. Not merely scarlet fever. Scarlet fever *and* mumps. Not to mention housemaid's knee, diabetes, measles, shingles, and the botts. We're onto a big thing, my Susan. Let us push it along."

7

I

SUNSHINE calling to all right-thinking men to come out and revel in its heartening warmth, poured in at the windows of the great library of Blandings Castle. But to Clarence, ninth Earl of Emsworth, much as he liked sunshine as a rule, it brought no cheer. His face drawn, his pince-nez askew, his tie drooping away from its stud like a languorous lily, he sat staring sightlessly before him. He looked like something that had just been prepared for stuffing by a taxidermist.

A moralist, watching Lord Emsworth in his travail, would have reflected smugly that it cuts both ways, this business of being a peer of the realm with large private means and a good digestion. Unalloyed prosperity, he would have pointed out in his offensive way, tends to enervate: and in this world of ours, full of alarms and uncertainties, where almost anything is apt to drop suddenly on top of your head without warning at almost any moment, what one needs is to be tough and alert.

When some outstanding disaster happens to the ordinary man, it finds him prepared. Years of missing the eight-forty-five, taking the dog for a run on rainy nights, endeavouring to abate smoky chimneys, and coming down to breakfast and discovering that they have burned the bacon again, have given his soul a protective hardness, so that by the time his wife's relations arrive for a long visit he is ready for them.

Lord Emsworth had had none of this salutary training. Fate, hitherto, had seemed to spend its time thinking up ways of pampering him. He ate well, slept well, and had no money troubles. He grew the best roses in Shropshire. He had won a first prize for pumpkins at that county's agricultural show, a thing no Earl of Emsworth had ever done before. And, just previous to the point at which this chronicle opens, his younger son Frederick had married the daughter of an American millionaire and had gone to live three thousand miles away from Blandings Castle, with lots of good, deep water in between him and it. He had come to look on himself as Fate's spoiled darling.

Can we wonder, then, that in the agony of this sudden treacherous blow he felt stunned and looked eviscerated? Is it surprising that the sunshine made no appeal to him? May we not consider him justified, as he sat there, in swallowing a lump in his throat like an ostrich gulping down a brass door knob?

The answer to these questions, in the order given, is No, No, and Yes.

The door of the library opened, revealing the natty person of his brother Galahad. Lord Emsworth straightened his pince-nez and looked at him apprehensively. Knowing how little reverence there was in the Hon. Galahad's composition and how tepid was his interest in the honourable struggles for supremacy of Fat Pigs, he feared that the other was about to wound him in his bereavement with some jarring flippancy. Then his gaze softened and he was conscious of a soothing feeling of relief. There was no frivolity in his brother's face, only a gravity which became him well. The Hon. Galahad sat down, hitched up the knees of his trousers, cleared his throat, and spoke in a tone that could not have been more sympathetic or in better taste.

"Bad business, this, Clarence."

"Appalling, my dear fellow."

"What are you going to do about it?"

Lord Emsworth shrugged his shoulders hopelessly. He generally did when people asked him what he was going to do about things.

"I am at a loss," he confessed. "I do not know how to act. What young Carmody tells me has completely upset all my plans."

"Carmody?"

"I sent him to the Argus Enquiry Agency in London to engage the services of a detective. It is a firm that Sir Gregory Parsloe once mentioned to me, in the days when we were on better terms. He said, in rather a meaning way, I thought, that if ever I had any trouble of any sort that needed expert and tactful handling, these were the people to go to. I gathered that they had assisted him in some matter, the details of which he did not confide to me, and had given complete satisfaction."

"Parsloe!" said the Hon. Galahad, and sniffed.

"So I sent young Carmody to London to approach them about finding the Empress. And now he tells me that his errand proved fruitless. They were firm in their refusal to trace missing pigs."

"Just as well."

"What do you mean?"

"Save you a lot of unnecessary expense. There's no need for you to waste money employing detectives."

"I thought that possibly the trained mind—"

"I can tell you who's got the Empress. I've known it all along."

"What!"

"Certainly."

"Galahad!"

"It's as plain as the nose on your face."

Lord Emsworth felt his nose.

"Is it?" he said doubtfully.

"I've just been talking to Constance—"

"Constance?" Lord Emsworth opened his mouth feebly. "She hasn't got my pig?"

"I've just been talking to Constance," repeated the Hon. Galahad, "and she called me some very unpleasant names."

"She does, sometimes. Even as a child, I remember—"

"Most unpleasant names. A senile mischief maker, among others, and a meddling old penguin. And all because I told her that the man who had stolen Empress of Blandings was young Gregory Parsloe."

"Parsloe!"

"Parsloe. Surely it's obvious? I should have thought it would have been clear to the meanest intelligence."

From boyhood up, Lord Emsworth had possessed an intelligence about as mean as an intelligence can be without actually being placed under restraint. Nevertheless, he found his brother's theory incredible.

"Parsloe?"

"Don't keep saying 'Parsloe.'"

"But, my dear Galahad—"

"It stands to reason."

"You don't really think so?"

"Of course I think so. Have you forgotten what I told you the other day?"

"Yes," said Lord Emsworth. He always forgot what people told him the other day.

"About young Parsloe," said the Hon. Galahad impatiently. "About his nobbling my dog Towser."

Lord Emsworth started. It all came back to him. A hard expression crept into the eyes behind the pince-nez, which emotion had just jerked crooked again.

"To be sure. Towser. Your dog. I remember."

"He nobbled Towser, and he's nobbled the Empress. Dash it, Clarence, use your intelligence. Who else except young Parsloe had any interest in getting the Empress out of the way? And if he hadn't known there was some dirty work being planned would that pig man of his, Brotherhood or whatever his name is, have been going about offering three to one on Pride of Matchingham? I told you at the time it was fishy."

The evidence was damning, and yet Lord Emsworth found himself once more a prey to doubt. Of the blackness of Sir Gregory Parsloe-Parsloe's soul he had, of course, long been aware. But could the man actually be capable of the Crime of the Century. A fellow landowner? A justice of the peace? A man who grew pumpkins? A baronet?

"But, Galahad—a man in Parsloe's position . . . ?"

"What do you mean, a man in his position? Do you suppose a fellow changes his nature just because a cousin of his dies and he comes into a baronetcy? Haven't I told you a dozen times that I've known young Parsloe all his life? Known him intimately. He was always as hot as mustard and as wide as Leicester Square. Ask anyboy who used to go around town in those days. When they saw young Parsloe coming strong men winced and hid their valuables. He hadn't a penny except what he could get by tell-

111

ing the tale, and he always did himself like a prince. When I knew him first he was living down on the river at Shepperton. His old father, the Dean, had made an arrangement with the keeper of the pub there to give him breakfast and bed and nothing else. 'If he wants dinner he must earn it,' the old boy said. And do you know how he he used to earn it? He trained that mongrel of his, Banjo, to go and do tricks in front of parties that came to the place in steam launches. And then he would stroll up and hope his dog was not annoying them and stand talking till they went in to dinner and then go in with them and pick up the wine list, and before they knew what was happening he would be bursting with their champagne and cigars. That's the sort of fellow young Parsloe was."

"But even so—"

"I remember him running up to me outside that pub one afternoon—the Jolly Miller, it was called—his face shining with positive ecstasy. 'Come in, quick!' he said. 'There's a new barmaid, and she hasn't found out yet I'm not allowed credit.'"

"But, Galahad—"

"And if young Parsloe thinks I've forgotten a certain incident that occurred in the early summer of the year '95 he's very much mistaken. He met me in the Haymarket and took me into the Two Goslings for a drink—there's a hat shop now where it used to be—and after we'd had it he pulls a sort of dashed little top affair out of his pocket, a thing with numbers written round it. Said he'd found it in the street and wondered who thought of these ingenious little toys and insisted on our spinning it for half-crowns. 'You take the odd numbers, I'll take the even,' says young Parsloe. And before I could fight my way into the fresh air I was ten pounds seven and sixpence in the hole. And I discovered next morning that they make those beastly things so that if you push the stem through and spin them the wrong way up you're bound to get an even number. And when I asked him the following afternoon to show me that top again he said he'd lost it. That's the sort of fellow young Parsloe was. And you expect me to believe that inheriting a baronetcy and settling down in the country has made him so dashed pure and highminded that he wouldn't stoop to nobbling a pig."

Lord Emsworth uncoiled himself. Cumulative evidence had done its work. His eyes glittered, and he breathed stertorously.

"The scoundrel!"

"Tough nut, always was."

"What shall I do?"

"Do? Why, go to him right away and tax him."

"Tax him?"

"Yes. Look him squarely in the eye and tax him with his crime."

"I will! Immediately."

"I'll come with you."

"Look him squarely in the eye!"

"And tax him!"

"And tax him." Lord Emsworth had reached the hall and was peering agitatedly to right and left. "Where the devil's my hat? I can't find my hat. Somebody's always hiding my hat. I will not have my hats hidden."

"You don't need a hat to tax a man with stealing a pig," said the Hon. Galahad, who was well versed in the manners and rules of good society.

II

In his study at Matchingham Hall in the neighbouring village of Much Matchingham, Sir Gregory Parsloe-Parsloe sat gazing at the current number of a weekly paper. We have seen that weekly paper before. On that occasion it was in the plump hands of Beach. And, oddly enough, what had attracted Sir Gregory's attention was the very item which had interested the butler.

The Hon. Galahad Threepwood, brother of the Earl of Emsworth. A little bird tells us that "Gally" is at Blandings Castle, Shropshire, the ancestral seat of the family, busily engaged in writing his Reminiscences. As every member of the Old Brigade will testify, they ought to be as warm as the weather, if not warmer!

113

But whereas Beach, perusing this, had chuckled, Sir Gregory Parsloe-Parsloe shivered, like one who on a country ramble suddenly perceives a snake in his path.

Sir Gregory Parsloe-Parsloe of Matchingham Hall, seventh baronet of his line, was one of those men who start their lives well, skid for a while, and then slide back onto the straight and narrow path and stay there. That is to say, he had been up to the age of twenty a blameless boy and from the age of thirty-one, when he had succeeded to the title, a practically blameless bart. So much so that now, in his fifty-second year, he was on the eve of being accepted by the local Unionist Committee as their accredited candidate for the forthcoming by-election in the Bridgeford and Shifley Parliamentary Division of Shropshire.

But there had been a decade in his life, that dangerous decade of the twenties, when he had accumulated a past so substantial that a less able man would have been compelled to spread it over a far longer period. It was an epoch in his life to which he did not enjoy looking back, and years of irreproachable barthood had enabled him, as far as he personally was concerned, to bury the past. And now, it seemed, this pestilential companion of his youth was about to dig it up again.

The years had turned Sir Gregory into a man of portly habit; and, as portly men do in moments of stress, he puffed. But, puff he never so shrewdly, he could not blow away that paragraph. It was still there, looking up at him, when the door opened and the butler announced Lord Emsworth and Mr. Galahad Threepwood.

Sir Gregory's first emotion on seeing the taxing party file into the room was one of pardonable surprise. Aware of the hard feelings which George Cyril Wellbeloved's transference of his allegiance had aroused in the bosom of that gifted pig man's former employer, he had not expected to receive a morning call from the Earl of Emsworth. As for the Hon. Galahad, he had ceased to be on cordial terms with him as long ago as the winter of the year nineteen hundred and six.

Then, following quickly on the heels of surprise, came indignation. That the author of the Reminiscences should be writing scurrilous stories about him with one hand and strolling calmly into his private study with, so to speak, the other occasioned him the keenest resentment. He drew himself up and was in the very act of staring haughtily when the Hon. Galahad broke the silence.

"Young Parsloe," said the Hon. Galahad, speaking in a sharp, unpleasant voice, "your sins have found you out!"

It had been the baronet's intention to inquire to what he was indebted for the pleasure of this visit, and to inquire it icily; but at this remarkable speech the words halted on his lips.

"Eh?" he said blankly.

The Hon. Galahad was regarding him through his monocle rather as a cook eyes a black beetle on discovering it in the kitchen sink. It was a look which would have aroused pique in a slug, and once more the Squire of Matchingham's bewilderment gave way to wrath.

"What the devil do you mean?" he demanded.

"See his face?" asked the Hon. Galahad in a rasping aside.

"I'm looking at it now," said Lord Emsworth.

"Guilt written upon it."

"Plainly," agreed Lord Emsworth.

The Hon. Galahad, who had folded his arms in a menacing manner, unfolded them and struck the desk a smart blow.

"Be very careful, Parsloe! Think before you speak. And when you speak, speak the truth. I may say, by way of a start, that we know all."

How low an estimate Sir Gregory Parsloe had formed of his visitors' collective sanity was revealed by the fact that it was actually to Lord Emsworth that he now turned as the more intelligent one of the pair.

"Emsworth! Explain! What the deuce are you doing here? And what the devil is that old image talking about?"

Lord Emsworth had been watching his brother with growing admiration. The latter's spirited opening of the case for the prosecution had won his hearty approval.

"You know," he said curtly.

"I should say he dashed well does know," said the Hon. Galahad. "Parsloe, produce that pig!"

115

Sir Gregory pushed his eyes back into their sockets a split second before they would have bulged out of his head beyond recovery. He did his best to think calm, soothing thoughts. He had just remembered that he was a man who had to be careful about his blood pressure.

"Pig?"

"Pig."

"Did you say pig?"

"Pig."

"What pig?"

"He says, 'What pig?'"

"I heard him," said Lord Emsworth.

Sir Gregory Parsloe again had trouble with his eyes.

"I don't know what you are talking about."

The Hon. Galahad unfolded his arms again and smote the desk a blow that unshipped the cover of the inkpot.

"Parsloe, you sheep-faced, shambling exile from hell," he cried, "disgorge that pig immediately!"

"My Empress," added Lord Emsworth.

"Precisely. Empress of Blandings. The pig you stole last night."

Sir Gregory Parsloe-Parsloe rose slowly from his chair. The Hon. Galahad pointed an imperious finger at him, but he ignored the gesture. His blood pressure was now hovering around the hundred-and-fifty mark.

"Do you mean to tell me that you seriously accuse—"

"Parsloe, sit down!"

Sir Gregory choked.

"I always knew, Emsworth, that you were as mad as a coot."

"As a what?" whispered his lordship.

"Coot," said the Hon. Galahad curtly. "Sort of duck." He turned to the defendant again. "Vituperation will do you no good, young Parsloe. We *know* that you have stolen that pig."

"I haven't stolen any damned pig. What would I want to steal a pig for?"

The Hon. Galahad snorted.

"What did you want to nobble my dog Towser for in the back

116

room of the Black Footman in the spring of the year '97?" he said. "To queer the favourite, that's why you did it. And that's what you're after now, trying to queer the favourite again. Oh, we can see through you all right, young Parsloe. We read you like a book."

Sir Gregory had stopped worrying about his blood pressure. No amount of calm, soothing thoughts could do it any good now.

"You're crazy! Both of you. Stark staring mad."

"Parsloe, will you or will you not cough up that pig?"

"I have not got your pig."

"That is your last word, is it?"

"I haven't seen the creature."

"Why a coot?" asked Lord Emsworth, who had been brooding for some time in silence.

"Very well," said the Hon. Galahad. "If that is the attitude you propose to adopt there is no course before me but to take steps. And I'll tell you the steps I'm going to take, young Parsloe. I see now that I have been foolishly indulgent. I have allowed my kind heart to get the better of me. Often and often, when I've been sitting at my desk, I've remembered a good story that simply cried out to be put into my Reminiscences, and every time I've said to myself, 'No,' I've said, 'that would wound young Parsloe. Good as it is, I can't use it. I must respect young Parsloe's feelings.' Well, from now on there will be no more forbearance. Unless you restore that pig I shall insert in my book every dashed thing I can remember about you—starting with our first meeting, when I came into Romano's and was introduced to you while you were walking round the supper table with a soup tureen on your head and stick of celery in your hand, saying that you were a sentry outside Buckingham Palace. The world shall know you for what you are—the only man who was ever thrown out of the Café de l'Europe for trying to raise the price of a bottle of champagne by raffling his trousers at the main bar. And, what's more, I'll tell the full story of the prawns."

A sharp cry escaped Sir Gregory. His face had turned a deep magenta. In these affluent days of his middle age he always looked rather like a Regency buck who has done himself well for years

117

among the fleshpots. He now resembled a Regency buck who, in addition to being on the verge of apoplexy, has been stung in the leg by a hornet.

"I will," said the Hon. Galahad firmly. "The full, true, and complete story of the prawns, omitting nothing."

"What was the story of the prawns, my dear fellow?" asked Lord Emsworth, interested.

"Never mind. I know. And young Parsloe knows. And if Empress of Blandings is not back in her sty this afternoon, you will find it in my book."

"But I keep telling you," cried the suffering baronet, "that I know nothing whatever about your pig."

"Ha!"

"I've not seen the animal since last year's agricultural show."

"Ho!"

"I didn't know it had disappeared till you told me."

The Hon. Galahad stared fixedly at him through the black-rimmed monocle. Then, with a gesture of loathing, he turned to the door.

"Come, Clarence!" he said.

"Are we going?"

"Yes," said the Hon. Galahad with quiet dignity. "There is nothing more that we can do here. Let us get away from this house before it is struck by a thunderbolt."

III

The gentlemanly office boy who sat in the outer room of the Argus Enquiry Agency read the card which the stout visitor had handed to him and gazed at the stout visitor with respect and admiration. A polished lad, he loved the aristocracy. He tapped on the door of the inner office.

"A gentleman to see me?" asked Percy Pilbeam.

"A *baronet* to see you, sir," corrected the office boy. "Sir Gregory Parsloe-Parsloe, Matchingham Hall, Salop."

"Show him in immediately," said Pilbeam with enthusiasm.

He rose and pulled down the lapels of his coat. Things he felt,

118

were looking up. He remembered Sir Gregory Parsloe. One of his first cases. He had been able to recover for him some letters which had fallen into the wrong hands. He wondered, as he heard the footsteps outside, if his client had been indulging in correspondence again.

From the baronet's sandbagged expression as he entered such might well have been the case. It is the fate of Sir Gregory Parsloe-Parsloe to come into this chronicle puffing and looking purple. He puffed and looked purple now.

"I have called to see you, Mr. Pilbeam," he said, after the preliminary civilities had been exchanged and he had lowered his impressive bulk into a chair, "because I am in a position of serious difficulty."

"I am sorry to hear that, Sir Gregory."

"And because I remember with what discretion and resource you once acted on my behalf."

Pilbeam glanced at the door. It was closed. He was now convinced that his visitor's little trouble was the same as on that previous occasion, and he looked at the indefatigable man with frank astonishment. Didn't these old bucks, he was asking himself, ever stop writing compromising letters? You would have thought they would get writer's cramp.

"If there is any way in which I can assist you, Sir Gregory . . . Perhaps you will tell me the facts from the beginning?"

"The beginning?" Sir Gregory pondered. "Well, let me put it this way. At one time, Mr. Pilbeam, I was younger than I am to-day."

"Quite."

"Poorer."

"No doubt."

"And less respectable. And during that period of my life I unfortunately went about a good deal with a man named Threepwood."

"Galahad Threepwood?"

"You know him?" said Sir Gregory, surprised.

Pilbeam chuckled reminiscently.

"I know his name. I wrote an article about him once, when

119

I was editing a paper called *Society Spice*. Number One of the Thriftless Aristocrats series. The snappiest thing I ever did in my life. They tell me he called twice at the office with a horse-whip, wanting to see me."

Sir Gregory exhibited concern.

"You have met him, then?"

"I have not. You are probably not familiar with the inner workings of a paper like *Society Spice*, Sir Gregory, but I may tell you that it is foreign to the editorial policy ever to meet visitors who call with horsewhips."

"Would he have heard your name?"

"No. There was a very strict rule in the *Spice* office that the names of the editorial staff were not to be divulged."

"Ah!" said Sir Gregory, relieved.

His relief gave place to indignation. There was an inconsistency about the Hon. Galahad's behaviour which revolted him.

"He cut up rough, did he, because you wrote things about him in your paper? And yet he doesn't seem to mind writing things himself about other people, damn him. That's quite another matter. A different thing altogether. Oh, yes!"

"Does he write? I didn't know."

"He's writing his Reminiscences at this very moment. He's down at Blandings Castle, finishing them now. And the book's going to be full of stories about me. That's why I've come to see you. Dashed, infernal, damaging stories, which'll ruin my reputation in the county. There's one about some prawns—"

Words failed Sir Gregory. He sat puffing. Pilbeam nodded gravely. He understood the position now. As to what his client expected him to do about it, however, he remained hazy.

"But if these stories you speak of are libellous—"

"What has that got to do with it? They're true."

"The greater the truth, the greater the—"

"Oh, I know all about that," interrupted Sir Gregory impatiently. "And a lot of help it's going to be to me. A jury could give me the heaviest damages on record and it wouldn't do me a bit of good. What about my reputation in the county? What about know-

120

ing that every damned fool I met was laughing at me behind my back? What about the Unionist Committee? I may tell you, Mr. Pilbeam, apart from any other consideration, that I am on the point of being accepted by our local Unionist Committee as their candidate at the next election. And if that old pest's book is published they will drop me like a hot coal. Now do you understand?"

Pilbeam picked up a pen, and with it scratched his chin thoughtfully. He liked to take an optimistic view with regard to his clients' affairs, but he could not conceal from himself that Sir Gregory appeared to be out of luck.

"He is determined to publish this book?"

"It's the only object he's got in life, the miserable old fossil."

"And he is resolved to include the stories?"

"He called on me this morning expressly to tell me so. And I caught the next train to London to put the matter in your hands."

Pilbeam scratched his left cheek bone.

"H'm!" he said. "Well, in the circumstances, I really don't see what is to be done except—"

"—Get hold of the manuscript and destroy it, you were about to say? Exactly. That's precisely what I've come to ask you to do for me."

Pilbeam opened his mouth, startled. He had not been about to say anything of the kind. What he had been intending to remark was that, the situation being as described, there appeared no course to pursue but to fold the hands, set the teeth, and await the inevitable disaster like a man and a Briton. He gazed blankly at this lawless bart. Baronets are proverbially bad, but surely, felt Percy Pilbeam, there was no excuse for them to be as bad as all that.

"Steal the manuscript?"

"Only possible way."

"But that's rather a tall order, isn't it, Sir Gregory?"

"Not," replied the baronet ingratiatingly, "for a clever young fellow like you."

The flattery left Pilbeam cold. His distant, unenthusiastic manner underwent no change. However clever a man is, he was thinking, he cannot very well abstract the manuscript of a book of Reminiscences from a house unless he is first able to enter that house.

"How could I get into the place?"

"I should have thought you would have found a dozen ways."

"Not even one," Pilbeam assured him.

"Look how you recovered those letters of mine."

"That was easy."

"You told them you had come to inspect the gas meter."

"I could scarcely go to Blandings Castle and say I had come to inspect the gas meter and hope to be invited to make a long visit on the strength of it. You do not appear to realize, Sir Gregory, that the undertaking you suggest would not be a matter of a few minutes. I might have to remain in the house for quite a considerable time."

Sir Gregory found his companion's attitude damping. He was a man who, since his accession to the baronetcy and its accompanying wealth, had grown accustomed to seeing people jump smartly to it when he issued instructions. He became peevish.

"Why couldn't you go there as a butler or something?"

Percy Pilbeam's only reply to this was a tolerant smile. He raised the pen and scratched his head with it.

"Scarcely feasible," he said. And again that rather pitying smile flitted across his face.

The sight of it brought Sir Gregory to the boil. He felt an irresistible desire to say something to wipe it away. It reminded him of the smiles he had seen on the faces of bookmakers in his younger days when he had suggested backing horses with them on credit and in a spirit of mutual trust.

"Well, have it your own way," he snapped. "But it may interest you to know that to get that manuscript into my possession I am willing to pay a thousand pounds."

It did, as he had foreseen, interest Pilbeam extremely. So much so that in his emotion he jerked the pen wildly, inflicting a nasty scalp wound.

"A thuth?" he stammered.

Sir Gregory, a prudent man in money matters, perceived that he had allowed his sense of the dramatic to carry him away.

"Well, five hundred," he said, rather quickly. "And five hundred pounds is a lot of money, Mr. Pilbeam."

The point was one which he had no need to stress. Percy Pilbeam had grasped it without assistance, and his face grew wan with thought. The day might come when the proprietor of the Argus Enquiry Agency would remain unmoved by the prospect of adding five hundred pounds to his bank balance, but it had not come yet.

"A check for five hundred the moment that old weasel's manuscript is in my hands," said Sir Gregory insinuatingly.

Nature had so arranged it that in no circumstances could Percy Pilbeam's face ever become really beautiful; but at this moment there stole into it an expression which did do something to relieve, to a certain extent, its normal unpleasantness. It was an expression of rapture, of joy, of almost beatific happiness—the look, in short, of a man who sees his way clear to laying his hands on five hundred pounds.

There is about the mention of any substantial sum of money something that seems to exercise a quickening effect on the human intelligence. A moment before Pilbeam's mind had been an inert mass. Now, abruptly, it began to function like a dynamo.

Get into Blandings Castle? Why, of course he could get into Blandings Castle. And not sneak in, either, with a trousers seat itching in apprehension of the kick that should send him out again, but bowl proudly up to the front door in his two-seater and hand his suitcase to the butler and be welcomed as the honoured guest. Until now he had forgotten, for he had deliberately set himself to forget, the outrageous suggestion of that young idiot whose name escaped him that he should come to Blandings and hunt about for lost pigs. It had wounded his self-respect so deeply at the time that he had driven it from his thoughts. When he had found himself thinking about Hugo he had immediately pulled himself together and started thinking about something else. Now it all came back to him. And Hugo's parting words, he recalled, had been that if ever he changed his mind the commission would still be open.

"I will take this case, Sir Gregory," he said.

"Woof?"

"You may rely on my being at Blandings Castle by to-morrow evening at the latest. I have thought of a way of getting there."

He rose from his desk and paced the room with knitted brows. That agile brain had begun to work under its own steam. He paused once to look in a distrait manner out of the window, and when Sir Gregory cleared his throat to speak, jerked an impatient shoulder at him. He could not have baronets, even with hyphens in their names, interrupting him at a moment like this.

"Sir Gregory," he said at length, "the great thing in matters like this is to be prepared with a plan. I have a plan."

"Woof!" said Sir Gregory.

This time he meant that he had thought all along that his companion would get one after pacing like that.

"When you arrive home I want you to invite Mr. Galahad Threepwood to dinner to-morrow night."

The baronet shook like a jelly. Wrath and amazement fought within him. Ask the man to dinner? After what had occured?

"As many others of the Blandings Castle party as you think fit, of course, but Mr. Threepwood without fail. Once he is out of the house my path will be clear."

Wrath and amazement died away. The baronet had grasped the idea. The beauty and simplicity of the stratagem stirred his admiration. But was it not, he felt, a simpler matter to issue such an invitation than to get it accepted? A vivid picture rose before his eyes of the Hon. Galahad as he had last seen him.

Then there came to him the blessed, healing thought of Lady Constance Keeble. He would send the invitation to her and—yes, dash it!—he would tell her the full facts, put his cards on the table, and trust to her sympathy and proper feeling to enlist her in the cause. He had long been aware that her attitude towards the Reminiscences resembled his own. He could rely on her to help him. He could also rely on her somehow—by what strange feminine modes of coercion he, being a bachelor, could only guess at—to deliver the Hon. Galahad Threepwood at Matchingham Hall in time for dinner. Women, he knew, had this strange power over their near relations.

"Splendid!" he said. "Excellent! Capital. Woof! I'll see it's done."

"Then you can leave the rest to me."

"You think, if I can get him out of the house, you will be able to secure the manuscript?"

"Certainly."

Sir Gregory rose and extended a trembling hand.

"Mr. Pilbeam," he said, with deep feeling, "coming to see you was the wisest thing I ever did in my life."

"Quite," said Percy Pilbeam.

8

HAVING reread the half-dozen pages which he had written since luncheon, the Hon. Galahad Threepwood attached them with a brass paper fastener to the main body of his monumental work and placed the manuscript in its drawer—lovingly, like a young mother putting her first born to bed. The day's work was done. Rising from the desk, he yawned and stretched himself.

He was ink stained but cheerful. Happiness, as solid thinkers have often pointed out, comes from giving pleasure to others; and the little anecdote that he had just committed to paper would, he knew, give great pleasure to a considerable number of his fellow men. All over England they would be rolling out of their seats when they read it. True, their enjoyment might possibly not be shared to its fullest extent by Sir Gregory Parsloe-Parsloe of Matchingham Hall, for what the Hon. Galahad had just written was the story of the prawns: but the first lesson an author has to learn is that he cannot please everybody.

He left the small library which he had commandeered as a private study and, descending the broad staircase, observed Beach in the hall below. The butler was standing mountainously beside the tea table, staring in a sort of trance at a platefull of anchovy sandwiches; and it struck the Hon. Galahad, not for the first time in the last few days, that he appeared to have something on his mind. A strained, haunted look he seemed to have, as if he had done a murder and was afraid somebody was going to find the body. A more practised physiognomist would have been able to interpret that look. It was the one that butlers always wear when they have allowed themselves to be persuaded against their better judgment into becoming accessories before the fact in the theft of their employers' pigs.

"Beach," he said, speaking over the banisters, for he had just remembered that there was a question he wanted to ask the man about the somewhat eccentric Major General Magnus in whose employment he had once been.

"What's the matter with you?" he added with some irritation. For the butler, jerked from his reverie, had jumped a couple of inches and shaken all over in a manner that was most trying to watch. A butler, felt the Hon. Galahad, is a butler, and a startled fawn is a startled fawn. He disliked the blend of the two in a single body.

"Why on earth do you spring like that when anyone speaks to you? I've noticed it before. He leaps," he said complainingly to his niece Millicent, who now came down the stairs with slow, listless steps; "when addressed he quivers like a harpooned whale."

"Oh?" said Millicent dully. She had drooped into a chair and picked up a book. She looked like something that might have occurred to Ibsen in one of his less frivolous moments.

"I am extremely sorry, Mr. Galahad."

"No use being sorry. Thing is not to do it. If you are practising the shimmy for the servants' ball be advised by an old friend and give it up. You haven't the build."

"I think I may have caught a chill, sir."

"Take a stiff whisky toddy. Put you right in no time. What's the car doing out there?"

"Her ladyship ordered it, sir. I understand that she and Mr. Baxter are going to Market Blandings to meet the train arriving at four-forty."

"Somebody expected?"

"The American young lady, sir, Miss Schoonmaker."

"Of course, yes. I remember. She arrives to-day, does she?"

"Yes, sir."

"Schoonmaker. I used to know old Johnny Schoonmaker well. A great fellow. Mixed the finest mint juleps in America. Have you ever tasted a mint julep, Beach?"

"Not to my recollection, sir."

"Oh, you'd remember all right if you had. Insidious things. They creep up to you like a baby sister and slide their little hands into yours, and the next thing you know the judge is telling you to pay the clerk of the court fifty dollars. Seen Lord Emsworth anywhere?"

"His lordship is at the telephone, sir."

"Don't do it, I tell you!" said the Hon. Galahad petulantly. For once again the butler had been affected by what appeared to be a kind of palsy.

"I beg your pardon, Mr. Galahad. It was something I was suddenly reminded of. There was a gentleman just after luncheon who desired to communicate with you on the telephone. I understood him to say that he was speaking from Oxford, being on his way from London to Blackpool in his automobile. Knowing that you were occupied with your literary work I refrained from disturbing you. And till I mentioned the word 'telephone' the matter slipped my mind."

"Who was he?"

"I did not get the gentleman's name sir. The wire was faulty. But he desired me to inform you that his business had to do with a dramatic entertainment."

"A play?"

"Yes, sir," said Beach, plainly impressed by this happy way of putting it. "I took the liberty of advising him that you might be able to see him later in the afternoon. He said that he would call after tea."

The butler passed from the hall with heavy haunted steps and the Hon. Galahad turned to his niece.

"I know who it is," he said. "He wrote to me yesterday. It's a theatrical manager fellow I used to go about with years ago. Man named Mason. He's got a play, adapted from the French, and he's had the idea of changing it into the period of the 'nineties and getting me to put my name to it."

"Oh?"

"On the strength of my book coming out at the same time. Not a bad notion, either. Galahad Threepwood's a name that's going to have box-office value pretty soon. The house'll be sold out for weeks to all the old buffers who'll come flocking up to London to see if I've put anything about them into it."

"Oh?" said Millicent.

The Hon. Galahad frowned. He sensed a lack of interest and sympathy.

"What's the matter with you?" he demanded.

"Nothing."

"Then why are you looking like that?"

"Like what?"

"Pale and tragic, as if you'd just gone into Tattersall's and met a bookie you owed money to."

"I am perfectly happy."

The Hon. Galahad snorted.

"Yes, radiant. I've seen fogs that were cheerier. What's that book you're reading?"

"It belongs to Aunt Constance." Millicent glanced wanly at the cover. "It seems to be about theosophy."

"Theosophy! Fancy a young girl in the springtime of life . . . What the devil has happened to everybody in this house? There's some excuse, perhaps, for Clarence. If you admit the possibility of a sane man getting so attached to a beastly pig he has a right to be upset. But what's wrong with all the rest of you? Ronald! Goes about behaving like a bereaved tomato. Beach! Springs up and down when you speak to him. And that young fellow Carmody—"

"I am not interested in Mr. Carmody."

"This morning," said the Hon. Galahad, aggrieved, "I told that boy one of the most humorous limericks I ever heard in my life—about an Old Man of—however, that is neither here nor there—and he just gaped at me with his jaw dropping, like a spavined horse looking over a fence. There are mysteries afoot in this house, and I don't like 'em. The atmosphere of Blandings Castle has changed all of a sudden from that of a normal, happy English home into something Edgar Allan Poe might have written on a rainy Sunday. It's getting on my nerves. Let's hope this girl of Johnny Schoonmaker's will cheer us up. If she's anything like her father she ought to be a nice lively girl. But I suppose, when she arrives, it'll turn out that she's in mourning for a great-aunt or brooding over the situation in Russia or something. I don't know what young people are coming to nowadays. Gloomy. Introspective. The old gay spirit seems to have died out altogether. In my young days a girl of your age would have been upstairs making an apple-pie bed for somebody instead of lolling on chairs reading books about theosophy."

Snorting once more, the Hon. Galahad disappeared into the smoking room, and Millicent, tight lipped, returned to her book. She had been reading for some minutes when she became aware of a long, limp, drooping figure at her side.

"Hullo," said Hugo, for this ruin of a fine young man was he.

Millicent's ear twitched, but she did not reply.

"Reading?" said Hugo.

He had been standing on his left leg. With a sudden change of policy he now shifted and stood on his right.

"Interesting book?"

Millicent looked up.

"I beg your pardon?"

"Only said—is that an interesting book?"

"Very," said Millicent.

Hugo decided that his right leg was not a success. He stood on his left again.

"What's it about?"

"Transmigration of souls."

"A thing I'm not very well up on."

"One of the many, I should imagine," said the haughty girl. "Every day you seem to know less and less about more and more." She rose and made for the stairs. Her manner suggested that she was disappointed in the hall of Blandings Castle. She had supposed it a nice place for a girl to sit and study the best literature, and now, it appeared, it was overrun by the underworld. "If you're really anxious to know what 'transmigration' means, it's simply that some people believe that when you die your soul goes into something else."

"Rum idea," said Hugo, becoming more buoyant. He began to draw hope from her chattiness. She had not said as many consecutive words as this to him for quite a time. "Into something

130

else, eh? Odd notion. What do you suppose made them think of that?"

"Yours, for instance, would probably go into a pig. And then I would come along and look into your sty, and I'd say, 'Good gracious! Why, there's Hugo Carmody. He hasn't changed a bit!'"

The spirit of the Carmodys had been a good deal crushed by recent happenings, but at this it flickered into feeble life.

"I call that a beastly thing to say."

"Do you?"

"Yes, I do."

"I oughtn't to have said it?"

"No, you oughtn't."

"Well, I wouldn't have if I could have thought of anything worse."

"And when you let a little thing like what happened the other night rot up a great love like ours, I—well, I call it a bit rotten. You know perfectly well that you're the only girl in the world I ever—"

"Shall I tell you something?"

"What?"

"You make me sick."

Hugo breathed passionately through his nose.

"So all is over, is it?"

"You can jolly well bet all is over. And if you're interested in my future plans I may mention I intend to marry the first man who comes along and asks me. And you can be a page at the wedding if you like. You couldn't look any sillier than you do now, even in a frilly shirt and satin kickerbockers."

Hugo laughed raspingly.

"Is that so?"

"It is."

"And once you said there wasn't another man like me in the world."

"Well, I should hate to think there was," said Millicent. And as the celebrated James-Thomas-Beach procession had entered with cakes and gate-leg tables and her last word seemed about

131

as good a last word as a girl might reasonably consider herself entitled to, she passed proudly up the stairs.

James withdrew. Thomas withdrew. Beach remained gazing with a hypnotized eye at the cake.

"Beach!" said Hugo.

"Sir?"

"Curse all women!"

"Very good, sir," said Beach.

He watched the young man disappear through the open front door, heard his footsteps crunch on the gravel, and gave himself up to meditation again. How gladly, he was thinking, if it not been for upsetting Mr. Ronald's plans, would he have breathed in his employer's ear as he filled his glass at dinner, "The pig is in the gamekeeper's cottage in the west wood, your lordship. Thank you, your lordship." But it was not to be. His face twisted, as if with sudden pain, and he was aware of the Hon. Galahad emerging from the smoking room.

"Just remembered something I wanted to ask you, Beach. You were with old General Magnus, weren't you, some years ago, before you came here?"

"Yes, Mr. Galahad."

"Then perhaps you can tell me the exact facts about that trouble in 1912. I know the old chap chased young Mandeville three times round the lawn in his pajamas, but did he merely try to stab him with the bread knife or did he actually get home?"

"I could not say, sir. He did not honour me with his confidence."

"Infernal nuisance," said the Hon. Galahad. "I like to get these things right."

He eyed the butler discontentedly as he retired. More than ever was he convinced that the fellow had something on his mind. The very way he walked showed it. He was about to return to the smoking room when his brother Clarence came into the hall. And there was in Lord Emsworth's bearing so strange a gaiety that he stood transfixed. It seemed to the Hon. Galahad years since he had seen anyone looking cheerful in Blandings Castle.

"Good God, Clarence! What's happened?"

"What, my dear fellow?"

132

"You're wreathed in smiles, dash it, and skipping like the high hills. Found that pig under the drawing-room sofa or something?"

Lord Emsworth beamed.

"I have had the most cheering piece of news, Galahad. That detective—the one I sent young Carmody to see—the Argus man, you know—he has come after all. He drove down in his car and is at this moment in Market Blandings, at the Emsworth Arms. I have been speaking to him on the telephone. He rang up to ask if I still required his services."

"Well, you don't."

"Certainly I do, Galahad. I consider his presence vital."

"He can't tell you any more than you know already. There's only one man who can have stolen that pig, and that's young Parsloe."

"Precisely. Yes. Quite true. But this man will be able to collect evidence and bring the thing home and—er—bring it home. He has the trained mind. I consider it most important that the case should be in the hands of a man with a trained mind. We should be seeing him very shortly. He is having what he describes as a bit of a snack at the Emsworth Arms. When he has finished he will drive over. I am delighted. Ah, Constance, my dear."

Lady Constance Keeble, attended by the Efficient Baxter, had appeared at the foot of the stairs. His lordship eyed her a little warily. The chatelaine of Blandings was apt sometimes to react unpleasantly to the information that visitors not invited by herself were expected at the castle.

"Constance, my dear, a friend of mine is arriving this evening to spend a few days. I forgot to tell you."

"Well, we have plently of room for him," replied Lady Constance, with surprising amiability. "There is something I forgot to tell you, too. We are dining at Matchingham to-night."

"Matchingham?" Lord Emsworth was puzzled. He could think of no one who lived in the village of Matchingham except Sir Gregory Parsloe-Parsloe. "With whom?"

"Sir Gregory, of course. Who else do you suppose it could be?"

"What?"

"I had a note from him after luncheon. It is short notice, of course, but that doesn't matter in the country. He took it for granted that we would not be engaged."

"Constance!" Lord Emsworth swelled slightly. "Constance, I will not—dash it, I will not—dine with that man. And that's final."

Lady Constance smiled a sort of lion tamer's smile. She had foreseen a reaction of this kind. She had expected sales resistance and was prepared to cope with it. Not readily, she knew, would her brother become Parsloe-conscious.

"Please do not be absurd, Clarence. I thought you would say that. I have already accepted for you, Galahad, myself, and Millicent. You may as well understand at once that I do not intend to be on bad terms with our nearest neighbour, even if a hundred of your pig men leave you and go to him. Your attitude in the matter has been perfectly childish from the very start. If Sir Gregory realizes that there has been a coolness and has most sensibly decided to make the first move toward a reconciliation, we cannot possibly refuse the overture."

"Indeed? And what about my friend? Arriving this evening."

"He can look after himself for a few hours, I should imagine."

"Abominable rudeness, he'll think it." This line of attack had occurred to Lord Emsworth quite suddenly. He found it good. Almost an inspiration, it seemed to him. "I invite my friend Pilbeam here to pay us a visit, and the moment he arrives we meet him at the front door, dash it, and say, 'Ah, here you are, Pilbeam! Well, amuse yourself, Pilbeam. We're off.' And this Miss—er—this American girl. What will she think?"

"Did you say Pilbeam?" asked the Hon. Galahad.

"It is no use talking, Clarence. Dinner is at eight. And please see that your dress clothes are nicely pressed. Ring for Beach and tell him now. Last night you looked like a scarecrow."

"Once and for all, I tell you—"

At this moment an unexpected ally took the arena on Lady Constance's side.

"Of course we must go, Clarence," said the Hon. Galahad, and Lord Emsworth, spinning round to face this flank attack, was surprised to see a swift, meaning wink come and go on his brother's face. "Nothing gained by having unpleasantness with your neighbours in the country. Always a mistake. Never pays."

"Exactly," said Lady Constance, a little dazed at finding this Saul among the prophets, but glad of the helping hand. "In the country one is quite dependent on one's neighbours."

"And young Parsloe—not such a bad chap, Clarence. Lots of good in Parsloe. We shall have a pleasant evening."

"I am relieved to find that you, at any rate, have sense, Galahad," said Lady Constance handsomely. "I will leave you to try and drive some of it into Clarence's head. Come, Mr. Baxter, we shall be late."

The sound of the car's engine had died away before Lord Emsworth's feelings found relief in speech.

"But, Galahad, my dear fellow!"

The Hon. Galahad patted his shoulder reassuringly.

"It's all right, Clarence, my boy. I know what I'm doing. I have the situation well in hand."

"Dine with Parsloe after what has occurred? After what occurred yesterday? It's impossibly. Why on earth the man is inviting us, I can't understand."

"I suppose he thinks that if he gives us a dinner I shall relent and omit the prawn story. Oh, I see Parsloe's motive all right. A clever move. Not that it'll work."

"But what do you want to go for?"

The Hon. Galahad raked the hall with a conspiratorial monocle. It appeared to be empty. Nevertheless, he looked under a settee and, going to the front door, swiftly scanned the gravel.

"Shall I tell you something, Clarence?" he said, coming back— "something that'll interest you?"

"Certainly, my dear fellow. Certainly. Most decidedly."

"Something that'll bring the sparkle to your eyes?"

"By all means. I should enjoy it."

"You know what we're going to do? To-night? After dining with Parsloe and sending Constance back in the car?"

"No."

The Hon. Galahad placed his lips to his brother's ear.

135

"We're going to steal his pig, my boy."

"What!"

"It came to me in a flash while Constance was talking. Parsloe stole the Empress. Very well, we'll steal Pride of Matchingham. Then we'll be in a position to look young Parsloe squarely in the eye and say, 'What about it?'"

Lord Emsworth swayed gently. His brain, never a strong one, had tottered perceptibly on its throne.

"Galahad!"

"Only thing to do. Reprisals. Recognized military manoeuvre."

"But how? Galahad, how can it be done?"

"Easily. If young Parsloe stole the Empress, why should we have any difficulty in stealing his animal? You show me where he keeps it, my boy, and I'll do the rest. Puffy Benger and I stole old Wivenhoe's pig at Hammers Easton in the year '95. We put it in Plug Basham's bedroom. And we'll put Parsloe's pig in a bedroom, too."

"In a bedroom?"

"Well, a sort of bedroom. Where are we to hide the animal— that's what you've been asking yourself, is it? I'll tell you. We're going to put it in that caravan that your flower-pot throwing friend Baxter arrived in. Nobody's going to think of looking there. Then we'll be in a position to talk terms to young Parsloe, and I think he will very soon see the game is up."

Lord Emsworth was looking at his brother almost devoutly. He had always known that Galahad's intelligence was superior to his own, but he had never realized it could soar to quite such lofty heights as this. It was, he supposed, the result of the life his brother had lived. He himself, sheltered through the peaceful, uneventful years at Blandings Castle, had allowed his brain to become comparatively atrophied. But Galahad, battling through these same years with hostile skittle-sharps and the sort of man that used to be a member of the old Pelican Club, had kept his clear and vigorous.

"You really think it would be feasible?"

"Trust me. By the way, Clarence, this man Pilbeam of yours. Do you know if he was ever anything except a detective?"

"I have no idea, my dear fellow. I know nothing of him. I have merely spoken to him on the telephone. Why?"

"Oh, nothing. I'll ask him when he arrives. Where are you going?"

"Into the garden."

"It's raining."

"I have my mackintosh. I really—I feel I really must walk about after what you have told me. I am in a state of considerable excitement."

"Well, work it off before you see Constance again. It won't do to have her start suspecting there's something up. If there's anything you want to ask me about you'll find me in the smoking room."

For some twenty minutes the hall of Blandings Castle remained empty. Then Beach appeared. At the same moment, from the gravel outside there came the purring of a high-powered car and the sound of voices. Beach posed himself in the doorway, looking, as he always did on these occasions, like the Spirit of Blandings welcoming the lucky guest.

137

9

LEAVE the door open, Beach," said Lady Constance.

"Very good, your ladyship."

"I think the smell of the wet earth and the flowers is so refreshing, don't you?"

The butler did not. He was not one of your fresh-air men. Rightly conjecturing, however, that the question had been addressed not to him but to the girl in the beige suit who had accompanied the speaker up the steps, he forbore to reply. He cast an appraising, bulging-eyed look at this girl and decided that she met with his approval. Smaller and slighter than the type of woman he usually admired, he found her, nevertheless, even by his own exacting standards of criticism, noticeably attractive. He liked her face and he liked the way she was dressed. Her frock was right, her shoes were right, her stockings were right, and her hat was right. As far as Beach was concerned Sue had passed the Censor.

Her demeanour pleased him, too. From the flush on her face and the sparkle in her eyes, she seemed to be taking her first entry into Blandings Castle in quite the proper spirit of reverential excitement. To be at Blandings plainly meant something to her, was an event in her life; and Beach, who after many years of residence within its walls had come to look on the Castle as a piece of personal property, felt flattered and gratified.

"I don't think this shower will last long," said Lady Constance.

"No," said Sue, smiling brightly.

"And now you must be wanting some tea after your journey."

"Yes," said Sue, smiling brightly.

It seemed to her that she had been smiling brightly for centuries. The moment she had alighted from the train and found her formidable hostess and this strangely sinister Mr. Baxter waiting to meet her on the platform, she had begun to smile brightly and had been doing it ever since.

"Usually we have tea on the lawn. It is so nice there."

"It must be."

"When the rain is over, Mr. Baxter, you must show Miss Schoonmaker the rose garden."

"I shall be delighted," said the Efficient Baxter.

He flashed gleaming spectacles in her direction, and a momentary panic gripped Sue. She feared that already this man had probed her secret. In his glance, it seemed to her, there shone suspicion.

Such, however, was not the case. It was only the combination of large spectacles and heavy eyebrows that had created the illusion. Although Rupert Baxter was a man who generally suspected everybody on principle, it so happened that he had accepted Sue without question. The glance was an admiring, almost a loving glance. It would be too much to say that Baxter had already fallen a victim to Sue's charms, but the good looks which he saw and the wealth which he had been told about were undeniably beginning to fan the hidden fire.

"My brother is a great rose grower."

"Yes, isn't he? I mean, I think roses are so lovely." The spectacles were beginning to sap Sue's morale. They seemed to be eating into her soul like some sort of corrosive acid. "How nice and old everything is here," she went on hurriedly. "What is that funny-looking gargoyle thing over there?"

What she actually referred to was a Japanese mask which hung from the wall, and it was unfortunate that the Hon. Galahad should have chosen this moment to come out of the smoking room. It made the question seem personal.

"My brother Galahad," said Lady Constance. Her voice lost some of the kindly warmth of the hostess putting the guest at her ease and took on the cold disapproval which the author of the Reminiscences always induced in her. "Galahad, this is Miss Schoonmaker."

"Really?" The Hon. Galahad trotted briskly up. "Is it? Bless my soul! Well, well, well!"

139

"How do you do?" said Sue, smiling brightly.

"How are you, my dear? I know your father intimately."

The bright smile faded. Sue had tried to plan this venture of hers carefully, looking ahead for all possible pitfalls, but that she would encounter people who knew Mr. Schoonmaker intimately she had not foreseen.

"Haven't seen him lately, of course. Let me see—must be twenty-five years since we met. Yes, quite twenty-five years."

A warm and lasting friendship was destined to spring up between Sue and the Hon. Galahad Threepwood but never in the whole course of it did she experience again quite the gush of whole-hearted affection which surged over her at these words.

"I wasn't born then," she said.

The Hon. Galahad was babbling on happily.

"A great fellow, old Johnny. You'll find some stories about him in my book. I'm writing my Reminiscences, you know. Fine sportsman, old Johnny. Great grief to him, I remember, when he broke his leg and had to go into a nursing home in the middle of the racing season. However, he made the best of it. Got the nurses interested in current form and used to make a book with them in fruit and cigarettes and things. I recollect coming to see him one day and findings him quite worried. He was a most conscientious man, with a horror of not settling up when he lost, and apparently one of the girls had had a suet dumpling on the winner of the three o'clock race at fifteen to eight, and he couldn't figure out what he had got to pay her."

Sue, laughing gratefully, was aware of a drooping presence at her side.

"My niece, Millicent," said Lady Constance. "Millicent, my dear, this is Miss Schoonmaker."

"How do you do?" said Sue, smiling brightly.

"How do you do?" said Millicent, like the silent tomb breaking its silence.

Sue regarded her with interest. So this was Hugo's Millicent. The sight of her caused Sue to wonder at the ardent nature of that young man's devotion. Millicent was pretty, but she would have thought that one of Hugo's exuberant disposition would have preferred something a little livelier.

She was startled to observe in the girl's eyes a look of surprise. In a situation as delicate as hers was, Sue had no wish to occasion surprise to anyone.

"Ronnie's friend?" asked Millicent. "The Miss Schoonmaker Ronnie met at Biarritz?"

"Yes," said Sue faintly.

"But I had the impression that you were very tall. I'm sure Ronnie told me so."

"I suppose almost anyone seems tall to that boy," said the Hon. Galahad.

Sue breathed again. She had had a return of the unpleasant feeling of being boneless which had come upon her when the Hon. Galahad had spoken of knowing Mr. Schoonmaker intimately. But though she breathed she was still shaken. Life at Blandings Castle was plainly going to be a series of shocks. She sat back with a sensation of dizziness. Baxter's spectacles seemed to her to be glittering more suspiciously than ever.

"Have you seen Ronald anywhere, Millicent?" asked Lady Constance.

"Not since lunch. I suppose he's out in the grounds somewhere."

"I saw him half an hour ago," said the Hon. Galahad. "He came mooning along under my window while I was polishing up some stuff I wrote this afternoon. I called him, but he just grunted and wandered off."

"He will be surprised to find you here," said Lady Constance, turning to Sue. "Your telegram did not arrive till after lunch, so he does not know that you were planning to come to-day. Unless you told him, Galahad."

"I didn't tell him. Never occurred to me that he knew Miss Schoonmaker. Forgot you'd met at Biarritz. What was he like then? Reasonably cheerful?"

"Yes, I think so."

"Didn't scowl and jump and gasp and quiver all over the place?"

"No."

"Then something must have happened when he went up to London. It was after he came back that I remember noticing that he seemed upset about something. Ah, the rain's stopped."

Lady Constance looked over her shoulder.

"The sky still looks very threatening," she said, "but you might be able to get out for a few minutes. Mr. Baxter," she explained, "is going to show Miss Schoonmaker the rose garden."

"No, he isn't," said the Hon. Galahad, who had been scrutinizing Sue through his monocle with growing appreciation. "I am. Old Johnny Schoonmaker's little girl—why, there are a hundred things I want to discuss."

The last thing Sue desired was to be left alone with the intimidating Baxter. She rose quickly.

"I should love to come," she said.

The prospect of discussing the intimate affairs of the Schoonmaker family was not an agreeable one, but anything was better than the society of the spectacles.

"Perhaps," said the Hon. Galahad, as he led her to the door, "you'll be able to put me right about that business of old Johnny and the mysterious woman at the New Year's Eve party. As I got the story, Johnny suddenly found this female—a perfect stranger, mind you—with her arms round his neck, telling him in a confidential undertone that she had made up her mind to go straight back to Des Moines, Iowa, and stick a knife into Fred. What he had done to win her confidence and who Fred was and whether she ever did stick a knife into him, your father hadn't found out by the time I left for home."

His voice died away, and a moment later the Efficient Baxter, starting as if a sudden thought had entered his powerful brain, rose abruptly and made quickly for the stairs.

10

I

THE ROSE garden of Blandings Castle was a famous beauty spot. Most people who visited it considered it deserving of a long and leisurely inspection. Enthusiastic horticulturists frequently went pottering and sniffing about it for hours on end. The tour through its fragrant groves personally conducted by the Hon. Galahad Threepwood lasted some six minutes.

"Well, that's what it is, you see," he said, as they emerged, waving a hand vaguely. "Roses and—er—roses, and all that sort of thing. You get the idea. And now, if you don't mind, I ought to be getting back. I want to keep in touch with the house. It slipped my mind, but I'm expecting a man to call to see me at any moment on some rather important business."

Sue was quite willing to return. She liked her companion, but she had found his company embarrassing. The subject of the Schoonmaker family history showed a tendency to bulk too largely in his conversation for comfort. Fortunately, his practice of asking a question and answering it himself and then rambling off into some anecdote of the person or persons involved had enabled her so far to avoid disaster: but there was no saying how long this happy state of things would last. She was glad of the opportunity of being alone.

Besides, Ronnie was somewhere out in these grounds. At any moment, if she went wandering through them, she might come upon him. And then, she told herself, all would be well. Surely he could not preserve his sullen hostility in the face of the fact that she had come all this way, pretending dangerously to be Miss Schoonmaker of New York, simply in order to see him?

Her companion, she found, was still talking.

"He wants to see me about a play. This book of mine is going to make a stir, you see, and he thinks that if he can get me to put my name to the play . . ."

Sue's thoughts wandered again. She gathered that the caller he was expecting had to do with the theatrical industry, and wondered for a moment if it was anyone she had ever heard of. She was not sufficiently interested to make inquires. She was too busy thinking of Ronnie.

"I shall be quite happy," she said, as the voice beside her ceased. "It's such a lovely place. I shall enjoy just wandering about by myself."

The Hon. Galahad seemed shocked at the idea.

"Wouldn't dream of leaving you alone. Clarence will look after you, and I shall be back in a few minutes."

The name seemed to Sue to strike a familiar chord. Then she remembered. Lord Emsworth. Ronnie's Uncle Clarence. The man who held Ronnie's destinies in the hollow of his hand.

"Hi! Clarence!" called the Hon. Galahad.

Sue perceived pottering toward them a long, stringy man of mild and benevolent aspect. She was conscious of something of a shock. In Ronnie's conversation the Earl of Emsworth had always appeared in the light of a sort of latter-day ogre, a man at whom the stoutest nephew might well shudder. She saw nothing formidable in this newcomer.

"Is that Lord Emsworth?" she asked, surprised.

"Yes. Clarence, this is Miss Schoonmaker."

His lordship had pottered up and was beaming amiably.

"Is it, indeed? Oh, ah, yes, to be sure. Delighted. How are you? How are you? Miss Who?"

"Schoonmaker. Daughter of my old friend Johnny Schoonmaker. You knew she was arriving. Considering that you were in the hall when Constance went to meet her—"

"Oh, yes." The cloud was passing from what, for want of a better word, must be called Lord Emsworth's mind. "Yes, yes, yes. Yes, to be sure."

"I've got to leave you to look after her for a few minutes, Clarence."

144

"Certainly, certainly."

"Take her about and show her things. I wouldn't go too far from the house, if I were you. There's a storm coming up."

"Exactly. Precisely. Yes, I will take her about and show her things. Are you fond of pigs?"

Sue had never considered this point before. Hers had been an urban life, and she could not remember ever having come into contact with a pig on what might be termed a social footing. But, remembering that this was the man whom Ronnie had described as being wrapped up in one of these animals, she smiled her bright smile.

"Oh, yes. Very."

"Mine has been stolen."

"I'm so sorry."

Lord Emsworth was visibly pleased at this womanly sympathy.

"But I now have strong hopes that she may be recovered. The trained mind is everything. What I always say—"

What is was that Lord Emsworth always said was unfortunately destined to remain unrevealed. It would probably have been something good, but the world was not to hear it; for at this moment, completely breaking his train of thought, there came from above, from the direction of the window of the small library, an odd scrabbling sound. Something shot through the air. And the next instant there appeared in the middle of a flower bed containing lobelias something that was so manifestly not a lobelia that he stared at it in stunned amazement, speech wiped from his lips as with a sponge.

It was the Efficient Baxter. He was on all fours, and seemed to be groping about for his spectacles, which had fallen off and got hidden in the undergrowth.

II

Properly considered, there is no such thing as an insoluble mystery. It may seem puzzling at first sight when ex-secretaries start falling as the gentle rain from heaven upon the lobelias beneath, but there is always a reason for it. That Baxter did not immediately give the reason was due to the fact that he had private and personal motives for not doing so.

We have called Rupert Baxter efficient, and efficient he was. The word, as we interpret it, implies not only a capacity for performing the ordinary tasks of life with a smooth firmness of touch but in addition a certain alertness of mind, a genius for opportunism, a gift for seeing clearly, thinking swiftly, and Doing It Now. With these qualities Rupert Baxter was preeminently equipped; and it had been with him the work of a moment to perceive, directly the Hon. Galahad had left the house with Sue, that here was his chance of popping upstairs, nipping into the small library, and abstracting the manuscript of the Reminiscences. Having popped and nipped, as planned, he was in the very act of searching the desk when the sound of a footstep outside froze him from his spectacles to the soles of his feet. The next moment fingers began to turn the door handle.

You may freeze a Baxter's body, but you cannot numb his active brain. With one masterful, lightning-like flash of clear thinking he took in the situation and saw the only possible way out. To reach the door leading to the large library he would have to circumnavigate the desk. The window, on the other hand, was at his elbow. So he jumped out of it.

All these things Baxter could have explained in a few words. Refraining from doing so, he rose to his feet and began to brush the mould from his knees.

"Baxter! What on earth—?"

The ex-secretary found the gaze of his late employer trying to nerves which had been considerably shaken by his fall. The occasions on which he disliked Lord Emsworth most intensely were just these occasions when the other gaped at him open-mouthed like a surprised halibut.

"I overbalanced," he said curtly.

"Overbalanced?"

"Slipped."

"Slipped?"

"Yes. Slipped."

"How? Where?"

It now occurred to Baxter that by a most fortunate chance the window of the small library was not the only one that looked out onto this arena into which he had precipitated himself. He might equally well have descended from the larger library which adjoined it.

"I was leaning out of the library window."

"Why?"

"Inhaling the air."

"What for?"

"And I lost my balance."

"Lost your balance?"

"I slipped."

"Slipped?"

Baxter had the feeling—it was one which he had often had in the old days when conversing with Lord Emsworth—that an exchange of remarks had begun which might go on forever. A keen desire swept over him to be—and that right speedily—in some other place. He did not care where it was. So long as Lord Emsworth was not there it would be Paradise enow.

"I think I will go indoors and wash my hands," he said.

"And face," suggested the Hon. Galahad.

"My face also," said Rupert Baxter coldly.

He started to move round the angle of the house, but long before he had got out of hearing Lord Emsworth's high and penetrating tenor was dealing with the situation. His lordship, as so often happened on these occasions, was under the impression that he spoke in a hushed whisper.

"Mad as a coot!" he said. And the words rang out through the still summer air like a public oration.

They cut Baxter to the quick. They were not the sort of words to which a man with an inch and a quarter of skin off his left shin bone ought ever to have been called upon to listen. With flushed ears and glowing spectacles, the Efficient Baxter passed on his way. Statistics relating to madness among coots are not to hand, but we may safely doubt whether even in the ranks of these notoriously unbalanced birds there could have been found at this moment one who was feeling half as mad as he was.

III

Lord Emsworth continued to gaze at the spot where his late secretary had passed from sight.

"Mad as a coot," he repeated.

In his brother Galahad he found a ready supporter.

"Madder," said the Hon. Galahad.

"Upon my word, I think he's actually worse than he was two years ago. Then, at least, he never fell out of windows."

"Why on earth do you have that fellow here?"

Lord Emsworth sighed.

"It's Constance, my dear Galahad. You know what she is. She insisted on inviting him."

"Well, if you take my advice you'll hide the flower pots. One of the things this fellow does when he gets these attacks," explained the Hon. Galahad, taking Sue into the family confidence, "is to go about hurling flower pots at people."

"Really?" said Sue.

"I assure you. Looking for me, Beach?"

The careworn figure of the butler had appeared, walking as one pacing behind the coffin of an old friend.

"Yes, sir. The gentleman has arrived, Mr. Galahad. I looked in the small library, thinking that you might possibly be there, but you were not."

"No, I was out here."

"Yes, sir."

"That's why you couldn't find me. Show him up to the small library, Beach, and tell him I'll be with him in a moment."

"Very good, sir."

The Hon. Galahad's temporary delay in going to see his visitor was due to his desire to linger long enough to tell Sue, to whom he had taken a warm fancy and whom he wished to shield as far as it was in his power from perils of life, what every girl ought to know about the Efficient Baxter.

"Never let yourself be alone with that fellow in a deserted spot, my dear," he counselled. "If he suggests a walk in the woods call for help. Been off his head for years. Ask Clarence."

Lord Emsworth nodded solemnly.

"And it tooks to me," went on the Hon. Galahad, "as if his mania had now taken a suicidal turn. Overbalanced, indeed! How the deuce could he have overbalanced? Flung himself out bodily, that's what he did. I couldn't think who it was he reminded me of till this moment. He's the living image of a man I used to know in the 'nineties. The first intimation any of us had that this chap had anything wrong with him was when he turned up to supper at the house of a friend of mine—George Pallant. You remember George, Clarence?—with a couple of days' beard on him. And when Mrs. George, who had known him all her life, asked him why he hadn't shaved—'Shaved?' says this fellow, surprised.—Packleby, his name was. One of the Leicestershire Packlebys.—'Shaved, dear lady?' he says. 'Well, considering that they even hide the butter knife when I come down to breakfast for fear I'll try to cut my throat with it, is it reasonable to suppose they'd trust me with a razor?' Quite stuffy about it, he was, and it spoiled the party. Look after Miss Schoonmaker, Clarence. I shan't be long."

Lord Emsworth had little experience in the art of providing diversion for young girls. Left thus to his native inspiration, he pondered a while. If the Empress had not been stolen, his task would, of course, have been simple. He could have given this Miss Schoonmaker a half hour of sheer entertainment by taking her down to the piggeries to watch the superb animal feed. As it was, he was at something of a loss.

"Perhaps you would care to see the rose garden?" he hazarded.

"I should love it," said Sue.

"Are you fond of roses?"

"Tremendously."

Lord Emsworth found himself warming to this girl. Her personality pleased him. He seemed dimly to recall something his sister Constance had said about her—something about wishing that her nephew Ronald would settle down with some nice girl with money like that Miss Schoonmaker whom Julia had met at Biarritz. Feeling so kindly toward her, it occurred to him that a word in season, opening her eyes to his nephew's true character, might prevent the girl making a mistake which she would regret forever when it was too late.

"I think you know my nephew Ronald?" he said.

"Yes."

Lord Emsworth paused to smell a rose. He gave Sue a brief biography of it before returning to the theme.

"That boy's an ass," he said.

"Why?" said Sue sharply. She began to feel less amiable toward this stringy old man. A moment before she had been thinking that it was rather charming, that funny, vague manner of his. Now she saw him clearly for what he was—a dodderer, and a Class A dodderer at that.

"Why?" His lordship considered the point. "Well, heredity, probably, I should say. His father, old Miles Fish, was the biggest fool in the Brigade of Guards." He looked at her impressively through slanting pince-nez, as if to call her attention to the fact that this was something of an achievement. "The boy throws tennis ball at pigs," he went on, getting down to the ghastly facts.

Sue was surprised. The words, if she had caught them correctly, seemed to present a side of Ronnie's character of which she had been unaware.

"Does what?"

"I saw him with my own eyes. He threw a tennis ball at Empress of Blandings. And not once but repeatedly."

The motherly instinct which all girls feel toward the men they love urged Sue to say something in Ronnie's defence. But apart from suggesting that the pig had probably started it she could not think of anything. They left the rose garden and began to walk back to the lawn, Lord Emsworth still exercised by the thought of his nephew's shortcomings. For one reason and another Ronnie had always been a source of vague annoyance to him since boyhood. There had even been times when he had felt that he would almost have preferred the society of his younger son, Frederick.

"Aggravating boy," he said. "Most aggravating. Always up to something or other. Started a night club the other day. Lost a lot of money over it. Just the sort of thing he would do. My brother Galahad started some kind of a club many years ago. It cost my old father nearly a thousand pounds, I recollect. There is something about Ronald that reminds me very much of Galahad at the same age."

Although Sue had found much in the author of the Reminiscences to attract her she was able to form a very fair estimate of the sort of young man he must have been in the middle twenties. This charge, accordingly, struck her as positively libellous.

"I don't agree with you, Lord Emsworth."

"But you never knew my brother Galahad as a young man," his lordship pointed out cleverly.

"What is the name of that hill over there?" asked Sue in a cold voice, changing the unpleasant subject.

"That hill? Oh, that one?" It was the only one in sight. "It is called the Wrekin."

"Oh?" said Sue.

"Yes," said Lord Emsworth.

"Ah," said Sue.

They had crossed the lawn and were on the broad terraces that looked out over the park. Sue leaned on the low stone wall that bordered it and gazed before her into the gathering dusk.

The castle had been built on a knoll of rising ground, and on this terrace one had the illusion of being perched up at a great height. From where she stood, Sue got a sweeping view of the park and of the dim, misty Vale of Blandings that dreamed beyond. In the park rabbits were scuttling to and fro. In the shrubberies birds called sleepily. From somewhere out across the fields there came the faint tinkling of sheep bells. The lake shone like old silver, and there was a river in the distance, dull gray between the dull green of the trees.

It was a lovely sight, age-old, orderly, and English, but it was spoiled by the sky. The sky was overcast and looked bruised. It seemed to be made of dough, and one could fancy it pressing down on the world like a heavy blanket. And it was muttering to itself. A single heavy drop of rain splashed on the stone beside Sue, and there was a low growl far away as if some powerful and unfriendly beast had spied her.

She shivered. She had been gripped by a sudden depression,

151

a strange foreboding that chilled the spirit. That muttering seemed to say that there was no happiness anywhere and never could be any. The air was growing close and clammy. Another drop of rain fell, squashily like a toad, and spread itself over her hand.

Lord Emsworth was finding his companion unresponsive. His stream of prattle slackened and died away. He began to wonder how he was to escape from a girl who, though undeniably pleasing to the eye, was proving singularly difficult to talk to. Raking the horizon in search of aid, he perceived Beach approaching, a silver salver in his hand. The salver had a card on it and an envelope.

"For me, Beach?"

"The card, your lordship. The gentleman is in the hall."

Lord Emsworth breathed a sigh of relief.

"You will excuse me, my dear? It is most important that I should see this fellow immediately. My brother Galahad will be back very shortly, I have no doubt. He will entertain you. You don't mind?"

He bustled away, glad to go, and Sue became conscious of the salver, thrust deferentially toward her.

"For you, miss."

"For me?"

"Yes, miss," moaned Beach, like a winter wind wailing through dead trees.

He inclined his head sombrely and was gone. She tore open the envelope. For one breath-taking instant she had thought it might be from Ronnie. But the writing was not Ronnie's familiar scrawl. It was bold, clear, decisive writing, the writing of an efficient man.

She looked at the last page.

Yours sincerely

R. J. Baxter

Sue's heart was beating faster as she turned back to the beginning. When a girl in the position in which she had placed herself has been stared at through steel-rimmed spectacles in the way this R. J. Baxter had stared at her through his spectacles, her initial reaction to mysterious notes from the man behind the lenses can not but be a panic fear that all has been discovered.

The opening sentence dispelled her alarm. Purely personal motives, it appeared, had caused Rupert Baxter to write these few lines. The mere fact that the letter began with the words "Dear Miss Schoonmaker" was enough in itself to bring comfort.

At the risk of annoying you by the intrusion of my private affairs [wrote the Efficient Baxter, rather in the manner of one beginning an after-dinner speech], I feel that I must give you an explanation of the incident which occurred in the garden in your presence this afternoon. From the observation—in the grossest taste—which Lord Emsworth let fall in my hearing, I fear you may have placed a wrong construction on what took place. (I allude to the expresion "Mad as a coot," which I distinctly heard Lord Emsworth utter as I moved away.)

The facts were precisely as I stated. I was leaning out of the library window, and, chancing to lean too far, I lost my balance and fell. That I might have received serious injuries and was entitled to expect sympathy, I overlook. But the words "Mad as a coot" I resent extremely.

Had this incident not occurred, I would not have dreamed of saying anything to prejudice you against your host. As it is, I feel that in justice to myself I must tell you that Lord Emsworth is a man to whose utterances no attention should be paid. He is to all intents and purposes half-witted. Life in the country, with its lack of intellectual stimulus, has caused his natural feebleness of mind to reach a stage which borders closely on insanity. His relatives look on him as virtually an imbecile and have, in my opinion, every cause to do so.

In these circumstances, I think I may rely on you to attach no importance to his remarks this afternoon.

Yours sincerely
R. J. BAXTER

P.S. You will, of course, treat this as entirely confidential.
P.P.S. If you are fond of chess and would care for a game after dinner I am a good player.
P.P.S.S. Or bezique.

Sue thought it a good letter, neat and well expressed. Why it had been written she could not imagine. It had not occurred to her that love—or, at any rate, a human desire to marry a wealthy heiress—had begun to burgeon in R. J. Baxter's bosom. With no particular emotions other than the feeling that if he was counting on playing bezique with her after dinner he was due for a disappointment, she put the letter in her pocket, and looked out over the park again.

The object of all good literature is to purge the soul of its petty troubles. This, she was pleased to discover, Baxter's letter had succeeded in doing. Recalling its polished phrases, she found herself smiling appreciatively.

That muttering sky did not look so menacing now. Everything, she told herself, was going to be all right. After all, she did not ask much from Fate—just an uninterrupted five minutes with Ronnie. And if Fate so far had denied her this very moderate demand—

"All alone?"

Sue turned, her heart beating quickly. The voice, speaking close behind her, had had something of the effect of a douche of iced water down her back. For, restorative though Baxter's letter had been, it had not left her in quite the frame of mind to enjoy anything so sudden and jumpy as an unexpected voice.

It was the Hon. Galahad, back from his interview with the gentleman, and the sight of him did nothing to calm her agitation. He was eying her, she thought, with a strange and sinister intentness. And though his manner, as he planted himself beside her and began to talk, seemed all that was cordial and friendly, she could not rid herself of a feeling of uneasiness. That look still lingered in her mind's eye. With the air all heavy and woolly and the sky growling pessimistic prophecies it had been a look to alarm the bravest girl.

Chattering amiably, the Hon. Galahad spoke of this and that:

154

of scenery and the weather; of birds and rabbits; of friends of his who had served terms in prison, and of other friends who, one would have said on the evidence, had been lucky to escape. Then his monocle was up again and that look was back on his face.

The air was more breathless than ever.

"You know," said the Hon. Galahad, "it's been a great treat to me, meeting you, my dear. I haven't seen any of your people for a number of years, but your father and I correspond pretty regularly. He tells me all the news. Did you leave your family well?"

"Quite well."

"How was your Aunt Edna?"

"Fine," said Sue feebly.

"Ah," said the Hon. Galahad. "Then your father must have been mistaken when he told me she was dead. But perhaps you thought I meant your Aunt Edith?"

"Yes," said Sue gratefully.

"She's all right, I hope?"

"Oh, yes."

"What a lovely woman!"

"Yes."

"You mean she still is?"

"Oh, yes."

"Remarkable! She must be well over seventy by now. No doubt you mean beautiful considering she is over seventy?"

"Yes."

"Pretty active?"

"Oh, yes."

"When did you see her last?"

"Oh—just before I sailed."

"And you say she's active? Curious! I heard two years ago that she was paralyzed. I suppose you mean active for a paralytic."

The little puckers at the corners of his eyes deepened into wrinkles. The monocle gleamed like the eye of a dragon. He smiled genially.

"Confide in me, Miss Brown," he said. "What's the game?"

11

I

SUE DID not answer. When the solid world melts abruptly beneath the feet one feels disinclined for speech. Avoiding the monocle, she stood looking with wide blank eyes at a thrush which hopped fussily about the lawn. Behind her the sky gave a low chuckle, as if this was what it had been waiting for.

"Up there," proceeded the Hon. Galahad, pointing to the small library, "is the room where I work. And sometimes, when I'm not working, I look out of the window. I was looking out a short while back when you were down here talking to my brother Clarence. There was a fellow with me. He looked out, too." His voice sounded blurred and far away. "A theatrical manager fellow I used to know very well in the old days. A man named Mason."

The thrush had flown away. Sue continued to gaze at the spot where it had been. Across the years, for the mind works oddly in times of stress, there had come to her vivid recollection of herself at the age of ten, taken by her mother to the Isle of Man on her first steamer trip and just beginning to feel the motion of the vessel. There had been a moment then, just before the supreme catastrophe, when she had felt exactly as she was feeling now.

"We saw you, and he said, 'Why there's Sue!' I said, 'Sue? Sue Who?' 'Sue Brown,' said this fellow Mason. He said you were one of the girls at his theatre. He didn't seem particularly surprised to see you here. He said he took it that everything had been fixed up all right and he was glad, because you were one of the best. He wanted to come and have a chat with you, but I headed him off. I thought you might prefer to talk over this matter of your being Miss Sue Brown alone with me. Which brings me back to my original question. What, Miss Brown, is the game?"

Sue felt dizzy, helpless, hopeless.

"I can't explain," she said.

The Hon. Galahad tut-tutted protestingly.

"You don't mean to say you propose to leave the thing as just another of those historic mysteries? Don't you want me ever to get a good night's sleep again?"

"Oh, it's so long."

"We have the evening before us. Take it bit by bit, a little at a time. To begin with, what did Mason mean by saying that everything was all right?"

"I had told him about Ronnie."

"Ronnie? My nephew Ronald?"

"Yes. And, seeing me here, he naturally took it for granted that Lord Emsworth and the rest of you had consented to the engagement and invited me to the castle."

"Engagement?"

"I used to be engaged to Ronnie."

"What! That young Fish?"

"Yes."

"Good God!" said the Hon. Galahad.

Suddenly Sue began to feel conscious of a slackening of the tension. Mysteriously, the conversation was seeming less difficult. In spite of the fact that Reason scoffed at the absurdity of such an idea, she felt just as if she were talking to a potential friend and ally. The thought had come to her at the moment when, looking up, she caught sight of her companion's face. It is an unpleasant thing to say of any man, but there is no denying that the Hon. Galahad's face, when he was listening to the confessions of those who had behaved as they ought not to have behaved, very frequently lacked the austerity and disapproval which one likes to see in faces on such occasions.

"But however did Pa Mason come to be here?" asked Sue.

"He came to discuss some business in connection with—Never mind about that," said the Hon. Galahad, calling the meeting to order. "Kindly refrain from wandering from the point. I'm beginning to see daylight. You are engaged to Ronald you say?"

"I was."

"But you broke it off?"

"He broke it off."

"He did?"

"Yes. That's why I came here. You see, Ronnie was here and I was in Lo.idon, and you can't put things properly in letters, so I thought that if I could get down to Blandings I could see him and explain and put everything right—and I'd met Lady Constance in London one day when I was with Ronnie, and he had introduced me as Miss Schoonmaker, so that part of it was all right—so—well, so I came."

If this chronicle has proved anything it has proved by now that the moral outlook of the Hon. Galahad Threepwood was fundamentally unsound. A man to shake the head at. A man to view with concern. So felt his sister, Lady Constance Keeble, and she was undoubtedly right. If final evidence were needed, his next words supplied it.

"I never heard," said the Hon. Galahad, beaming like one listening to a tale of virtue triumphant, "anything so dashed sporting in my life."

Sue's heart leaped. She had felt all along that Reason, in denying the possibility that this man could ever approve of what she had done, had been mistaken. These pessimists always are.

"You mean," she cried, "you won't gave me away?"

"Me?" said the Hon. Galahad, aghast at the idea. "Of course I won't. What do you take me for?"

"I think you're an angel."

The Hon. Galahad seemed pleased at the compliment, but it was plain that there was something that worried him. He frowned a little.

"What I can't make out," he said, "is why you want to marry my nephew Ronald."

"I love him, bless his heart."

"No, seriously!" protested the Hon. Galahad. "Do you know that he once put tin-tacks on my chair?"

"And he throws tennis balls at pigs. All the same, I love him."

"You can't!"

"I do."

"How can you possibly love a fellow like that?"

"That's just what he always used to say," said Sue softly. "And I think that's why I love him."

The Hon. Galahad sighed. Fifty years' experience had taught him that it was no use arguing with women on this particular point, but he had conceived a warm affection for this girl, and it shocked him to think of her madly throwing herself away.

"Don't you go doing anything in a hurry, my dear. Think it over carefully. I've seen enough of you to know that you're a very exceptional girl."

"I don't believe you like Ronnie."

"I don't dislike him. He's improved since he was a boy. I'll admit that. But he isn't worthy of you."

"Why not?"

"Well, he isn't."

She laughed.

"It's funny that you of all people should say that. Lord Emsworth was telling me just now that Ronnie is exactly like what you used to be at his age."

"What!"

"That's what he said."

The Hon. Galahad stared incredulously.

"That boy like me?" He spoke with indignation, for his pride had been sorely touched. "Ronald like me? Why, I was twice the man he is. How many policemen do you think it used to take to shift me from the Alhambra to Vine Street when I was in my prime? Two! Sometimes three. And one walking behind carrying my hat. Clarence ought to be more careful what he says, dash it. It's just this kind of loose talk that makes trouble. The fact of the matter is, he's gone and got his brain so addled with pigs he doesn't know what he is saying half the time."

He pulled himself together with a strong effort. He became calmer.

"What did you and that young poop quarrel about?" he asked.

"He is not a poop!"

159

"He is. It's astonishing to me that any one individual can be such a poop. You'd have thought it would have required a large syndicate. How long have you known him?"

"About nine months."

"Well, I've known him all his life. And I say he's a poop. If he wasn't he wouldn't have quarrelled with you. However, we won't split straws. What did you quarrel about?"

"He found me dancing."

"What's wrong with that?"

"I had promised him I wouldn't."

"And is that all the trouble?"

"It's quite enough for me."

The Hon. Galahad made light of the tragedy.

"I don't see what you're worrying about. If you can't smooth a little thing like that over you're not the girl I take you for."

"I thought I might be able to."

"Of course you'll be able to. Girls were always doing that sort of thing to me in my young days, and I never held out for five minutes once the crying started. Go and sob on the boy's waistcoat. How are you as a sobber?"

"Not very good, I'm afraid."

"Well, there are all sorts of other tricks you can try. Every girl knows a dozen. Falling on your knees, fainting, laughing hysterically, going rigid all over—scores of them."

"I think it will be all right if I can just talk to him. The difficulty is to get an opportunity."

The Hon. Galahad waved a hand spaciously.

"Make an opportunity! Why, I knew a girl years ago—she's a grandmother now—who had a quarrel with the fellow she was engaged to, and a week or so later she found herself staying at the same country house with him—Heron's Hill, it was, the Matchelow's place in Sussex—and she got him into her room one night and locked the door and said she was going to keep him there all night and ruin both their reputations unless he handed back the ring and agreed that the engagement was on again. And she'd have done it, too. Her name was Frederica Something. Red-haired girl."

160

"I suppose you have to have red hair to do a thing like that. I was thinking of a quiet meeting in the rose garden."

The Hon. Galahad seemed to consider this tame, but he let it pass.

"Well, whatever you do, you'll have to be quick about it, my dear. Suppose old Johnny Schoonmaker's girl really turns up? She said she was going to."

"Yes, but I made Ronnie send her a telegram, signed with Lady Constance's name, saying that there was scarlet fever at the castle and she wasn't to come."

One dislikes the necessity of perpetually piling up the evidence against the Hon. Galahad Threepwood, to show ever more and more clearly how warped was his moral outlook. Nevertheless, the fact must be stated that at these words he threw his head up and uttered a high, piercing laugh that sent the thrush, which had just returned to the lawn, starting back as if a bullet had hit it. It was a laugh which, when it had rung out in days of yore in London's more lively night resorts, had caused commissionaires to leap like war horses at the note of the bugle, to spit on their hands, feel their muscles, and prepare for action.

"It's the finest thing I ever heard!" cried the Hon. Galahad. "It restores my faith in the younger generation. And a girl like you seriously contemplates marrying a boy like—Oh, well!" he said resignedly, seeming to brace himself to make the best of a distasteful state of affairs, "it's your business, I suppose. You know your own mind best. After all, the great thing is to get you into the family. A girl like you is what this family has been needing for years."

He patted her kindly on the shoulder, and they started to walk toward the house. As they did so two men came out of it.

One was Lord Emsworth. The other was Percy Pilbeam.

II

There is about a place like Blandings Castle something which, if you are not in the habit of visiting country houses planned on the grand scale, tends to sap the morale. At the moment when Sue caught sight of him the proprietor of the Argus Enquiry Agency was not feeling his brightest and best.

Beach, ushering him through the front door, had started the trouble. He had merely let his eye rest upon Pilbeam, but it had been enough. The butler's eye, through years of insufficient exercise and too hearty feeding, had acquired in the process of time a sort of glaze which many people found trying when they saw it. In Pilbeam it created an inferiority complex of the severest kind.

He could not know that to this godlike man he was merely a blur. To Beach, tortured by the pangs of a guilty conscience, almost everything nowadays was merely a blur. Misinterpreting his gaze, Pilbeam had read into it a shocked contempt, a kind of wincing agony at the thought that things like himself should be creeping into Blandings Castle. He felt as if he had crawled out from under a flat stone.

And it was at this moment that somebody in the dimness of the hall had stepped forward and revealed himself as the young man, name unknown, who had showed such a lively disposition to murder him on the dancing floor of Mario's restaurant. And from the violent start which he gave it was plain that the young man's memory was as good as his own.

So far things had not broken well for Percy Pilbeam. But now his luck turned. There had appeared in the nick of time an angel from heaven, effectively disguised in a shabby shooting coat and an old hat. He had introduced himself as Lord Emsworth, and he had taken Pilbeam off with him into the garden. Looking back over his shoulder, Pilbeam saw that the young man was still standing there, staring after him—wistfully, it seemed to him; and he was glad, as he followed his host out into the fresh air, to be beyond the range of his eye. Between it and the eye of Beach, the butler, there seemed little to choose.

Relief, however, by the time he arrived on the terrace, had not completely restored his composure. That inferiority complex was still at work, and his surroundings intimidated him. At any moment, he felt, on a terrace like this, there might suddenly appear to confront him and complete his humiliation some brilliant shattering creature indigenous to this strange and disturbing world — a Duchess, perhaps — a haughty hunting woman, it might be — the dashing daughter of a hundred earls, possibly, who would look at him as Beach had looked at him and, raising beautifully pencilled eyebrows in aristocratic disdain, turn away with a murmured "Most extraordinary!" He was prepared for almost anything.

One of the few things he was not prepared for was Sue. And at the sight of her he leaped three clear inches and nearly broke a collar stud.

"Gaw!" he said.

"I beg your pardon?" said Lord Emsworth. He had not caught his companion's remark and hoped he would repeat it. The lightest utterance of a detective with the trained mind is something not to be missed. "What did you say, my dear fellow?"

He, too, perceived Sue; and with a prodigious effort of the memory, working by swift stages through Schofield, Maybury, Coolidge, and Spooner, recalled her name.

"Mr. Pilbeam, Miss Schoonmaker," he said. "Galahad, this is Mr. Pilbeam. Of the Argus, you remember."

"Pilbeam?"

"How do you do?"

"Pilbeam?"

"My brother," said Lord Emsworth, exerting himself to complete the introduction. "This is my brother Galahad."

"Pilbeam?" said the Hon. Galahad, looking intently at the proprietor of the Argus. "Were you ever connected with a paper called *Society Spice*, Mr. Pilbeam?"

The gardens of Blandings Castle seemed to the detective to rock gently. There had, he knew, been a rigid rule to the office of that bright but frequently offensive paper that the editor's name was never to be revealed to callers; but it now appeared only too sickeningly evident that a leakage had occurred. Underlings, he realize too late, can be bribed.

He swallowed painfully. Force of habit had come within a hair's breadth of making him say "Quite."

"Never," he gasped. "Certainly not. No! Never."

"A fellow of your name used to edit it. Uncommon name, too."

"Relation, perhaps. Distant."

"Well, I'm sorry you're not the man," said the Hon. Galahad regretfully. "I've been wanting to meet him. He wrote a very offensive thing about me once. Most offensive thing."

Lord Emsworth, who had been according the conversation the rather meagre interest which he gave to all conversations that did not deal with pigs, created a diversion.

"I wonder," he said, "if you would like to see some photographs?"

It seemed to Pilbeam, in his disordered state, strange that anyone should suppose that he was in a frame of mind to enjoy the Family Album, but he uttered a strangled sound which his host took for acquiescence.

"Of the Empress, I mean, of course. They will give you some idea of what a magnificent animal she is. They will—" he sought for the *mot juste*—"stimulate you. I'll go to the library and get them out."

The Hon. Galahad was now his old affable self again.

"You doing anything after dinner?" he asked Sue.

"There was some talk," said Sue, "of a game of bezique with Mr. Baxter."

"Don't dream of it," said the Hon. Galahad vehemently. "The fellow would probably try to brain you with the mallet. I was thinking that if I hadn't got to go out to dinner I'd like to read you some of my book. I think you would appreciate it. I wouldn't read it to anybody except you. I somehow feel you've got the right sort of outlook. I let my sister Constance see a couple of pages once, and she was too depressing for words. An author can't work if people depress him. I'll tell you what I'll do—I'll give you the thing to read. Which is your room?"

"The Garden Room, I think it's called."

"Oh, yes. Well, I'll bring the manuscript to you before I leave."

He sauntered off. There was a moment's pause. Then Sue turned to Pilbeam. Her chin was tilted. There was defiance in her eye.

"Well?" she said.

164

III

Percy Pilbeam breathed a sigh of relief. At the first moment of their meeting all that he had ever read about doubles had raced through his mind. This question clarified the situation. It put matters on a firm basis. His head ceased to swim. It was Sue Brown and no other who stood before him.

"What on earth are you doing here?" he asked.

"Never mind."

"What's the game?"

"Never mind."

"There's no need to be so dashed unfriendly."

"Well, if you must know, I came here to see Ronnie and try to explain about that night at Mario's."

There was a pause.

"What was the name the old boy called you?"

"Schoonmaker."

"Why did he call you that?"

"Because that's who he thinks I am."

"What on earth made you choose a name like that?"

"Oh, don't keep asking questions."

"I don't believe there is such a name. And when it comes to asking questions," said Pilbeam warmly, "what do you expect me to do? I never got such a shock in my life as when I met you just now. I thought I was seeing things. Do you mean to say you're here under a false name, pretending to be somebody else?"

"Yes."

"Well, I'm hanged! And as friendly as you please with everybody."

"Yes."

"Everybody except me."

"Why should I be friendly with you? You've done your best to ruin my life."

"Eh?"

"Oh, never mind," said Sue impatiently.

There was another pause.

165

"Chatty!" said Pilbeam, wounded again.

He fidgeted his fingers along the wall.

"The Galahad fellow seems to look on you as a daughter or something."

"We are great friends."

"So I see. And he's going to give you his book to read."

"Yes."

A keen, purposeful, Argus-Enquiry-Agency sort of look shot into Pilbeam's face.

"Well, this is where you and I get together," he said.

"What do you mean?"

"I'll tell you what I mean. Do you want to make some money?"

"No," said Sue.

"What! Of course you do. Everybody does. Now, listen. Do you know why I'm here?"

"I've stopped wondering why you're anywhere. You just seem to pop up."

She started to move away. A sudden disturbing thought had come to her. At any moment Ronnie might appear on the terrace. If he found her here, closeted, so to speak, with the abominable Pilbeam, what would he think? What, rather, would he not think?

"Where are you going?"

"Into the house."

"Come back," said Pilbeam urgently.

"I'm going."

"But I've got something important to say."

"Well?"

She stopped.

"That's right," said Pilbeam approvingly. "Now, listen. You'll admit that, if I liked, I could give you away and spoil whatever game it is that you're up to in this place?"

"Well?"

"But I'm not going to do it if you'll be sensible."

"Sensible?"

Pilbeam look cautiously up and down the terrace.

"Now, listen," he said. "I want your help. I'll tell you why I'm

166

here. The old boy thinks I've come down to find his pig, but I haven't. I've come to get that book your friend Galahad is writing."

"What!"

"I thought you'd be surprised. Yes, that's what I'm after. There's a man living near here who's scared stiff that there's going to be a lot of stories about him in that book, and he came to see me at my office yesterday and offered me—" he hesitated a moment—"offered me," he went on, "a hundred pounds if I'd get into the house somehow and snitch the manuscript. And you being friendly with the old buster has made everything simple."

"You think so?"

"Easy," he assured her. "Especially now he's going to give you the thing to read. All you have to do is hand it over to me and there's fifty quid for you. For doing practically nothing."

Sue's eyes lit up. Pilbeam had expected that they would. He could not conceive of a girl whose eyes would not light up at such an offer.

"Oh?" said Sue.

"Fifty quid," said Pilbeam. "I'm going halves with you."

"And if I don't do what you want I suppose you will tell them who I really am?"

"That's it," said Pilbeam, pleased at her ready intelligence.

"Well, I'm not going to do anything of the kind."

"What!"

"And if," said Sue, "you want to tell these people who I am, go ahead and tell them."

"I will."

"Do. But just bear in mind that the moment you do I shall tell Mr. Threepwood that it was you who wrote that thing about him in *Society Spice*."

Percy Pilbeam swayed like a sapling in the breeze. The blow had unmanned him. He found no words with which to reply.

"I will," said Sue.

Pilbeam continued speechless. He was still trying to recover from his deadly thrust through an unexpected chink in his armour when the opportunity for speech passed. Millicent had ap-

167

peared and was walking along the terrace toward them. She wore her customary air of settled gloom. On reaching them she paused.

"Hullo," said Millicent, from the depths.

"Hullo," said Sue.

The library window framed the head and shoulders of Lord Emsworth.

"Pilbeam, my dear fellow, will you come up to the library? I have found the photographs."

Millicent eyed the detective's retreating back with a mournful curiosity.

"Who's he?"

"A man named Pilbeam."

"Pill, I should say, is right. What makes him waddle like that?"

Sue was unable to supply a solution to this problem. Millicent came and stood beside her and, leaning on the stone parapet, gazed disparagingly at the park. She gave the impression of disliking all parks but this one particularly.

"Ever read Schopenhauer?" she asked, after a silence.

"No."

"You should. Great stuff."

She fell into a heavy silence again, her eyes peering into the gathering gloom. Somewhere in the twilight world a cow had begun to emit long, nerve-racking bellows. The sound seemed to sum up and underline the general sadness.

"Schopenhauer says that all the suffering in the world can't be mere chance. Must be meant. He says life's a mixture of suffering and boredom. You've got to have one or the other. His stuff's full of snappy cracks like that. You'd enjoy it. Well, I'm going for a walk. You coming?"

"I don't think I will, thanks."

"Just as you like. Schopenhauer says suicide's absolutely O.K. He says Hindoos do it instead of going to church. They bung themselves into the Ganges and get eaten by crocodiles and call it a well-spent day."

"What a lot you seem to know about Schopenhauer."

"I've been reading him up lately. Found a copy in the library. Schopenhauer says we are like lambs in a field, disporting themselves under the eye of the butcher, who chooses first one and then another for his prey. Sure you won't come for a walk?"

"No, thanks, really, I think I'll go in."

"Just as you like," said Millicent. "Liberty Hall."

She moved off a few steps, then returned.

"Sorry if I seem loopy," she said. "Something on my mind. Been giving it a spot of thought. The fact is, I've just got engaged to be married to my cousin Ronnie."

The trees that stood out against the banking clouds seemed to swim before Sue's eyes. An unseen hand had clutched her by the throat and was crushing the life out of her.

"Ronnie!"

"Yes," said Millicent, rather in the tone of voice which Schopenhauer would have used when announcing the discovery of a caterpillar in his salad. "We fixed it up just now."

She wandered away, and Sue clung to the terrace wall. That at least was solid in a world that rocked and crashed.

"I say!"

It was Hugo. She was looking at him through a mist, but there was never any mistaking Hugo Carmody.

"I say! Did she tell you?"

Sue nodded.

"She's engaged."

Sue nodded.

"She's going to marry Ronnie."

"Death, where is thy sting?" said Hugo, and vanished in the direction taken by Millicent.

12

I

THE FIRM and dignified note in which Rupert Baxter had expressed his considered opinion of the Earl of Emsworth had been written in the morning room immediately upon the ex-secretary's return to the house and delivered into Beach's charge with hands still stained with garden mould. Only when this urgent task had been performed did he start to go upstairs in quest of the wash and brush-up which he so greatly needed. He was mounting the stairs to his bedroom and had reached the first floor when a door opened and his progress was arrested by what in a lesser woman would have been a yelp. Proceeding, as it did, from the lips of Lady Constance Keeble, we must call it an exclamation of surprise.

"Mr. Baxter!"

She was standing in the doorway of her boudoir, and she eyed his dishevelled form with such open-mouthed astonishment that for an instant the ex-secretary came near to including her with the head of the family in the impromptu commination service which was taking shape in his mind. He was in no mood for wide-eyed looks of wonder.

"May I come in?" he said curtly. He could explain all, but did not wish to do so on the first-floor landing of a house where almost anybody might be listening with flapping ears.

"But, Mr. Baxter!" said Lady Constance.

He paused for a moment to grit his teeth, then closed the door.

"What *have* you been doing, Mr. Baxter?"

"Jumping out of window."

"Jumping out of *win*-dow?"

He gave a brief synopsis of the events which had led up to his

170

spirited act. Lady Constance drew in her breath with a remorseful hiss.

"Oh, dear!" she said. "How foolish of me. I should have told you."

"I beg your pardon?"

Even though she was in the safe retirement of her boudoir Lady Constance Keeble looked cautiously over her shoulder. In the stirring and complicated state into which life had got itself at Blandings Castle practically everybody in the place, except Lord Emsworth, had fallen into the habit nowadays of looking cautiously over his or her shoulder before he or she spoke.

"Sir Gregory Parsloe said in his note," she explained, "that this man Pilbeam who is coming here this evening is acting for him."

"Acting for him?"

"Yes. Apparently Sir Gregory went to see him yesterday and has promised him a large sum of money if he will obtain possession of my brother Galahad's manuscript. That is why he has invited us to dinner to-night, to get Galahad out of the house. So there was no need for you to have troubled."

There was silence.

"So there was no need," repeated the Efficient Baxter slowly, wiping from his eye the remains of a fragment of mould which had been causing him some inconvenience, "for me to have troubled."

"I am so sorry, Mr. Baxter."

"Pray do not mention it, Lady Constance."

His eye, now that the mould was out of it, was able to work again with its customary keennees. His spectacles, as he surveyed the remorseful woman before him, had a cold, steely look.

"I see," he said. "Well, it might perhaps have spared me some little inconvenience had you informed me of this earlier, Lady Constance. I have bruised my left shin somewhat severely and, as you see, made myself rather dirty."

"I am so sorry."

"Furthermore, I gathered from the remark he let fall that the impression my actions have made upon Lord Emsworth is that I am insane."

"Oh, dear!"

"He even specified the precise degree of insanity. As mad as a coot, were his words."

He softened a little. He reminded himself that this woman before him, who was so nearly doing what is described as wringing the hands, had always been his friend, had always wished him well, had never slackened her efforts to restore him to the secretarial duties which he had once enjoyed.

"Well, it cannot be helped," he said. "The thing now is to think of some way of recovering the lost ground."

"You mean, if you could find the Empress?"

"Exactly."

"Oh, Mr. Baxter, if you only could!"

"I can."

Lady Constance stared at his dark, purposeful, efficient face in dumb admiration. To another man who had spoken those words she would have replied "How?" or even "How on earth?" But, as they had proceeded from Rupert Baxter, she merely waited silently for enlightenment.

"Have you given this matter any consideration, Lady Constance?"

"Yes."

"To what conclusions have you come?"

Lady Constance felt dull and foolish. She felt like Doctor Watson—almost like a Scotland Yard Bungler.

"I don't think I have come to any," she said, avoiding the spectacle guiltily. "Of course," she added, "I think it is absurd to suppose that Sir Gregory—"

Baxter waved aside the notion. It was not even worth a "Tchah!"

"In any matter of this kind," he said, "the first thing to do is to seek motive. Who is there in Blandings Castle who could have had a motive for stealing Lord Emsworth's pig?"

Lady Constance would have given a year's income to have been able to make some reasonably intelligent reply, but all she could do was look and listen. Baxter was not annoyed. He would not have had it otherwise. He preferred his audiences dumb and expectant.

172

"Carmody."

"Mr. Carmody!"

"Precisely. He is Lord Emsworth's secretary, and a most inefficient secretary, a secretary who stands hourly in danger of losing his position. He sees me arrive at the Castle, a man who formerly held the post he holds. He is alarmed. He suspects. He searches wildly about in his mind for means of consolidating himself in Lord Emsworth's regard. Then he has an idea, the sort of wild, motion-picture-bred idea which would come to a man of his stamp. He thinks to himself that if he removes the pig and conceals it somewhere and then pretends to have found it and restores it to its owner, Lord Emsworth's gratitude will be so intense that all danger of his dismissal will be at an end."

He removed his spectacles and wiped them. Lady Constance uttered a low cry. In anybody else it would have been a squeak. Baxter replaced his spectacles.

"I have no doubt the pig is somewhere in the grounds at this moment," he said.

"But, Mr. Baxter—"

The ex-secretary raised a compelling hand.

"But he would not have undertaken a thing like this single-handed. A secretary's time is not his own, and it would be necessary to feed the pig at regular intervals. He would require an accomplice. And I think I know who that accomplice is—Beach!"

This time not even the chronicler's desire to place Lady Constance's utterances in the best and most attractive light can hide the truth. She bleated.

"Bee-ee-ee-ee-ech!"

The spectacles raked her keenly.

"Have you observed Beach closely of late?"

She shook her head. She was not a woman who observed butlers closely.

"He has something on his mind. He is nervous. Guilty. Conscience stricken. He jumps when you speak to him."

"Does he?"

"Jumps," repeated the Efficient Baxter. "Just now I gave him a—I happened to address him, and he sprang in the air." He

173

paused. "I have half a mind to go and question him."

"Oh, Mr. Baxter! Would that be wise?"

Rupert Baxter's intention of interrogating the butler had been merely a nebulous one, a sort of idle dream, but these words crystallized it into a resolve. He was not going to have people asking him if things would be wise.

"A few searching questions should force him to reveal the truth."

"But he'll give notice!"

This interview had been dotted with occasions on which Baxter might reasonably have said, "Tchah!" but, as we have seen, until this moment he had refrained. He now said it.

"Tchah!" said the Efficient Baxter. "There are plenty of other butlers."

And with this undeniable truth he stalked from the room. The wash and brush-up were still as necessary as they had been ten minutes before, but he was too intent on the chase to think about washes and brushes-up. He hurried down the stairs. He crossed the hall. He passed through the green baize door that led to the quarters of the Blandings Castle staff. And he was making his way along the dim passage to the pantry where at this hour Beach might be supposed to be when its door opened abruptly and a vast form emerged.

It was the butler. And from the fact that he was wearing a bowler hat it was plain that he was seeking the great outdoors.

Baxter stopped in mid-stride and remained on one leg, watching. Then, as his quarry disappeared in the direction of the back entrance, he followed quickly.

Out in the open it was almost as dark as it had been in the passage. That gray, threatening sky had turned black by now. It was a swollen mass of inky clouds, heavy with the thunder, lightning, and rain which so often come in the course of an English summer to remind the island race that they are hardy Nordics and must not be allowed to get their fibre all sapped up by eternal sunshine like the less favoured dwellers in more southerly climes. It bayed at Baxter like a bloodhound.

But it took more than dirty weather to quell the Efficient Baxter when duty called. Like the character in Tennyson's poem who followed the gleam, he followed the butler. There was but one point about Beach which even remotely resembled a gleam, but it happened to be only one which at this moment really mattered. He was easy to follow.

The shrubbery swallowed the butler. A few seconds later it had swallowed the Efficient Baxter.

II

There are those who maintain—and make a nice income by doing so in the evening papers—that in these degenerate days the old hardy spirit of the Briton has died out. They represent themselves as seeking vainly for evidence of the survival of those qualities of toughness and endurance which once made Englishmen what they were. To such, the spectacle of Rupert Baxter braving the elements could not have failed to bring cheer and consolation. They would have been further stimulated by the conduct of Hugo Carmody.

It had not escaped Hugo's notice, as he left Sue on the terrace and started out in the wake of Millicent, that the weather was hotting up for a storm. He saw the clouds. He heard the fast-approaching thunder. For neither did he give a hoot. Let it rain, was Hugo's verdict. Let it jolly well rain as much as it dashed well wanted to. As if encouraged, the sky sent down a fat, wet drop which insinuated itself just between his neck and collar.

He hardly noticed it. The information confided to him by his friend Ronald Fish had numbed his sense so thoroughly that water down the back of the neck was merely an incident. He was feeling as he had not felt since the evening some years ago when, boxing for his university in the light-weight division, he had incautiously placed the point of his jaw in the exact spot at the moment occupied by his opponent's right fist. When you have done this or—equally—when you have just been told that the girl you love is definitely betrothed to another, you begin to understand how anarchists must feel when the bomb goes off too soon.

In all the black days through which he had been living recently,

175

Hugo had never really lost hope. It had been dim sometimes, but it had always been there. It was his opinion that he knew women, just as it was Sue's idea that she knew men. Like Sue, he had placed his trust in the thought that true love conquers all obstacles; that coldness melts; that sundered hearts may at long last be brought together again by a little judicious pleading and reasoning. Even the fact that Millicent stared at him when they met, with large, scornful eyes that went through him like stilettos, unpleasant though it was, had not caused him to despair. He had look forward to the moment when he should contrive to get her alone and do a bit of snappy talking along the right lines.

But this was final. This was the end. This put the tin hat on it. She was engaged to Ronnie. Soon she would be married to Ronnie. Lake a gadfly the hideous thought sent Hugo Carmody reeling on through the gloom.

It was so dark now that he could scarcely see before him. And, looking about him, he discovered that the reason for this was that he had made his way into a wood of sorts. The west wood, he deduced dully, taking into consideration the fact that there was no other in this particular part of the estate. Well, he might just as well be in the west wood as anywhere. He trudged on.

The ground beneath his feet was spongy and equipped with low-lying brambles which pricked through his thin flannels and would have caused him discomfort if he had been in the frame of mind to notice brambles. There were trees against which he bumped, and logs over which he tripped. And ahead of him, in a small clearing, there was a dilapidated-looking cottage. He noticed this because it seemed the sort of place where a man, now that a warm, gusty wind had sprung up, might shelter and light a cigarette. The need for tobacco had become imperative.

He was surprised to find that it was raining, and had apparently, from the state of his clothes, been raining for quite some time. It was also thundering. The storm had broken, and the boom of it seemed to be all round him. A flash of lightning reminded him that he was in just the kind of place, among all these trees, where blokes get struck. At dinner time they are missed, and later on search parties come out with lanterns. Somebody stumbles over something soft, and the rays of the lantern fall on a charred and blackened form. Here, quickly, we have found him! Where? Over here. Is *that* Hugo Carmody? Well, well! Pick him up, boys, and bring him along. He was a good chap once. Moody, though, of late. Some trouble about a girl, wasn't it? She will be sorry when she hears of this. Drove him to it, you might almost say. Steady with that stretcher. Now, when I say, *"To me."* Right!

There was something about this picture which quite cheered Hugo up. Ajax defied the lightning. Hugo Carmody rather encouraged it than otherwise. He looked approvingly at a more than usually vivid flash that seemed to dart among the treetops like a snake. All the same, he was forced to reflect, he was getting dashed wet. No sense, when you came right down to it, in getting dashed wet. After all, a man could be struck by lightning just as well in that cottage sort of place over there. Ho! for the cottage, felt Hugo, and headed for it at a gallop.

He had just reached the door when it was flung open. There was a noise rather like that made by a rising pheasant, and the next moment something white had flung itself into his arms and was weeping emotionally on his chest.

"Hugo! Hugo darling!"

Reason told Hugo it could scarcely be Millicent who was clinging to him like this and speaking to him like this. And yet Millicent it most certainly appeared to be. She continued to speak, still in the same friendly, even chatty strain.

"Hugo! Save me!"

"Right ho!"

"I wur-wur-went in thur-thur-there to shush-shush-shelter from the rain, and it's all pitch dark."

Hugo squeezed her fondly and with the sort of relief that comes to men who find themselves squeezing where they had not thought to squeeze. No need for that snappy bit of talking now. No need for arguments and explanations, for pleadings and entreaties. No need for anything but a good biceps.

He was bewildered. But mixed with his bewilderment had come

177

a certain feeling of complacency. There was no denying that it was enjoyable, this exhibition of tremulous weakness in one who, if she had had the shadow of a fault, had always been inclined to matter-of-factness and the display of that rather hard, bright self-sufficiency which is so characteristic of the modern girl. If this melting mood was due to the fact that Millicent, while in the cottage, had seen a ghost, Hugo wanted to meet that ghost and shake its hand. Every man likes to be in a position to say, "There, there, little woman!" to the girl of his heart, particularly if for the last few days she has been treating him like a more than ordinarily unpleasant worm, and Hugo Carmody felt that he was in that position now.

"There, there!" he said, not quite feeling up to risking the "little woman." "It's all right."

"But it tut-tut-tut—"

"It what?" said Hugo, puzzled.

"It tut-tut-tut-tisn't. There's a man in there!"

"A man?"

"Yes. I didn't know there was anyone there, and it was pitch dark, and I heard something move, and I said, 'Who's that?' and then he suddenly spoke to me in German."

"In German?"

"Yes."

Hugo released her gently. His face was determined.

"I'm going to have a look."

"Hugo! Stop! You'll be killed."

She stood there, rigid. The rain lashed about her, but she did not heed it. The lightning gleamed. She paid it no attention. For the minute that lasts an hour she waited, straining her ears for sounds of the death struggle. Then a dim form appeared.

"I say, Millicent."

"Hugo! Are you all right?"

"Yes, I'm all right. I say, Millicent, do you know what?"

"No, what?"

A chuckle came to her through the darkness.

"It's the pig."

"It's what?"

178

"The pig."

"Who's a pig?"

"This is. Your friend in here. It's Empress of Blandings, as large
as life. Come and have a look."

III

Millicent had a look. She came to the door of the cottage and
peered in. Yes, just as he had said, there was the Empress. In the
feeble light of the match that Hugo was holding, the noble animal's
attractive face was peering up at her—questioningly, as if wondering if she might be the bearer of the evening snack which would
be so exceedingly welcome. The picture was one which would
have set Lord Emsworth screaming with joy. Millicent merely
gaped.

"How on earth did she get here?"

"That's what I'm going to find out," said Hugo. "One always
knew she must be cached somewhere, of course. What is this place,
anyway?"

"It used to be a gamekeeper's cottage, I believe."

"Well, there seems to be a room up above," said Hugo, striking another match. "I'm going to go up there and wait. It's quite
likely that somebody will be along soon to feed the animal, and
I'm going to see who it is."

"Yes, that's what we'll do. How clever of you!"

"Not you. You get back home."

"I won't."

There was a pause. A strong man would, no doubt, have asserted himself. But Hugo, though feeling better than he had done
for days, was not feeling quite so strong as all that.

"Just as you like." He shut the door. "Well, come on. We'd better be making a move. The fellow may be here at any moment."

They climbed the crazy stairs and lowered themselves cautiously
to a floor which smelled of mice and mildew. Below, all was in
darkness, but there were holes through which it would be possible to look when the time should come for looking. Millicent
could feel one near her face.

179

"You don't think this floor will give way?" she asked rather nervously.

"I shouldn't think so. Why?"

"Well, I don't want to break my neck."

"You don't, don't you? Well, I would jolly well like to break mine," said Hugo, speaking tensely in the darkness. It had just occurred to him that now would be a good time for a heart-to-heart talk. "If you suppose I'm keen on going on living with you and Ronnie doing the Wedding Glide all over the place you're dashed well mistaken. I take it you're aware that you've broken my bally heart, what?"

"Oh, Hugo!" said Millicent.

Silence fell. Below, the Empress rustled. Aloft, something scuttered.

"Oo!" cried Millicent. "Was that a rat?"

"I hope so."

"What!"

"Rats gnaw you," explained Hugo. "They cluster round and chew you to the bone and put an end to your misery."

There was silence again. Then Millicent spoke in a small voice.

"You're being beastly," she said.

Remorse poured over Hugo in a flood.

"I'm frightfully sorry. Yes, I know I am, dash it! But look here, you know—I mean, all this getting engaged to Ronnie. A bit thick, what? You don't expect me to give three hearty cheers, do you? Wouldn't want me to break into a few care-free dance steps?"

"I can't believe it's really happened."

"Well, how did it happen?"

"It sort of happened all of sudden. I was feeling miserable and very angry with you and—and all that. And I met Ronnie and he took me for a stroll and we went down by the lake and started throwing little bits of stick at the swans, and suddenly Ronnie sort of grunted and said, 'I say!' and I said, 'Hullo?' and he said, 'Will you marry me?' and I said, 'All right,' and he said 'I ought to warn you, I despise all women,' and I said, 'And I loathe all men,' and he said 'Right-o, I think we shall be very happy.' "

"I see."

"I only did it to score off you."

"You succeeded."

A trace of spirit crept into Millicent's voice.

"You never really loved me," she said. "You know jolly well you didn't."

"Is that so?"

"Well, what did you want to go sneaking off to London for, then, and stuffing that beastly girl of yours with food?"

"She isn't my girl. And she isn't beastly."

"She is."

"Well, you seem to get on with her all right. I saw you chatting on the terrace together as cosily as dammit."

"What!"

"Miss Schoonmaker."

"I don't know what you're talking about. What's Miss Schoonmaker got to do with it?"

"Miss Schoonmaker isn't Miss Schoonmaker. She's Sue Brown."

For a moment it seemed to Millicent that the crack in her companion's heart had spread to his head. Futile though the action was, she stared in the direction from which his voice had proceeded. Then, suddenly, his words took on a meaning. She gasped.

"She's followed you down here!"

"She hasn't followed me down here. She's followed Ronnie down here. Can't you get it into your nut," said Hugo, with justifiable exasperation, "that you've been making floaters and bloomers and getting everything mixed up all along? Sue Brown has never cared a curse for me, and I've never thought anything about her, except that she's a jolly girl and nice to dance with. That's absolutely and positively the only reason I went out with her. I hadn't had a dance for six weeks, and my feet had begun to itch so that I couldn't sleep at night. So I went to London and took her out, and Ronnie found her talking to that pestilence Pilbeam and thought he had taken her out, and she had told him she didn't even know the man, which was quite true, but Ronnie cut up rough and said he was through with her and came down here, and she wanted to get a word with him, so she came down here, pretending to be Miss Schoonmaker, and the moment she gets here she finds Ronnie is engaged to you. A nice surprise for the poor girl!"

Millicent's head had begun to swim long before the conclusion of this recital.

"But what is Pilbeam doing down here?"

"Pilbeam?"

"He was on the terrace talking to her."

A low snarl came through the darkness.

"Pilbeam here? Ah! So he came, after all, did he? He's the fellow Lord Emsworth sent me to about the Empress. He runs the Argus Enquiry Agency. It was Pilbeam's minions that dogged my steps that night, at your request. So he's here, is he? Well, let him enjoy himself while he can. Let him sniff the country air while the sniffing is good. A bitter reckoning awaits that bloke."

From the disorder of Millicent's mind another point emerged insistently demanding explanation.

"You said she wasn't pretty!"

"Who?"

"Sue Brown."

"Nor is she."

"You don't call her pretty? She's fascinating."

"Not to me," said Hugo doggedly. "There's only one girl in the world that I call pretty, and she's going to marry Ronnie." He paused. "If you haven't realized by this time that I love you and always shall love you and have never loved anybody else and never shall love anybody else, you're a fathead. If you brought me Sue Brown or any other girl in the world on a plate with watercress round her, I wouldn't so much as touch her hand."

Another rat—unless it was an exceptionally large mouse—had begun to make its presence felt in the darkness. It seemed to be enjoying an early dinner off a piece of wood. Millicent did not even notice it. She had reached out, and her hand had touched Hugo's arm. Her fingers closed on it desperately.

"Oh, Hugo!" she said.

The arm became animated. It clutched her. drew her along the mouse-and-mildew scented floor. And time stood still.

182

Hugo was the first to break the silence.

"And to think that not so long ago I was wishing that a flash of lightning would strike me amidships!" he said.

The aroma of mouse and mildew had passed away. Violets seemed to be spreading their fragrance through the cottage. Violets and roses. The rat, a noisy feeder, had changed into an orchestra of harps, dulcimers, and sackbuts that played soft music.

And then, jarring upon these sweet strains, there came the sound of the cottage door opening. And a moment later light shone through the holes in the floor.

Millicent gave Hugo's arm a warning pinch. They looked down. On the floor below stood a lantern, and beside it a man of massive build who, from the galloping noises that floated upward, appeared to be giving the Empress those calories and proteins which a pig of her dimensions requires so often and in such large quantities.

This Good Samaritan had been stooping. Now he straightened himself and looked about him with an apprehensive eye. He raised the lantern, and its light fell upon his face.

And, as she saw that face, Millicent, forgetting prudence, uttered in a high, startled voice a single word.

"Beach!" cried Millicent.

Down below, the butler stood congealed. It seemed to him that the Voice of Conscience had spoken.

IV

Conscience, besides having a musical voice, appeared also to be equipped with feet. Beach could hear them clattering down the stairs, and the volume of noise was so great that it seemed as if Conscience must be a centipede. But he did not stir. It would have required at that moment a derrick to move him, and there was no derrick in the gamekeeper's cottage in the west wood. He was still standing like a statue when Hugo and Millicent arrived. Only when the identity of the newcomers impressed itself on his numbed senses did his limbs begin to twitch and show some signs of relaxing. For he looked on Hugo as a friend. Hugo, he felt, was one of the few people in his world who finding him in his present questionable position might be expected to take the broad and sympathetic view.

He nerved himself to speak.

"Good-evening, sir. Good-evening, miss."

"What's all this?" said Hugo.

Years ago, in his hot and reckless youth, Beach had once heard that question from the lips of a policeman. It had disconcerted him then. It disconcerted him now.

"Well, sir," he replied.

Millicent was staring at the Empress, who, after one courteous look of inquiry at the intruders, had given a brief grunt of welcome and returned to the agenda.

"*You* stole her, Beach? *You!*"

The butler quivered. He had known this girl since her long hair and rompers days. She had sported in his pantry. He had cut elephants out of paper for her and taught her tricks with bits of string. The shocked note in her voice seared him like vitriol. To her, he felt, niece to the Earl of Emsworth and trained by his lordship from infancy in the best traditions of pig worship, the theft of the Empress must seem the vilest of crimes. He burned to reestablish himself in her eyes.

There comes in the life of every conspirator a moment when loyalty to his accomplices wavers before the urge to make things right for himself. We can advance no more impressive proof of the nobility of the butler's soul than that he did not obey this impulse. Millicent's accusing eyes were piercing him, but he remained true to his trust. Mr. Ronald had sworn him to secrecy, and even to square himself he could not betray him.

And, as if by way of a direct reward from Providnece for this sterling conduct, inspiration decended upon Beach.

"Yes, miss," he replied.

"Oh, Beach!"

"Yes, miss. It was I who stole the animal. I did it for your sake, miss."

Hugo eyed him sternly.

"Beach," he said, "this is pure apple sauce."

"Sir?"

"Apple sauce, I repeat. Why endeavour to swing the lead, Beach? What do you mean, you stole the pig for her sake?"

"Yes," said Millicent. "Why for my sake?"

The butler was calm now. He had constructed his story and he was going to stick to it.

"In order to remove the obstacles in your path, miss."

"Obstacles?"

"Owing to the fact that you and Mr. Carmody have frequently entrusted me with your—may I say surreptitious correspondence, I have long been cognizant of your sentiments toward one another, miss. I am aware that it is your desire to contract a union with Mr. Carmody, and I knew that there would be objections raised on the part of certain members of the family."

"So far," said Hugo critically, "this sounds to me like drivel of the purest water. But go on."

"Thank you, sir. And then it occurred to me that, were his lordship's pig to disappear, his lordship would, on recovering the animal, be extremely grateful to whoever restores it. It was my intention to apprise you of the animal's whereabouts and suggest that you should inform his lordship that you had discovered it. In his gratitude, I fancied, his lordship would consent to the union."

There could never be complete silence in any spot where Empress of Blandings was partaking of food; but something as near silence as was possible followed this speech. In the rays of the lantern Hugo's eyes met Millicent's. In hers, as in his, there was a look of stunned awe. They had heard of faithful old servitors. They had read about faithful old servitors. They had seen faithful old servitors on the stage. But never had they dreamed that faithful old servitors could be as faithful as this.

"Oh, Beach!" said Millicent.

She had used the words before. But how different this "Oh, Beach!" was from that other, earlier "Oh, Beach!" On that occasion the exclamation had been vibrant with reproach, pain, disillusionment. Now it contained gratitude, admiration, and affection almost too deep for speech.

And the same may be said of Hugo's "Gosh!"

"Beach," cried Millicent, "you're an angel!"

"Thank you, miss."

"A topper!" agreed Hugo.

"Thank you, sir."

"However did you get such a corking idea?"

"It came to me, miss."

"I'll tell you what it is, Beach," said Hugo earnestly. "When you hand in your dinner pail in due course of time—and may the moment be long distant!—you've got to leave your brain to the nation. You've simply got to. Have it pickled and put in the British Museum, because it's the outstanding brain of the century. I never heard of anything so brilliant in my life. Of course the old boy will be all over us."

"He'll do anything for us," said Millicent.

"This is not merely a scheme. It is more. It is an egg. Pray silence for your chairman. I want to think."

Outside, the storm had passed. Birds were singing. Far away, the thunder still rumbled. It might have been the sound of Hugo's thoughts, leaping and jostling one another.

"I've worked it all out," said Hugo at length. "Some people might say, Rush to the old boy now and tell him we've found his pig. I say, no. In my opinion we ought to hold this pig for a rising market. The longer we wait, the more grateful he will be. Give him another forty-eight hours, I suggest, and he will have reached the stage where he will deny us nothing."

"But—"

"No! Act precipitately and we are undone. Don't forget that it is not merely a question of getting your uncle's consent to our union. We've got to break it to him that you aren't going to marry Ronnie. And the family have always been pretty keen on your marrying Ronnie. To my mind, another forty-eight hours at the very least is essential."

"Perhaps you're right."

"I know I'm right."

"Then we'll simply leave the Empress here?"

"No," said Hugo decidedly. "This place doesn't strike me safe.

186

If we found her here, anybody might. We require a new safe deposit, and I know the very one. It's—"

Beach came out of the silence. His manner betrayed agitation.

"If it is all the same to you, sir, I would much prefer not to hear it."

"Eh?"

"It would be a great relief to me, sir, to be able to expunge the entire matter from my mind. I have been under a considerable mental strain of late, sir, and I really don't think I could bear any more of it. Besides, supposing I were questioned, sir. It may be my imagination, but I have rather fancied from the way he has looked at me occasionally that Mr. Baxter harbours suspicions."

"Baxter always harbours suspicions about something," said Millicent.

"Yes, miss. But in this case they are well grounded, and if it is all the same to you and Mr. Carmody I would greatly prefer that he was not in a position to go on harbouring them."

"All right, Beach," said Hugo. "After what you have done for us, your lightest wish is law. You can be out of this, if you want to. Though I was going to suggest that, if you cared to go on feeding the animal—"

"No, sir—really—if you please . . ."

"Right ho, then. Come along, Millicent. We must be shifting."

"Are you going to take her away now?"

"This very moment. I pass this handkerchief through the handy ring which you observe in the nose and—Ho! Allez-oop! Goodbye, Beach. It is a far, far better thing that I do than I have ever done, I think."

"Good-bye, Beach," said Millicent. "I can't tell you how grateful we are."

"I am glad to have given satisfaction, miss, I wish you every success and happiness, sir."

Left alone, the butler drew in his breath till he swelled like a balloon, then poured it out again in a long, sighing puff. He picked up the lantern and left the cottage. His walk was the walk of a butler from whose shoulders a great weight has rolled.

187

V

It is a fact not generally known, for a nice sense of the dignity of his position restrained him from exercising it, that Beach possessed a rather attractive singing voice. It was a mellow baritone, in timbre not unlike that which might have proceeded from a cask of very old, dry sherry, had it had vocal chords: and we cannot advance a more striking proof of the lightness of heart which had now come upon him than by mentioning that, as he walked home through the wood, he broke his rigid rule and definitely warbled. "There's a light in thy bow-er," sang Beach. "A light in thy BOW-er . . ."

He felt more like a gay young second footman than a butler of years' standing. He listened to the birds with an uplifted heart. Upon the rabbits that sported about his path he bestowed a series of indulgent smiles. The shadow that had darkened his life had passed away. His conscience was at rest.

So completely was this so that when, on reaching the house, he was informed by Footman James that Lord Emsworth had been inquiring for him and desired his immediate presence in the library, he did not even tremble. A brief hour ago, and what menace this announcement would have seemed to him to hold. But now it left him calm. It was with some little difficulty that, as he mounted the stairs, he kept himself from resuming his song.

"Er—Beach."

"Your lordship?"

The butler now became aware that his employer was not alone. Dripping in an unpleasant manner on the carpet, for he seemed somehow to have got himself extremely wet, stood the Efficient Baxter. Beach regarded him with a placid eye. What was Baxter to him or he to Baxter now?

"Your lordship?" he said again, for Lord Emsworth appeared to be experiencing some difficulty in continuing the conversation.

"Eh? What? What? Oh, yes."

The ninth earl braced himself with a visible effort.

"Er—Beach."

"Your lordship?"

"I—er—I sent for you, Beach—"

"Yes, your lordship?"

At this moment Lord Emsworth's eye fell on a volume on the desk dealing with Diseases in Pigs. He seemed to draw strength from it.

"Beach," he said, in quite a crisp, masterful voice, "I sent for you because Mr. Baxter has made a remarkable charge against you. Most extraordinary."

"I should be glad to be acquainted with the gravamen of the accusation, your lordship."

"The what?" asked Lord Emsworth, starting.

"If your lordship would be kind enough to inform me of the substance of Mr. Baxter's charge?"

"Oh, the substance? Yes. You mean the substance? Precisely. Quite so. The substance. Yes, to be sure. Quite so. Quite so. Yes. Exactly. No doubt."

It was plain to the butler that his employer had begun to dodder. Left to himself this human cuckoo clock would go maundering on like this indefinitely. Respectfully, but with the necessary firmness, he called him to order.

"What is it that Mr. Baxter says, your lordship?"

"Eh? Oh, tell him, Baxter. Yes, tell him, dash it."

The Efficient Baxter moved a step closer and began to drip on another part of the carpet. His spectacles gleamed determinedly. Here was no stammering, embarrassed peer of the realm, but a man who knew his own mind and could speak it.

"I followed you to the gamekeeper's cottage in the west wood just now, Beach."

"Sir?"

"You heard what I said."

"Undoubtedly, sir. But I fancied I must be mistaken. I have not been to the spot you mention, sir."

"I saw you with my own eyes."

"I can only repeat my asseveration, sir," said the butler with a saintly meekness.

189

Lord Emsworth, who had taken another look at Diseases in Pigs, became brisk again.

"He says he peeped through the window, dash it."

Beach raised a respectful eyebrow. It was as if he had said that it was not his place to comment on the pastimes of the Castle's guests, however childish. If Mr. Baxter wished to go out into the woods in the rain and play solitary games of Peep-bo, that, said the eyebrow, was a matter that concerned Mr. Baxter alone.

"And you were in there, he says, feeding the Empress."

"Your lordship?"

"And you were in there—Dash it, you heard."

"I beg your pardon, your lordship, but I really fail to comprehend."

"Well, if you want it in a nutshell, Mr. Baxter says it was you who stole my pig."

There were few things in the world that the butler considered worth raising both eyebrows at. This was one of the few. He stood for a moment, exhibiting them to Lord Emsworth: then turned to Baxter, so that he could see them, too. This done, he lowered them and permitted about three-eighths of a smile to play for a moment about his lips.

"Might I speak frankly, your lordship?"

"Dash it, man, we want you to speak frankly. That's the whole idea. That's why I sent for you. We want a full confession and the name of your accomplice and all that sort of thing."

"I hesitate only because what I should like to say may possibly give offence to Mr. Baxter, your lordship, which would be the last thing I should desire."

The prospect of offending the Efficient Baxter which caused such concern to Beach appeared to disturb his lordship not at all.

"Get on. Say what you like."

"Well, then, your lordship, I think it possible that Mr. Baxter, if he will pardon my saying so, may have been suffering from a hallucination."

"Tchah!" said the Efficient Baxter.

"You mean he's potty?" said Lord Emsworth, struck with the

idea. In this excitement of his late secretary's information, he had overlooked this simple explanation. Now there came surging back to him all the evidence that went to support such a theory. Those flower pots—that leap from the library window. He looked at Baxter keenly. There *was* a sort of wild gleam in his eyes. The old coot glitter.

"Really, Lord Emsworth!"

"Oh, I'm not saying you are, my dear fellow. Only—"

"It is quite obvious to me," said Baxter stiffly, "that this man is lying. Wait!" he continued, raising a hand. "Are you prepared to come with his lordship and me to the cottage now, at this very moment, and let his lordship see for himself?"

"No, sir."

"Ha!"

"I should first," said Beach, "wish to go downstairs and get my hat."

"Quite right," agreed Lord Emsworth cordially. "Very sensible. Might catch a nasty cold in the head. Certainly, get your hat, Beach, and meet us at the front door."

"Very good, your lordship."

A bystander, observing the little party that was gathered some five minutes later on the gravel outside the great door of Blandings Castle, would have noticed about it a touch of chill, a certain restraint. None of its three members seemed really in the mood for a ramble through the woods. Beach, though courtly, was not cordial. The face under his bowler hat was the face of a good man misjudged. Baxter was eying the sullen sky as though he suspected it of something. As for Lord Emsworth, he had just become conscious that he was about to accompany through dark and deserted ways one who, though on this afternoon's evidence the trend of his tastes seemed to be toward suicide, might quite possibly become homicidal.

"One moment," said Lord Emsworth.

He scuttled into the house again and came out looking happier. He was carrying a stout walking stick with an ivory knob on it.

13

I

BLANDINGS CASTLE basked in the afterglow of a golden summer evening. Only a memory now was the storm which, two hours since, had raged with such violence through its parks, pleasure grounds, and messuages. It had passed, leaving behind it peace and bird song and a sunset of pink and green and orange and opal and amethyst. The air was cool and sweet, and the earth sent up a healing fragrance. Little stars were peeping down from a rain-washed sky.

To Ronnie Fish, slumped in an armchair in his bedroom on the second floor, the improved weather conditions brought no spiritual uplift. He could see the sunset, but it left him cold. He could hear the thrushes calling in the shrubberies, but did not think much of them. It is, in short, in no sunny mood that we re-introduce Ronald Overbury Fish to the reader of this chronicle.

The meditation of a man who has recently proposed to and been accepted by a girl some inches taller than himself, for whom he entertains no warmer sentiment than a casual feeling that, take her for all in all, she isn't a bad sort of egg, must of necessity tend toward the sombre: and the surroundings in which Ronnie had spent the latter part of the afternoon had not been of a kind to encourage optimism. At the moment when the skies suddenly burst asunder and the world became a shower bath, he had been walking along the path that skirted the wall of the kitchen garden; and the only shelter that offered itself was a gloomy cave or dugout that led to the heating apparatus of the hothouses. Into this he had dived like a homing rabbit, and here, sitting on a heap of bricks, he had remained for the space of fifty minutes with no company but one small green frog and his thoughts.

The place was a sort of Sargasso Sea into which had drifted all the flotsam and jetsam of the kitchen-garden which adjoined. There was a wheelbarrow, lacking its wheel and lying drunkenly on its side. There were broken pots in great profusion. There were a heap of withered flowers, a punctured watering can, a rake with large gaps in its front teeth, some potatoes unfit for human consumption, and half a dead blackbird. The whole effect was extraordinarily like hell, and Ronnie's spirits, not high at the start, had sunk lower and lower.

Sobered by rain, wheelbarrows, watering cans, rakes, potatoes, and dead blackbirds, not to mention the steady, supercilious eye of a frog which resembled that of a bishop at the Athenaeum inspecting a shy new member, Ronnie had begun definitely to repent of the impulse which had led him to ask Millicent to be his wife. And now, in the cosier environment of his bedroom, he was regretting it more than ever.

Like most people who have made a defiant and dramatic gesture and then have leisure to reflect, he was oppressed by a feeling that he had gone considerably farther than was prudent. Samson, as he heard the pillars of the temple begin to crack, must have felt the same. Gestures are all very well while the intoxication lasts. The trouble is that it lasts such a very little while.

In asking Millicent to marry him he had gone, he now definitely realized, too far. He had overdone it. It was not that he had any objection to Millicent as a wife. He had none whatever—provided she were somebody else's wife. What was so unpleasant was the prospect of being married to her himself.

He groaned in spirit and became aware that he was no longer alone. The door had opened, and his friend Hugo Carmody was in the room. He noted with a dull surprise that Hugo was in the conventional costume of the English gentleman about to dine. He had not supposed the hour so late.

"Hullo," said Hugo. "Not dressed? That gong's gone"

It now became clear to Ronnie that he simply was not equal

to facing his infernal family at the dinner table. He supposed that Millicent had spread the news of their engagement by this time, and that meant discussion, wearisome congratulations, embraces from his Aunt Constance, chaff of the vintage of 1895 from his Uncle Galahad—in short, fuss and gabble. And he was in no mood for fuss and gabble. Pot luck with a tableful of Trappist monks he might just have endured, but not a hearty feed with the family.

"I don't want any dinner."

"No dinner?"

"No."

"Ill or something?"

"No."

"But you don't want any dinner? I see. Rummy! However, your affair, of course. It begins to look as if I should have to don the nosebag alone. Beach tells me that Baxter also will be absent from the trough. He's upset about something, it seems, and has asked for a snort and sandwiches in the smoking room. And as for the pustule Pilbeam," said Hugo grimly, "I propose to interview him at the earliest possible date, and after that he won't want any dinner, either."

"Where are the rest of them?"

"Didn't you know?" said Hugo, surprised. "They're dining over at old Parsloe's. Your aunt, Lord Emsworth, old Galahad, and Millicent." He coughed. A moment of some slight embarrassment impended. "I say, Ronnie, old man, while on the subject of Millicent—"

"Well?"

"You know that engagement of yours?"

"What about it?"

"It's off."

"Off?"

"Right off. A washout. She's changed her mind."

"What!"

"Yes. She's going to marry me. I may tell you we have been engaged for weeks—one of those secret betrothals—but we had a row. Row now over. Complete reconciliation. So she asked

194

me to break it to you gently that in the circs she proposes to return you to store."

A thrill of ecstasy shot through Ronnie. He felt as men on the scaffold feel when the messenger bounds in with the reprieve.

"Well, that's the first bit of good news I've had for a long time," he said.

"You mean you didn't want to marry Millicent?"

"Of course I didn't."

"Not so much of the 'of course,' laddie," said Hugo, offended. "She's an awfully nice girl—"

"An angel. Shropshire's leading seraph."

"—but I'm not in love with her any more than she's in love with me."

"In that case," said Hugo, with justifiable censure, "why propose to her? A goofy proceeding, it seems to me." He clicked his tongue. "Of course, this is what happened. You grabbed Millicent to score off Sue, and she grabbed you to score off me. And now, I suppose, you've fixed it up with Sue again. Very sound. Couldn't have made a wiser move. She's obviously the girl for you."

Ronnie winced. The words had touched a nerve. He had been trying not to think of Sue, but without success. Her picture insisted on rising before him. Not being able to exclude her from his thoughts he had tried to think of her bitterly.

"I haven't," he cried.

Extraordinary how difficult it was, even now, to think bitterly of Sue. Sue was Sue. That was the fundamental fact that hampered him. Try as he might to concentrate it on the tragedy of Mario's restaurant, his mind insisted on slipping back to earlier scenes of sunshine and happiness.

"You haven't?" said Hugo, damped.

That Ronnie could possibly be in ignorance of Sue's arrival at the castle never occurred to him. Long ere this, he took it for granted, they must have met. And he assumed, from the equanimity with which his friend had received the news of the loss of Millicent, that Sue and he must have had just such another heart-to-heart talk as had taken place in the room above the gamekeeper's cottage. The dour sullenness of Ronnie's face made his kindly heart sink.

"You mean you haven't fixed things up?"

"No."

Ronnie writhed. Sue in his ear. Sue up the river. Sue in his arms to the music of sweet saxophones. Sue laughing. Sue smiling. Sue in the springtime, with the little breezes ruffling her hair . . .

He forced his mind away from these weakening visions. Sue at Mario's. . . . That was better. . . . Sue letting him down. . . . Sue hobnobbing with the blister Pilbeam. . . . That was much better.

"I think you're being very hard on that poor little girl, Ronnie."

"Don't call her a poor little girl."

"I will call her a poor little girl," said Hugo firmly. "To me she is a poor little girl, and I don't care who knows it. I don't mind telling you that my heart bleeds for her. Bleeds profusely. And I must say I should have thought—"

"I don't want to talk about her."

"—after her doing what she has done—"

"I don't want to talk about her, I tell you."

Hugo sighed. He gave it up. The situation was what they called an *impasse*. Too bad. His best friend and a dear little girl like that parted forever. Two jolly good eggs sundered for all eternity. Oh, well, that was Life.

"If you want to talk about anything," said Ronnie, "you had much better talk about this engagement of yours."

"Only too glad, old man. Was afraid it might bore you, or would have touched more freely on subject."

"I suppose you realize the family will squash it flat?"

"Oh, no, they won't."

"You think my Aunt Constance is going to leap about and bang the cymbals?"

"The Keeble, I admit," said Hugo, with a faint shiver, "may make her presence felt to some extent. But I rely on the ninth earl's support and patronage. Before long, I shall be causing the ninth to look on me as a son."

"How?"

For a moment Hugo almost yielded to the temptation to confide in this friend of his youth. Then he realized the unwisdom of such a course. By an odd coincidence, he was thinking exactly the same of Ronnie as Ronnie at an earlier stage of this history had thought of him. Ronnie, he considered, though a splendid chap, was not fitted to be a repository of secrets. A babbler. A sieve. The sort of fellow who would spread a secret hither and thither all over the place before nightfall.

"Never mind," he said. "I have my methods."

"What are they?"

"Just methods," said Hugo, "and jolly good ones. Well, I'll be pushing off. I'm late. Sure you won't come down to dinner? Then I'll be going. It is imperative that I get hold of Pilbeam with all possible speed. Don't want the sun to go down on my wrath. All has ended happily in spite of him, but that's no reason why he shouldn't be massacred. I look on myself as a man with a public duty."

For some minutes after the door had closed Ronnie remained humped in his chair. Then, it spite of everything, there began to creep upon him a desire for food, too strong to be resisted. Perfect health and a tealess afternoon spent in the open had given him a compelling appetite. He still shrank from the thought of the dining room. Fond at he was of Hugo, he simply could not stand his conversation to-night. A chop at the Emsworth Arms would meet the case. He could get down there in five minutes in his two-seater.

He rose. His mind, as he moved to the door, was not entirely occupied with thoughts of food. Hugo's parting words had turned it in the direction of Pilbeam again.

What had brought Pilbeam to the castle, he did not know. But, now that he was here, let him look out for himself! A couple of minutes alone with P. Frobisher Pilbeam was just the medicine his bruised soul required. Apparently, from what he had said, Hugo also entertained some grievances against the man. It could be nothing compared with his own.

Pilbeam! The cause of all his troubles. Pilbeam! The snake in the grass. Pilbeam! . . . Yes. . . . His heart might be broken,

197

his life a wreck, but he could still enjoy the faint consolation of dealing faithfully with Pilbeam.

He went out into the corridor. And, as he did so, Percy Pilbeam came out of the room opposite.

II

Pilbeam had dressed for dinner with considerable care. Owing to the fact that Lord Emsworth, in his woolen-headed way, had completely forgotten to inform him of the exodus to Matchingham Hall, he was expecting to meet a gay and glittering company at the meal and had prepared himself accordingly. Looking at the result in the mirror, he had felt a glow of contentment. This glow was still warming him as he passed into the corridor. As his eyes fell on Ronnie it faded abruptly.

In the days of his editorship of *Society Spice*, that frank and fearless journal, P. Frobisher Pilbeam had once or twice had personal encounters with people having no cause to wish him well. They had not appealed to him. He was a man who found no pleasure in physical violence. And that physical violence threatened now was only too sickeningly plain. It was foreshadowed in the very manner in which this small but sturdy young man confronting him had begun to creep forward. Pilbeam, who was an F.R.Z.S., had seen leopards at the Zoo creep just like that.

Years of conducting a weekly scandal sheet, followed by a long period of activity as a private inquiry agent, undoubtedly train a man well for the exhibition of presence of mind in sudden emergencies. One finds it difficult in the present instance to overpraise Percy Pilbeam's ready resource. Had a great military strategist been present he would have nodded approval. With the grim menace of Ronnie Fish coming closer and closer, Percy Pilbeam did exactly what Napoleon, Hannibal, or the great Duke of Marlborough would have done. Reaching behind him for the handle and twisting it sharply, he slipped through the door of his bedroom, banged it, and was gone. Many an eel has disappeared into the mud with less smoothness and celerity.

If the leopard which he resembled had seen its prey vanish

into the undergrowth just before dinner time it would probably have expressed its feelings in exactly the same kind of short, rasping cry as proceeded from Ronnie Fish, witnessing this masterly withdrawal. For an instant he was completely taken aback. Then he plunged for the door and into the room.

He stood, baffled. Pilbeam had vanished. To Ronnie's astonished eyes the apartment appeared entirely free from detectives in any shape or form whatsoever. There was the bed. There were the chairs. There were the carpet, the dressing table, and the bookshelf. But of private inquiry agents there was a complete shortage.

How long this miracle would have continued to afflict him, one cannot say. His mind was still dealing dazedly with it, when there came to his ears a sharp click, as of a key being turned in the lock. It seemed to proceed from a hanging cupboard at the other side of the room.

Old Miles Fish, Ronnie's father, might, as Lord Emsworth had asserted, have been the biggest fool in the Brigade of Guards, but his son could reason and deduce. Springing forward, he tugged at the handle of the cupboard door. The door stood fast.

At the same moment there filtered through it the sound of muffled breathing.

Ronnie was already looking grim. He now looked grimmer. He placed his lips to the panel.

"Come out of that!"

The breathing stopped.

"All right," said Ronnie, with a hideous calm. "Right jolly ho! I can wait."

For some moments there was silence. Then from the beyond a voice spoke in reply.

"Be reasonable!" said the voice.

"Reasonable?" said Ronnie thickly. "Reasonable, eh?" He choked. "Come out! I only want to pull your head off," he added, with a note of appeal.

The voice became conciliatory.

"I know what you're upset about," it said.

"You do, eh?"

"Yes, I quite understand. But I can explain everything."

"What?"

"I say I can explain everything."

"You can, can you?"

"Quite," said the voice.

Up till now Ronnie had been pulling. It now occurred to him that pushing might possibly produce more satisfactory results. So he pushed. Nothing, however, happened. Blandings Castle was a house which rather prided itself on its solidity. Its walls were walls and its doors, doors. No jimcrack work here. The cupboard creaked but did not yield.

"I say!"

"Well?"

"I wish you'd listen. I tell you I can explain everything. About that night at Mario's, I mean. I know exactly how it is. You think Miss Brown is fond of me. I give you my solemn word she can't stand the sight of me. She told me so herself."

A pleasing thought came to Ronnie.

"You can't stay in there all night," he said.

"I don't want to stay in here all night."

"Well, come on out, then."

The voice became plaintive.

"I tell you she had never set eyes on me before that night at Mario's. She was dining with that fellow Carmody, and he went out and I came over and introduced myself. No harm in that, was there?"

Ronnie wondered if kicking would do any good. A tender feeling for his toes, coupled with the reflection that his Uncle Clarence might have something to say if he started breaking up cupboard doors, caused him to abandon the scheme. He stood, breathing tensely.

"Just a friendly word, that's all I came over to say. Why shouldn't a fellow introduce himself to a girl and say a friendly word?"

"I wish I'd got there earlier."

"I'd have been glad to see you," said Pilbeam courteously.

"Would you?"

"Quite."

"I shall be glad to see *you*," said Ronnie, "when I can get this damned door open."

Pilbeam began to fear asphyxiation. The air inside the cupboard was growing closer. Peril lent him the inspiration which it so often does.

"Look here," he said, "are you Ronnie?"

Ronnie turned pinker.

"I don't want any of your dashed cheek."

"No, but listen. Is your name Ronnie?"

Silence without.

"Because if it is," said Pilbeam, "you're the fellow she's come here to see."

More silence.

"She told me so. In the garden this evening. She came here calling herself Miss Shoemaker, or some such name, just to see you. That ought to show you that I'm not the man she's keen on."

The silence was broken by a sharp exclamation.

"What's that?"

Pilbeam repeated his remark. A growing hopefulness lent an almost finicky clearness to his diction.

"Come out!" cried Ronnie.

"That's all very well, but—"

"Come out, I want to talk to you."

"You are talking to me."

"I don't want to bellow this through a door. Come on out. I swear I won't touch you."

It was not so much Pilbeam's faith in the knightly word of the Fishes that caused him to obey the request as a feeling that, if he stayed cooped up in this cupboard much longer, he would get a rush of blood to the head. Already he was beginning to feel as if he were breathing a solution of dust and mothballs. He emerged. His hair was rumpled, and he regarded his companion warily. He had the air of a man who has taken his life in his hands. But the word of the Fishes held good. As far as Ronnie was concerned the war appeared to be over.

"What did you say? She's here?"

"Quite."

201

"What do you mean, quite?"

"Certainly. Quite. She got here just before I did. Haven't you seen her?"

"No."

"Well, she's here. She's in the room they call the Garden Room. I heard her tell that old bird Galahad so. If you go there now," said Pilbeam insinuatingly, "you could have a quiet word with her before she goes down to dinner."

"And she said she had come here to see me?"

"Yes. To explain about that night at Mario's. And what I say," proceeded Pilbeam warmly, "is, if a girl didn't love a fellow, would she came to a place like this, calling herself Miss Shoolbred or something, simply to see him? I ask you!" said Pilbeam.

Ronnie did not answer. His feelings held him speechless. He was too deep in a morass of remorse to be able to articulate. Indeed, he was in a frame of mind so abased that he almost asked Pilbeam to kick him. The thought of how he had wronged his blameless Sue was almost too bitter to be borne. It bit like a serpent and stung like an adder.

From the surge and riot of his reflections one thought now emerged clearly, shining like a beacon on a dark night. The Garden Room!

Turning without a word, he shot out of the door as quickly as Percy Pilbeam a short while ago had shot in. And Percy Pilbeam, with a deep sigh, went to the dressing table, took up the brush, and started to restore his hair to a state fit for the eyes of the nobility and gentry. This done, he smoothed his moustache and went downstairs to the drawing room.

III

The drawing room was empty. And to Pilbeam's surprise it continued to be empty for quite a considerable time. He felt puzzled. He had expected to meet a reproachful host with an eye on the clock and a haughty hostess clicking her tongue. As the minutes crept by and his solitude remained unbroken, he began to grow restless.

202

He wandered about the room, staring at the pictures, straightening his tie and examining the photographs on the little tables. The last of these was one of Lord Emsworth, taken apparently at about the age of thirty, in long whiskers and the uniform of the Shropshire Yeomanry. He was gazing at this with the fascinated horror which it induced in everyone who saw it suddenly for the first time, when the door at last opened, and with a sinking sensation of apprehension Pilbeam beheld the majestic form of Beach.

For an instant he stood eying the butler with that natural alarm which comes to all of us when in the presence of a man who a few short hours earlier has given us one look and made us feel like a condemned food product. Then his tension relaxed.

It has been well said that for every evil in this world nature supplies an antidote. If butlers come, can cocktails be far behind? Beach was carrying a tray with glasses and a massive shaker on it; and Pilbeam, seeing these, found himself regarding their formidable bearer almost with equanimity.

"A cocktail, sir?"

"Thanks."

He accepted a brimming glass. The darkness of its contents suggested a welcome strength. He drank. And instantaneously all through his system beacon fires seemed to burst into being.

He drained the glass. His whole outlook on life was now magically different. Quite suddenly he had begun to feel equal to a dozen butlers, however glazed their eyes might be.

And it might have been an illusion caused by gin and vermouth, but this butler seemed to have changed considerably for the better since their last meeting. His eye, though still glassy, had lost the old basilisk quality. There appeared now, in fact, to be something so positively light-hearted about Beach's whole demeanour that the proprietor of the Argus Enquiry Agency was emboldened to plunge into conversation.

"Nice evening."

"Yes, sir."

"Nice after the storm."

"Yes, sir."

"Came down a bit, didn't it?"

"The rain was undoubtedly extremely heavy, sir. Another cocktail?"

"Thanks."

The relighting of the beacons had the effect of removing from Pilbeam the last trace of diffidence and shyness. He saw now that he had been entirely mistaken in this butler. Encountering him in the hall at the moment of his arrival, he had supposed him supercilious and hostile. He now perceived that he was a butler and a brother. More like Old King Cole, that jolly old soul, indeed, than anybody Pilbeam had met for months.

"I got caught in it," he said affably.

"Indeed, sir?"

"Yes. Lord Emsworth had been showing me some photographs of that pig of his. . . . By the way, in strict confidence—what's your name?"

"Beach, sir."

"In strict confidence, Beach, I know something about that pig."

"Indeed, sir?"

"Yes. Well, after I had seen the photographs I went for a walk in the park and the rain came on and I got pretty wet. In fact, I don't mind telling you I had to get under cover and take my trousers off to dry."

He laughed merrily.

"Another cocktail, sir?"

"Making three in all?"

"Yes, sir."

"Perhaps you're right," said Pilbeam.

For some moments he sat, pensive and distrait, listening to the strains of a brass band which seemed to have started playing somewhere in the vicinity. Then his idly floating thoughts drifted back to the mystery which had been vexing him before this delightful butler's entry.

"I say, Beach, I've been waiting here hours and hours. Where's this dinner I heard you beating gongs about?"

"Dinner is ready, sir, but I put it back some little while, as gentlemen aren't punctual in the summertime."

Pilbeam considered this statement. It sounded to him as if it would make rather a good song title. Gentlemen aren't punctual in the summertime, in the summertime (I said, in the summertime). So take me back to that Old Kentucky Shack. . . . He tried to fit it to the music which the brass band was playing, but it did not go very well, and he gave it up.

"Where is everybody?" he asked.

"His lordship and her ladyship and Mr. Galahad and Miss Threepwood are dining at Matchingham Hall."

"What! With old Pop Parsloe?"

"With Sir Gregory Parsloe-Parsloe, yes, sir."

Pilbeam chuckled.

"Well, well, well! Quick worker, old Parsloe. Don't you think so Beach? I mean, you advise him to do a thing, to act in a certain way, to adopt a certain course of action, and he does it right away. You agree with me, Beach?"

"I fear my limited acquaintance with Sir Gregory scarcely entitles me to offer an opinion, sir."

"Talking of old Parsloe, Beach—you did say your name was Beach?"

"Yes, sir."

"With a capital B?"

"Yes, sir."

"Well, talking of old Parsloe, Beach, I could tell you something about him—something he's up to."

"Indeed, sir?"

"But I'm not going to. Respect client's confidence. Lips sealed. Professional secret."

"Yes, sir?"

"As you rightly say, yes. Any more of that stuff in the shaker, Beach?"

"A little, sir, if you consider it judicious."

"That's just what I do consider it. Start pouring."

The detective sipped luxuriously, fuller and fuller every moment of an uplifting sense of well-being. If the friendship which had sprung up between himself and the butler was possibly a little one-sided, on the one side on which it did exist it was warm, even fervent. It seemed to Pilbeam that for the first time since he had arrived at Blandings Castle he had found a real chum, a kindred soul in whom he might confide. And he was filled with an overwhelming desire to confide in somebody.

"As a matter of fact, Beach," he said, "I could tell you all sorts of things about all sorts of people. Practically everybody in this house I could tell you something about. What's the name of that chap with the light hair, for instance? The old boy's secretary."

"Mr. Carmody, sir?"

"Carmody! That's the name. I've been trying to remember it. Well, I could tell you something about Carmody."

"Indeed, sir?"

"Yes. Something about Carmody that would interest you very much. I saw Carmody this afternoon when Carmody didn't see me."

"Indeed, sir?"

"Yes. Where is Carmody?"

"I imagine he will be down shortly, sir. Mr. Ronald also."

"Ronald!" Pilbeam drew in his breath sharply. "There's a tough baby, Beach. That Ronnie. Do you know what he wanted to do just now? Murder me!"

In Beach's opinion, for he did not look on Percy Pilbeam as a very necessary member of society, this would have been a commendable act, and he regretted that its consummation had been prevented. He was also feeling that the conscientious butler he had always prided himself on being would long ere this have withdrawn and left this man to talk to himself. But even the best of butlers have human emotions, and the magic of Pilbeam's small-talk held Beach like a spell. It reminded him of the Gossip page of *Society Spice*, a paper to which he was a regular subscriber. He was piqued and curious. So far, it was true, his companion had merely hinted, but something seemed to tell him that, if he lingered on, a really sensational news item would shortly emerge.

He had never been more right in his life. Pilbeam by this time had finished the fourth cocktail, and the urge to confide had become overpowering. He looked at Beach, and it nearly made him cry to think that he was holding anything back from such a splendid fellow.

"And do you know why he wanted to murder me, Beach?"

It scarcely seemed to the butler that the action required anything in the nature of a reasoned explanation, but he murmured the necessary response.

"I could not say, sir."

"Of course you couldn't. How could you? You don't know. That's why I'm telling you. Well, listen. He's in love with a girl in the chorus at the Regal, a girl named Sue Brown, and he thought I had been taking her out to dinner. That's why he wanted to murder me, Beach."

"Indeed, sir?"

The butler spoke calmly, but he was deeply stirred. He had always flattered himself that the inmates of Blandings Castle kept few secrets from him, but this was something new.

"Yes. That was why. I had the dickens of a job holding him off, I can tell you. Do you know what saved me, Beach?"

"No, sir."

"Presence of mind. I put it to him—to Ronnie—I put it to Ronnie as a reasonable man that, if this girl loved me, would she have come to this place, pretending to be Miss Shoemaker, simply so as to see him?"

"Sir!"

"Yes, that's who Miss Shoemaker is, Beach. She's a chorus girl called Sue Brown, and she's come here to see Ronnie."

Beach stood transfixed. His eyes swelled bulbously from their sockets. He was incapable of even an "Indeed, sir?"

He was still endeavouring to assimilate this extraordinary revelation when Hugo Carmody entered the room.

"Ah!" said Hugo, his eye falling on Pilbeam. He stiffened. He stood looking at the detective like Schopenhauer's butcher at the selected lamb.

"Leave us, Beach," he said, in a grave, deep voice.

The butler came out of his trance.

"Sir?"

"Pop off."

"Very good, sir."

The door closed.

"I've been looking for you, viper," said Hugo.

"Have you, Carmody?" said Percy Pilbeam effervescently. "I've been looking for you, too. Got something I want to talk to you about. Each looking for each. Or am I thinking of a couple of other fellows? Come right in, Carmody, and sit down. Good old Carmody! Jolly old Carmody! Splendid old Carmody. Well, well, well, well, well!"

If the lamb mentioned above had suddenly accosted the above-mentioned butcher in a similar strain of hearty camaraderie, it could have hardly disconcerted him more than Pilbeam with these cheery words disconcerted Hugo. His stern, set gaze became a gaping stare.

Then he pulled himself together. What did words matter? He had no time to bother about words. Action was what he was after. Action!

"I don't know if you're aware of it, worm," he said, "but you came jolly near to blighting my life."

"Doing what, Carmody?"

"Blighting my life."

"List to me while I tell you of the Spaniard who blighted my life," sang Percy Pilbeam, letting it go like a lark in the spring-time. He had never felt happier or in more congenial society. "How did I blight your life, Carmody?"

"You didn't."

"You said I did."

"I said you tried to."

"Make up your mind, Carmody."

"Don't keep calling me Carmody."

"But, Carmody," protested Pilbeam, "it's your name, isn't it? Certainly it is. Then why try to hush it up, Carmody? Be frank and open. I don't mind people knowing my name. I glory in it. It's Pilbeam—Pilbeam—Pilbeam—that's what it is—Pilbeam!"

"In about thirty seconds," said Hugo, "it will be Mud."

It struck Percy Pilbeam for the first time that in his companion's manner there was a certain peevishness.

"Something the matter?" he asked, concerned.

"I'll tell you what's the matter."

"Do, Carmody, do," said Pilbeam. "Do, do, do. Confide in me. I like your face."

He settled himself in a deep armchair and, putting the tips of his fingers together after a little preliminary difficulty in making them meet, leaned back, all readiness to listen to whatever trouble it was that was disturbing this new friend of his.

"Some days ago, insect—"

Pilbeam opened his eyes.

"Speak up, Carmody," he said. "Don't mumble."

Hugo's fingers twitched. He regarded his companion with a burning eye and wondered why he was wasting time talking instead of at once proceeding to the main business of the day and knocking the fellow's head off at the roots. What saved Pilbeam was the reclining position he had assumed. If you are a Carmody and a sportsman, you cannot attack even a viper if it persists in lying back on its spine and keeping its eyes shut.

"Some days ago," he began again, "I called at your office. And after we had talked of this and that I left. I discovered later that immediately upon my departure you had set your foul spies on my trail and had instructed them to take notes of my movements and report on them. The result being that I came jolly close to having my bally life ruined. And, if you want to know what I'm going to do, I'm going to haul you out of that chair and turn you round and kick you hard and go on kicking you till I kick you out of the house. And if you dare to shove your beastly little nose back inside the place, I'll disembowel you."

Pilbeam unclosed his eyes.

"Nothing," he said, "could be fairer than that. Nevertheless, that's no reason why you should go about stealing pigs."

Hugo had often read stories in which people reeled and would have fallen had they not clutched at whatever it was that they clutched at. He had never expected to undergo that experience

209

himself. But it is undoubtedly the fact that, if he had not at this moment gripped the back of a chair, he would have been hard put to it to remain perpendicular.

"Pig pincher!" said Pilbeam austerely, and closed his eyes again.

Hugo, having established his equilibrium by means of the chair, had now moved away. He was making a strong effort to recover his morale. He picked up the photograph of Lord Emsworth in his Yeomanry uniform and looked at it absently; then, as if it had just dawned upon him, put it down with a shudder, like a man who finds that he has been handling a snake.

"What do you mean?" he said thickly.

Pilbeam's eyes opened.

"What do I mean? What do you think I mean? I mean you're a pig pincher. That's what I mean. You go to and fro, sneaking pigs and hiding them in caravans."

Hugo took up Lord Emsworth's photograph again, saw what he was doing, and dropped it quickly. Pilbeam had closed his eyes once more, and, looking at him, Hugo could not repress a reluctant thrill of awe. He had often read about the superhuman intuition of detectives, but he had never before been privileged to observe it in operation. Then an idea occurred to him.

"Did you see me?"

"What say, Carmody?"

"Did you see me?"

"Yes, I see you, Carmody," said Pilbeam playfully. "Peep-bo!"

"Did you see me put that pig in the caravan?"

Pilbeam nodded eleven times in rapid succession.

"Certainly I saw you, Carmody. Why shouldn't I see you, considering I'd been caught in the rain and taken shelter in the caravan and was in there with my trousers off, trying to dry them because I'm subject to lumbago?"

"I didn't see you."

"No, Carmody, you did not. And I'll tell you why, Carmody. Because I heard a girl's voice outside saying, 'Be quick, or somebody will come along!' and I hid. You don't suppose I would let a sweet girl see me in knee-length mesh-knit underwear, do you? Not done, Carmody," said Pilbeam severely. "Not cricket."

Hugo was experiencing the bitterness which comes to all criminals who discover too late that they have undone themselves by trying to be clever. It had seemed at the time such a good idea to remove the Empress from the gamekeeper's cottage in the west wood and place her in Baxter's caravan, where nobody would think of looking. How could he have anticipated that the caravan would be bulging with blighted detectives?

At this tense moment the door opened and Beach appeared.

"I beg your pardon, sir, but do you propose to wait any longer for Mr. Ronald?"

"Eh?"

"Certainly not," said Pilbeam. "Who the devil's Mr. Ronald, I should like to know? I didn't come to this place to do a fast-cure. I want my dinner, and I want it now. And if Mr. Ronald doesn't like it, he can do the other thing." He strode in a dominating manner to the door. "Come along, Carmody. Din-dins."

Hugo had sunk into a chair.

"I don't want any dinner," he said dully.

"You don't want any dinner?"

"No."

"No dinner?"

"No."

Pilbeam shrugged his shoulders impatiently.

"The man's an ass," he said.

He headed for the stairs. His manner seemed to indicate that he washed his hands of Hugo.

Beach lingered.

"Shall I bring you some sandwiches, sir?"

"No, thanks. What's that?"

A loud crash had sounded. The butler went to the door and looked out.

"It is Mr. Pilbeam, sir. He appears to have fallen downstairs."

For an instant a look of hope crept into Hugo's careworn face.

"Has he broken his neck?"

"Apparently not, sir."

"Ah," said Hugo regretfully.

14

I

THE EFFICIENT Baxter had retired to the smoking room shortly before half-past seven. He desired silence and solitude, and in this cosy haven he got both. For a few minutes nothing broke the stillness but the slow ticking of a clock on the mantelpiece. Then from the direction of the hall there came a new sound, faint at first but swelling and swelling to a frenzied blare, seeming to throb through the air with a note of passionate appeal like a woman wailing for her demon lover. It was that tocsin of the soul, the muezzin of the country house, the dressing-for-dinner gong.

Baxter did not stir. The summons left him unmoved. He had heard it, of course. Butler Beach was a man who swung a pretty gong stick. He had that quick forearm flick and wristy follow through which stamp the master. If you were anywhere within a quarter of a mile or so you could not help hearing him. But the sound had no appeal for Baxter. He did not propose to go in to dinner. He wanted to be alone with his thoughts.

They were not the sort of thoughts with which most men would have wished to be left alone, being both dark and bitter. That expedition to the gamekeeper's cottage in the west wood had not proved a pleasure trip for Rupert Baxter. Reviewing it in his mind, he burned with baffled rage.

And yet everybody had been very nice to him—very nice and tactful. True, at the moment of the discovery that the cottage contained no pig and appeared to have been pigless from its foundation, there had been perhaps just the slightest suspicion of constraint. Lord Emsworth had grasped his ivory-knobbed stick a little more tightly and had edged behind Beach in a rather noticeable way, his manner saying more plainly than was agreeable, "If he springs, be ready!" And there had come into the butler's face a look, hard to bear, which was a blend of censure and pity. But after that both of them had been charming.

Lord Emsworth had talked soothingly about light and shade effects. He had said—and Beach had agreed with him—that in the darkness of a thunderstorm anybody might have been deceived into supposing that he had seen a butler feeding a pig in the game-keeper's cottage. It was probably, said Lord Emsworth—and Beach thought so, too—a bit of wood sticking out of the wall or something. He went on to tell a longish story of how he himself, when a boy, had fancied he had seen a cat with flaming eyes. He had concluded by advising Baxter—and Beach said the suggestion was a good one—to hurry home and have a nice cup of hot tea and go to bed.

His attitude, in short, could not have been pleasanter or more considerate. Yet Baxter, as he sat in the smoking room, burned, as stated, with baffled rage.

The door handle turned. Beach stood on the threshold.

"If you have changed your mind, sir, about taking dinner, the meal is quite ready."

He spoke as friend to friend. There was nothing in his manner to suggest that the man he addressed had ever accused him of stealing pigs. As far as Beach was concerned, all was forgotten and forgiven.

But the milk of human kindness, of which the butler was so full, had not yet been delivered on Baxter's doorstep. The hostility in his eye, as he fixed it on his visitor, was so marked that a lesser man than Beach might have been disconcerted.

"I don't want any dinner."

"Very good, sir."

"Bring me that whisky-and-soda quick."

"Yes, sir."

The door closed as softly as it had opened, but not before a pang like a red-hot needle had pierced the ex-secretary's bosom. It was caused by the fact that he had distinctly heard the butler, as he withdrew, utter a pitying sigh.

213

It was the sort of sigh which a kind-hearted man would have given on peeping into a padded cell in which some old friend was confined, and Baxter resented it with all the force of an imperious nature. He had not ceased to wonder what, if anything, could be done about it when the refreshments arrived, carried by James the footman. James placed them gently on the table, shot a swift glance of respectful commiseration at the patient, and passed away.

The sigh had cut Baxter like a knife. The look stabbed him like a dagger. For a moment he thought of calling the man back and asking him what the devil he meant by staring at him like that, but wiser counsels prevailed. He contented himself with draining a glass of whisky-and-soda and swallowing two sandwiches.

This done, he felt a little—not much, but a little—better. Before, he would gladly have murdered Beach and James and danced on their graves. Now, he would have been satisfied with straight murder.

However, he was alone at last. That was some slight consolation. Beach had come and gone. Footman James had come and gone. Everybody else must by now be either at Matchingham Hall or assembled in the dining room. On the solitude which he so greatly desired there could be no further intrusion. He resumed his meditations.

For a time these dealt exclusively with the recent past, and were, in consequence, of a morbid character. Then, as the grateful glow of the whisky began to make itself felt, a softer mood came to Rupert Baxter. His mind turned to thoughts of Sue.

Men as efficient as Rupert Baxter do not fall in love in the generally accepted sense of the term. Their attitude toward the tender passion is more restrained than that of the ordinary feckless young man who loses his heart at first sight with a whoop and a shiver. Baxter approved of Sue. We cannot say more. But this approval, added to the fact that he had been informed by Lady Constance that the girl was the only daughter of a man who possessed sixty million dollars, had been enough to cause him to earmark her in his mind as the future Mrs. Baxter. In that capacity he had docketed her and filed her away at the first moment of their meeting.

Naturally, therefore, the remarks which Lord Emsworth had let fall in her hearing had caused him grave concern. It hampers a man in his wooing if the girl he has selected for his bride starts with the idea that he is as mad as a coot. He congratulated himself on the promptitude with which he had handled the situation. That letter which he had written her could not fail to put him right in her eyes.

Rupert Baxter was a man in whose lexicon there was no such word as failure. An heiress like this Miss Schoonmaker would not, he was aware, lack for suitors; but he did not fear them. If only she were making a reasonably long stay at the castle he felt that he could rely on his force of character to win the day. In fact, it seemed to him that he could almost hear the wedding bells ringing already. Then, coming out of his dreams, he realized that it was the telephone.

He reached for the instrument with a frown, annoyed at the interruption, and spoke with an irritated sharpness.

"Hullo?"

A ghostly voice replied. The storm seemed to have affected the wires.

"Speak up!" barked Baxter.

He banged the telephone violently on the table. The treatment, as is so often the case, proved effective.

"Blandings Castle?" said the voice, no longer ghostly.

"Yes."

"Post Office, Market Blandings, speaking. Telegram for Lady Constance Keeble."

"I will take it."

The voice became faint again. Baxter went through the movements as before.

"Lady Constance Keeble, Blandings Castle, Market Blandings, Shropshire, England," said the voice, recovering strength, as if it had shaken off a wasting sickness. "Handed in at Paris."

"Where?"

215

"Paris, France."

"Oh? Well?"

The voice gathered volume.

"'Terribly sorry hear news.'"

"What?"

"'News.'"

"Yes?"

"'Terribly sorry hear news Stop Quite understand Stop So disappointed shall be unable come to you later as going back America at end of Month Stop Do hope we shall be able arrange something when I return next year Stop Regards Stop!'"

"Yes?"

"Signed 'Myra Schoonmaker.'"

"Signed—*what?*"

"Myra Schoonmaker."

Baxter's mouth had fallen open. The forehead above the spectacles was wrinkled, the eyes behind them staring blankly and with a growing horror.

"Shall I repeat?"

"What?"

"Do you wish the message repeated?"

"No," said Baxter in a choking voice.

He hung up the receiver. There seemed to be something crawling down his back. His brain was numbed.

Myra Schoonmaker! Telegraphing from Paris!

Then who was this girl who was at the castle calling herself by that preposterous name? An impostor, an adventuress. She must be.

And if he made a move to expose her she would revenge herself by showing Lord Emsworth that letter of his.

In the agitation of the moment he had risen to his feet. He now sat down heavily.

That letter . . . !

He must recover it. He must recover it at once. As long as it remained in the girl's possession it was a pistol pointed at his head. Once let Lord Emsworth become acquainted with those very frank criticisms of himself which it contained and not even his ally, Lady Constance, would be able to restore him to his lost secretaryship. The ninth earl was a mild man, accustomed to bowing to his sister's decrees, but there were limits beyond which he could not be pushed.

And Baxter yearned to be back at Blandings Castle in the position he had once enjoyed. Blandings was his spiritual home. He had held other secretaryships—he held one now, at a salary far higher than that which Lord Emsworth had paid him—but never had he succeeded in recapturing that fascinating sense of power, of importance, of being the man who directed the destinies of one of the largest houses in England.

At all costs he must recover that letter. And the present moment, he perceived, was ideal for the venture. The girl must have the thing in her room somewhere, and for the next hour at least she would be in the dining room. He would have ample opportunity for a search.

He did not delay. Thirty seconds later he was mounting the stairs, his face set, his spectacles gleaming grimly. A minute later he reached his destination. No good angel, aware of what the future held, stood on the threshold to bar his entry. The door was ajar. He pushed it open and went in.

II

Blandings Castle, like most places of its size and importance, contained bedrooms so magnificent that they were never used. With their four-poster beds and their superb but rather oppressive tapestries they had remained untenanted since the time when Queen Elizabeth, dodging from country house to country house in that restless, snipe-like way of hers, had last slept in them. Of the guest rooms still in commission the most luxurious was that which had been given to Sue.

At the moment when Baxter stole cautiously in, it was looking its best in the gentle evening light. But Baxter was not in sight-seeing mood. He ignored the carved bedstead, the easy armchairs, the pictures, the decorations, and the soft carpet into which his feet sank. The beauty of the sky through the French windows

217

that gave onto the balcony drew but a single brief glance from him. Without delay he made for the writing desk which stood against the wall near the bed. It seemed to him a good point of departure for his search.

There were several pigeonholes in the desk. They contained single sheets of notepaper, double sheets of notepaper, postcards, envelopes, telegraph forms, and even a little pad on which the room's occupant was presumably expected to jot down any stray thoughts and reflections on Life which might occur to him or her before turning in for the night. But not one of them contained the fatal letter.

He straightened himself and looked about the room. The drawer of the dressing table now suggested itself as a possibility. He left the desk and made his way toward it.

The primary requisite of dressing tables being a good supply of light, they are usually placed in a position to get as much of it as possible. This one was no exception. It stood so near to the open windows that the breeze was ruffling the tassels on its lamp shades: and Baxter, arriving in front of it, was enabled for the first time to see the balcony in its entirety.

And as he saw it his heart seemed to side-slip. Leaning upon the parapet and looking out over the sea of gravel that swept up to the front door from the rhododendron-fringed drive stood a girl. And not even the fact that her back was turned could prevent Baxter identifying her.

For an instance he remained frozen. Even the greatest men congeal beneath the chill breath of the totally unexpected. He had assumed as a matter of course that Sue was down in the dining room, and it took him several seconds to adjust his mind to the unpleasing fact that she was up on her balcony. When he recovered his presence of mind sufficiently to draw noiselessly away from the line of vision, his first emotion was one of irritation. This chopping and changing, this eleventh-hour alteration of plans, these sudden decisions to remain upstairs when they ought to be downstairs, were what made women as a sex so unsatisfactory.

To irritation succeeded a sense of defeat. There was nothing

218

for it, he realized, but to give up his quest and go. He started to tiptoe silently to the door, agreeably conscious now of the softness and thickness of the Axminster pile that made it possible to move unheard, and had just reached it, when from the other side there came to his ears a sound of chinking and clattering — the sound, in fact, which is made by plates and dishes when they are carried on a tray to a guest who, after a long railway journey, has asked her hostess if she may take dinner in her room.

Practice makes perfect. This was the second time in the last three hours that Baxter had found himself trapped in a room in which it was vitally urgent that he should not be discovered, and he was getting the technique of the thing. On the previous occasion, in the small library, he had taken to himself wings like a bird and sailed out of window. In the present crisis such a course, he perceived immediately, was not feasible. The way of an eagle would profit him nothing. Soaring over the balcony, he would be observed by Sue and would, in addition, unquestionably break his neck. What was needed here was the way of a diving duck.

And so, as the door handle turned, Rupert Baxter, even in this black hour efficient, dropped on all-fours and slid under the bed as smoothly as if he had been practising for weeks.

III

Owing to the restricted nature of his position and the limited range of vision which he enjoys, virtually the only way in which a man who is hiding under a bed can entertain himself is by listening to what is going on outside. He may hear something of interest, or he may hear only the draught sighing along the floor; but, for better or for worse, that is all he is able to do.

The first sound that came to Rupert Baxter was that made by the placing of the tray on the table. Then, after a pause, a pair of squeaking shoes passed over the carpet and squeaked out of hearing. Baxter recognized them as those of Footman Thomas, a confirmed squeaker.

After this, somebody puffed, causing him to deduce the presence of Beach.

219

"Your dinner is quite ready, miss."

"Oh, thank you."

The girl had apparently come in from the balcony. A chair scraped to the table. A savoury scent floated to Baxter's nostrils, causing him acute discomfort. He had just begun to realize how extremely hungry he was and how rash he had been, first to attempt to dine off a couple of sandwiches and secondly to undertake a mission like his present one without a square meal inside him.

"That is chicken, miss—en casserole."

Baxter had deduced as much, and was trying not to let his mind dwell on it. He uttered a silent groan. In addition to the agony of having to smell food, he was beginning to be conscious of a growing cramp in his left leg. He turned on one side and did his best to emulate the easy nonchalance of those Indian fakirs who, doubtless from the best motives, spend the formative years of their lives lying on iron spikes.

"It looks very good."

"I trust you will enjoy it, miss. Is there anything further that I can do for you?"

"No, thank you. Oh, yes. Would you mind fetching that manuscript from the balcony? I was reading it out there, and I left it on the chair. It's Mr. Threepwood's book."

"Indeed, miss? An exceedingly interesting compilation, I should imagine?"

"Yes, very."

"I wonder if it would be taking a liberty, miss, to ask you to inform me later, at your leisure, if I made any appearance in its pages."

"You?"

"Yes, miss. From what Mr. Galahad has let fall from time to time I fancy it was his intention to give me printed credit as his authority for certain of the stories which appear in the book."

"Do you want to be in it?"

"Most decidedly, miss. I should consider it an honour. And it would please my mother."

"Have you a mother?"

"Yes, miss. She lives at Eastbourne."

The butler moved majestically onto the balcony, and Sue's mind had turned to speculation about his mother and whether she looked anything like him when there was a sound of hurrying feet without, the door flew open, and Beach's mother passed from her mind like the unsubstantial fabric of a dream. With a little choking cry she rose to her feet. Ronnie was standing before her.

15

AND MEANWHILE, if we may borrow an expression from a sister art, what of Hugo Carmody?

It is a defect unfortunately inseparable from any such document as this faithful record of events in and about Blandings Castle that the chronicler, in order to give a square deal to each of the individuals whose fortunes he has undertaken to narrate, is compelled to flit abruptly from one to the other in the manner popularized by the chamois of the Alps leaping from crag to crag. The activities of the Efficient Baxter seeming to him to demand immediate attention, he was reluctantly compelled some little while back to leave Hugo in the very act of reeling beneath a crushing blow. The moment has now come to return to him.

The first effect on a young man of sensibility and gentle upbringing of the discovery that an unfriendly detective has seen him placing stolen pigs in caravans is to induce a stunned condition of mind, a sort of mental coma. The face lengthens. The limbs grow rigid. The tie slips sideways and the cuffs recede into the coat sleeves. The subject becomes temporarily, in short, a total loss.

It is perhaps as well, therefore, that we did not waste valuable time watching Hugo in the process of digesting Percy Pilbeam's sensational announcement, for it would have been like looking at a statue. If the reader will endeavour to picture Rodin's Thinker in a dinner jacket and trousers with braid down the sides, he will have got the general idea. At the instant when Hugo Carmody makes his reappearance life has just begun to return to the stiffened frame.

And with life came the dawning of intelligence. This ghastly snag which had popped up in his path was too big, reflected Hugo, for any man to tackle. It called for a woman's keener wit. His first act on emerging from the depths, therefore, was to leave the drawing room and totter downstairs to the telephone. He got the number of Matchingham Hall and, establishing communication with Sir Gregory Parsloe-Parsloe's butler, urged him to summon Miss Millicent Threepwood from the dinner table. The butler said in rather a reproving way that Miss Threepwood was at the moment busy drinking soup. Hugo, with the first flash of spirit he had shown for a quarter of an hour, replied that he didn't care if she was bathing in it. "Fetch her," said Hugo, and almost added the words, "You scurvy knave." He then clung weakly to the receiver, waiting, and in a short while a sweet but agitated voice floated to him across the wire.

"Hugo?"

"Millicent?"

"Is that you?"

"Yes. Is that you?"

"Yes."

Anything in the nature of misunderstanding was cleared away. It was both of them.

"What's up?"

"Everything's up."

"How do you mean?"

"I'll tell you," said Hugo, and did so. It was not a difficult story to tell. Its plot was so clear that a few whispered words sufficed.

"You don't mean that?" said Millicent, the tale concluded.

"I do mean that."

"Oh, golly!" said Millicent.

Silence followed. Hugo waited palpitatingly. The outlook seemed to him black. He wondered if he had placed too much reliance in woman's wit. That "Golly!" had not been hopeful.

"Hugo!"

"Hullo?"

"This is a bit thick."

"Yes," agreed Hugo. The thickness had not escaped him.

"Well, there's only one thing to do."

A faint thrill passed through Hugo Carmody. One would be enough. Woman's wit was going to bring home the bacon after all.

"Listen!"

"Well?"

"The only thing to do is for me to go back to the dining room and tell Uncle Clarence you've found the Empress."

"Eh?"

"Found her, fathead."

"How do you mean?"

"Found her in the caravan."

"But weren't you listening to what I was saying?" There were tears in Hugo's voice. "Pilbeam saw us putting her there."

"I know."

"Well, what's our move when he says so?"

"Stout denial."

"Eh?"

"We stoutly deny it," said Millicent.

The thrill passed through Hugo again, stronger than before. It might work. Yes, properly handled, it would work. He poured broken words of love and praise into the receiver.

"That's right," he cried. "I see daylight. I will go to Pilbeam and tell him privily that if he opens his mouth I'll strangle him."

"Well, hold on. I'll go and tell Uncle Clarence. I expect he'll be out in a moment to have a word with you."

"Half a minute! Millicent!"

"Well?"

"When am I supposed to have found this ghastly pig?"

"Ten minutes ago, when you were taking a stroll before dinner. You happened to pass the caravan and you heard an odd noise inside and you looked to see what it was and there was the Empress, and you raced back to the house to telephone."

"But, Millicent! Half a minute!"

"Well?"

"The old boy will think Baxter stole her."

"So he will! Isn't that splendid? Well, hold on."

224

Hugo resumed his vigil. It was some moments later that a noise like the clucking of fowls broke out at the Matchingham Hall end of the wire. He deduced correctly that this was caused by the ninth Earl of Emsworth endeavouring to clothe his thoughts in speech.

"Kuk-kuk-kuk . . ."

"Yes, Lord Emsworth?"

"Kuk-Carmody!"

"Yes, Lord Emsworth?"

"Is this true?"

"Yes, Lord Emsworth."

"You've found the Empress?"

"Yes, Lord Emsworth."

"In that feller Baxter's caravan?"

"Yes, Lord Emsworth."

"Well, I'll be damned!"

"Yes, Lord Emsworth."

So far Hugo Carmody had found his share of the dialogue delightfully easy. On these lines he would have been prepared to continue it all night. But there was something else besides "Yes, Lord Emsowrth" that he must now endeavour to say. There is a tide in the affairs of men which, taken at the flood, leads on to fortune: and that tide, he knew, would never rise higher than at the present moment. He swallowed twice to unlimber his vocal chords.

"Lord Emsworth," he said, and, though his heart was beating fast, his voice was steady, "there is something I would like to take this opportunity of saying. It will come as a surprise to you, but I hope not as an unpleasant surprise. I love your niece Millicent, and she loves me, Lord Emsworth. We have loved each other for many weeks, and it is my hope that you will give your consent to our marriage. I am not a rich man, Lord Emsworth. In fact, strictly speaking, except for my salary I haven't a bean in the world. But my Uncle Lester owns Rudge Hall in Worcestershire—I dare say you have heard of the place? You turn to the left off the main road to Birmingham and go about a couple of miles—well, anyway, it's a biggish sort of place in Worcestershire, and my Uncle

225

Lester owns it, and the property is entailed, and I'm next in succession. . . . I won't pretend that my Uncle Lester shows any indications of passing in his checks—he was extremely fit last time I saw him—but, after all, he's getting on, and all flesh is as grass and, as I say, I'm next man in, so I shall eventually succeed to quite a fairish bit of the stuff and a house and park and rent roll and all that; so what I mean is, it isn't as if I wasn't in a position to support Millicent later on, and if you realized, Lord Emsworth, how we love one another I'm sure you would see that it wouldn't be playing the game to put any obstacles in the way of our happiness, so what I'm driving at, if you follow me, is, may we charge ahead?"

There was dead silence at the other end of the wire. It seemed as if this revelation of a good man's love had struck Lord Emsworth dumb. It was only some moments later, after he had said "Hullo!" six times and "I say, are you there?" twice that it was borne in upon Hugo that he had wasted two hundred and eighty words of the finest eloquence on empty space.

His natural chagrin at this discovery was sensibly diminished by the sudden sound of Millicent's voice in his ear.

"Hullo!"

"Hullo!"

"Hullo!"

"Hullo!"

"Hugo!"

"Hullo!"

"I say, Hugo!" She spoke with the joyous excitement of a girl who has just emerged from the centre of a family dog fight. "I say, Hugo, things are hotting up here properly. I sprung it on Uncle Clarence just now that I want to marry you!"

"So did I. Only he wasn't there."

"I said, 'Uncle Clarence, aren't you grateful to Mr. Carmody for finding the Empress?' and he said, 'Yes, yes, yes, yes, yes, to be sure. Capital boy! Capital boy! Always liked him.' And I said, 'I suppose you wouldn't by any chance let me marry him?' and he said, 'Eh, what? Marry him?' 'Yes,' I said. 'Marry him.' And he said, 'Certainly, certainly, certainly, certainly, by all means.'

226

And then Aunt Constance had a fit, and Uncle Gally said she was a kill-joy and ought to be ashamed of herself for throwing the gaff into love's young dream, and Uncle Clarence kept on saying 'Certainly, certainly.' I don't know what old Parsloe thinks of it all. He's sitting in his chair looking at the ceiling and drinking Hock. The butler left at the end of round one. I'm going back to see how it's all coming out. Hold the line."

A man for whom Happiness and Misery are swaying in the scales three miles away, and whose only medium of learning the result of the contest is a telephone wire, is not likely to ring off impatiently. Hugo sat tense and breathless, like one listening in on the radio to a championship fight in which he has a financial interest. It was only when a cheery voice spoke at his elbow that he realized that his solitude had been invaded, and by Percy Pilbeam at that.

Percy Pilbeam was looking rosy and replete. He swayed slightly, and his smile was rather wider and more pebble-beached than a total abstainer's would have been.

"Hullo, Carmody," said Percy Pilbeam. "What ho, Carmody. So here you are, Carmody."

It came to Hugo that he had something to say to this man.

"Here, you!" he cried.

"Yes, Carmody?"

"Do you want to be battered to a pulp?"

"No, Carmody."

"Then listen. You didn't see me put that pig in the caravan. Understand?"

"But I did, Carmody."

"You didn't—not if you want to go on living."

Percy Pilbeam appeared to be in a mood not only of keen intelligence but of the utmost reasonableness and amiability.

"Say no more, Carmody," he said agreeably. "I take your point. You want me not to tell anybody I saw you put that caravan in the pig. Quite, Carmody, quite."

"Well, bear it in mind."

"I will, Carmody. Oh, yes, Carmody, I will. I'm going for a stroll outside, Carmody. Care to join me?"

"Go to hell!"

"Quite," said Percy Pilbeam.

He tacked unsteadily to the door, aimed himself at it and passed through. And a moment later Millicent's voice spoke.

"Hugo?"

"Hullo?"

"Oh, Hugo, darling, the battle's over. We've won. Uncle Clarence has said 'Certainly' sixty-five times, and he's just told Aunt Constance that if she thinks she can bully him she's very much mistaken. It's a walk-over. They're all coming back right away in the car. Uncle Clarence is an angel."

"So are you."

"Me?"

"Yes, you."

"Not such an angel as you are."

"Much more of an angel than I am," said Hugo, in the voice of one trained to the appraising and classifying of angels.

"Well, anyway, you precious old thing, I'm going to give them the slip and walk home along the road. Get out Ronnie's two-seater and come and pick me up, and we'll go for a drive together, miles and miles through the country. It's the most perfect evening."

"You bet it is!" said Hugo fervently. "What I call something like an evening. Give me two minutes to get the car out and five to make the trip and I'll be with you."

"'At-a-boy'!" said Millicent.

"'At-a-baby'!" said Hugo.

16

SUE STOOD staring, wide eyed. This was the moment that she had tried to picture to herself a hundred times. And always her imagination had proved unequal to the task. Sometimes she had seen Ronnie in her mind's eye cold, aloof, hostile; sometimes gasping and tottering, dumb with amazement; sometimes pointing a finger at her like a character in a melodrama and denouncing her as an impostor. The one thing for which she had not been prepared was what happened now.

Eton and Cambridge train their sons well. Once they have grasped the fundamental fact of life that all exhibitions of emotion are bad form, bombshells cannot disturb their poise and earthquakes are lucky if they get so much as an "Eh, what?" from them. But Cambridge has its limitations, and so has Eton. And remorse had goaded Ronnie Fish to a point where their iron discipline had ceased to operate. He was stirred to his depths, and his scarlet face, his rumpled hair, his starting eyes, and his twitching fingers all proclaimed the fact.

"Ronnie!" cried Sue.

It was all she had time to say. The thought of what she had done for his sake; the thought that for love of him she had come to Blandings Castle under a false colours—an impostor—faced at every turn by the risk of detection—liable at any moment to be ignominiously exposed and looked at through a lorgnette by his Aunt Constance; the thought of the shameful way he had treated her—all these thoughts were racking Ronald Fish with a wearing anguish. They had brought the hot blood of the Fishes to the boil, and now, face to face with her, he did not hesitate.

He sprang forward, clasped her in his arms, hugged her to him. To Baxter's revolted ears, though he tried not to listen, there came in a husky cataract the sound of a Fish's self-reproaches. Ronnie was saying what he thought of himself, and his opinion appeared not to be high. He said he was a beast, a brute, a swine, a cad, a hound, and a worm. If he had been speaking of Percy Pilbeam he could scarely have been less complimentary.

Even up to this point Baxter had not liked the dialogue. It now became perfectly nauseating. Sue said it had all been her fault. Ronnie said, No, his. No, hers, said Sue. No, his, said Ronnie. No, hers, said Sue, No, altogether his, said Ronnie. It must have been his, he pointed out, because, as he had observed before, he was a hound and a worm. He now went further. He revealed himself as a blister, a tick, and a perishing outsider.

"You're not!"

"I am!"

"You're not!"

"I am!"

"Of course you're not!"

"I certainly am!"

"Well, I love you, anyway."

"You can't."

"I do!"

"You can't."

"I do."

Baxter writhed in silent anguish.

"How long?" said Baxter to his immortal soul. "How long?" The question was answered with a startling promptitude. From the neighbourhood of the French windows there sounded a discreet cough. The debaters sprang apart, two minds with but a single thought.

"Your manuscript, miss," said Beach sedately.

Sue looked at him. Ronnie looked at him. Sue until this moment had forgotten his existence. Ronnie had supposed him downstairs, busy about his butlerine duties. Neither seemed very glad to see him.

Ronnie was the first to speak.

"Oh—hullo, Beach!"

230

There being no answer to this except "Hullo, sir!" which is a thing that butlers do not say, Beach contented himself with a benignant smile. It had the unfortunate effect of making Ronnie think that the man was laughing at him, and the Fishes were men at whom butlers may not lightly laugh. He was about to utter a heated speech, indicating this, when the injudiciousness of such a course presented itself to his mind. Beach must be placated. He forced his voice to a note of geniality.

"So there you are, Beach?"

"Yes, sir."

"I suppose all this must seem tolerably rummy to you?"

"No, sir."

"No?"

"I had already been informed, Mr. Ronald, of the nature of your feelings toward this lady."

"What!"

"Yes, sir."

"Who told you?"

"Mr. Pilbeam, sir."

Ronnie uttered a gasp. Then he became calmer. He had suddenly remembered that this man was his ally, his accomplice, linked to him not only by a friendship dating back to his boyhood but by the even stronger bond of a mutual crime. Between them there need be no reserves. Delicate though the situation was, he now felt equal to it.

"Beach," he said, "how much do you know?"

"All, sir."

"All?"

"Yes, sir."

"Such as—"

Beach coughed.

"I am aware that this lady is a Miss Sue Brown. And, according to my informant, she is employed in the chorus of of the Regal Theatre."

"Quite the Encyclopaedia, aren't you?"

"Yes, sir."

231

"I want to marry Miss Brown, Beach."

"I can readily appreciate such a desire on your part, Mr. Ronald," said the butler with a paternal smile.

Sue caught at the smile.

"Ronnie! He's all right. I believe he's a friend."

"Of course he's a friend! Old Beach. One of my earliest and stoutest pals."

"I mean, he isn't going to give us away."

"Me, miss?" said Beach, shocked. "Certainly not."

"Splendid fellow, Beach!"

"Thank you, sir."

"Beach," said Ronnie, "the time has come to act. No more delay. I've got to make myself solid with Uncle Clarence at once. Directly he gets back to-night I shall go to him and tell him that Empress of Blandings is in the gamekeeper's cottage in the west wood, and then, while he's still weak, I shall spring on him the announcement of my engagement."

"Unfortunately, Mr. Ronald, the animal is no longer in the cottage."

"You've moved it?"

"Not I, sir. Mr. Carmody. By a most regrettable chance Mr. Carmody found me feeding it this afternoon. He took it away and deposited it in some place of which I am not cognizant, sir."

"But, good heavens, he'll dish the whole scheme. Where is he?"

"You wish me to find him, sir?"

"Of course I wish you to find him. Go at once and ask him where that pig is. Tell him it's vital."

"Very good, sir."

Sue had listened with bewilderment to this talk of pigs.

"I don't understand, Ronnie."

Ronnie was pacing the room in agitation. Once he came so close to where Baxter lay in his snug harbour that the ex-secretary had a flashing glimpse of a sock with a lavender clock. It was the first object of beauty that he had seen for a long time, and he should have appreciated it more than he did.

"I can't explain now," said Ronnie. "It's too long. But I can tell you this. If we don't get that pig back we're in the soup."

"Ronnie!"

Ronnie had ceased to pace the room. He was standing in a listening attitude.

"What's that?"

He sprang quickly to the balcony, looked over the parapet and came softly back.

"Sue!"

"What!"

"It's that blighter Pilbeam," said Ronnie in a guarded undertone. "He's climbing up the waterspout!"

17

From the moment when it left the door of Matchingham Hall and started on its journey back to Blandings Castle, a silence as of the tomb had reigned in the Antelope car which was bringing Lord Emsworth, his sister, Lady Constance Keeble, and his brother, the Hon. Galahad Threepwood, home from their interrupted dinner party. Not so much as a syllable proceeded from one of them.

In the light of what Millicent, an eyewitness at the front, had told Hugo over the telephone of the family battle which had been raging at Sir Gregory Parsloe's table this will appear strange. If ever three people with plenty to say to one another were assembled together in a small space, these three, one would have thought, were those three. Lady Constance alone might have been expected to provide enough conversation to keep the historian busy for hours.

The explanation, like all explanations, is simple. It is supplied by that one word Antelope.

Owing to the fact that some trifling internal ailment had removed from the active list the Hispano-Suiza in which Blandings Castle usually went out to dinner, Voules, the chauffeur, had had to fall back upon this secondary and inferior car; and anybody who has ever owned an Antelope is aware that there is no glass partition inside it, shutting off the driver from the cash customers. He is right there in their midst, ready and eager to hear everything that is said and to hand it on in due course to the Servants' Hall.

In these circumstances, though the choice seemed one between speech and spontaneous combustion, the little company kept their thoughts to themselves. They suffered, but they did it. It would be difficult to find a better illustration of all that is implied in the fine old phrase *Noblesse oblige*. At Lady Constance we point with particular pride. She was a woman, and silence weighed hardest on her.

There were times during the drive when even the sight of Voules's large, red ears all pricked up to learn the reason for this sudden and sensational return was scarcely sufficient to restrain Lady Constance Keeble from telling her brother Clarence just what she thought of him. From boyhood up he had not once come near to being her ideal man; but never had he sunk so low in her estimation as at the moment when she heard him giving his consent to the union of her niece Millicent with a young man who, besides being penniless, had always afflicted her with a nervous complaint for which she could find no name, but which is known to scientists as the heeby-jeebies.

Nor had he reestablished himself in any way by his outspoken remarks on the subject of the Efficient Baxter. He had said things about Baxter which no admirer of that energetic man could forgive. The adjectives mad, crazy, insane, gibbering—and worse, potty—had played in and out of his conversation like flashes of lightning. And from the look in his eye she gathered that he was still saying them all over again to himself.

Her surmise was correct. To Lord Emsworth the events of this day had come as a stunning revelation. On the strength of that flower-pot incident, two years ago, he had always looked on Baxter as mentally unbalanced; but, being a fair-minded man, he had recognized the possibility that a quiet, regular life and freedom from worries might, in the interval which had elapsed since his late secretary's departure from the castle, have affected a cure. Certainly the man had appeared quite normal on the day of his arrival. And now into the space of a few hours he had crammed enough variegated lunacy to equip all the March Hares in England and leave some over for the Mad Hatters.

The ninth Earl of Emsworth was not a man who was easily disturbed. His was a calm which, as a rule, only his younger son Frederick could shatter. But it was not proof against the sort of thing that had been going on to-day. No matter how placid you may

235

be, if you find yourself in close juxtaposition with a man who, when he is not hurling himself out of windows, is stealing pigs and trying to make you believe they were stolen by your butler, you begin to think a bit. Lord Emsworth was thoroughly upset. As the car bowled up the drive he was saying to himself that nothing could surprise him now.

And yet something did. As the car turned the corner by the rhododendrons and wheeled into the broad strip of gravel that faced the front door, he beheld a sight which brought the first sound he had uttered since the journey began bursting from his lips.

"Good God!"

The words were spoken in a high, penetrating tenor, and they made Lady Constance jump as if they had been pins running into her. This unexpected breaking of the great silence was agony to her taut nerves.

"What *is* the matter?"

"Matter? Look! Look at that fellow!"

Voules took it upon himself to explain. Never having met Lady Constance socially, as it were, he ought perhaps not to have spoken. He considered, however, that the importance of the occasion justified the solecism.

"A man is climbing the waterspout, m'lady."

"What! Where? I don't see him."

"He has just got into the balcony outside one of the bedrooms," said the Hon. Galahad.

Lord Emsworth went straight to the heart of the matter.

"It's that fellow Baxter!" he exclaimed.

The summer day, for all the artificial aid lent by daylight saving, was now definitely over, and gathering night had spread its mantle of dusk over the world. The visibility, therefore, was not good; and the figure which had just vanished over the parapet of the balcony of the Garden Room had been unrecognizable except to the eye of intuition. This, however, was precisely the sort of eye that Lord Emsworth possessed.

He reasoned closely. There were, he knew, on the premises

236

of Blandings Castle other male adults besides Rupert Baxter; but none of these would climb up waterspouts and disappear over balconies. To Baxter, on the other hand, such a pursuit would seem the normal, ordinary way of passing an evening. It would be his idea of wholesome relaxation. Soon, no doubt, he would come out onto the balcony again and throw himself to the ground. That was the sort of fellow Baxter was—a man of strange pleasures.

And so, going, as we say, straight to the heart of the matter, Lord Emsworth, jerking the pince-nez off his face in his emotion, exclaimed: "It's that fellow Baxter!"

Not since a certain day in their mutual nursery many years ago had Lady Constance gone to the length of actually hauling off and smiting her elder brother on the head with the flat of an outraged hand; but she came very near to doing it now. Perhaps it was the presence of Voules that caused her to confine herself to words.

"Clarence, you're an idiot!"

Even Voules could not prevent her saying that. After all, she was revealing no secrets. The chauffeur had been in service at the castle quite long enough to have formed the same impression for himself.

Lord Emsworth did not argue the point. The car had drawn up now outside the front door. The front door was open, as always of a summer evening, and the ninth earl, accompanied by his brother Galahad, hurried up the steps and entered the hall. And, as they did so, there came to their ears the sound of running feet. The next moment, the flying figure of Percy Pilbeam came into view, taking the stairs four at a time.

"God bless my soul!" said Lord Emsworth.

If Pilbeam heard the words or saw the speaker, he gave no sign of having done so. He was plainly in a hurry. He shot through the hall and, more like a startled gazelle than a private inquiry agent, vanished down the steps. His shirt front was dark with dirt stains, his collar had burst from its stud, and it seemed to Lord Emsworth, in the brief moment during which he was able to fo-

237

cus him, that he had a black eye. The next instant, there descended the stairs and flitted past with equal speed the form of Ronnie Fish.

Lord Emsworth got an entirely wrong conception of the affair. He had no means of knowing what had taken place in the Garden Room when Pilbeam, inspired by alcohol and flushed with the thought that now was the time to get into that apartment and possess himself of the manuscript of the Hon. Galahad's Reminiscences, had climbed the waterspout to put the plan into operation. He knew nothing of the detective's sharp dismay at finding himself unexpectedly confronted with the menacing form of Ronnie Fish. He was ignorant of the lively and promising mix-up which had been concluded by Pilbeam's tempestuous dash for life. All he saw was two men fleeing madly for the open spaces, and he placed the obvious interpretation upon this phenomenon.

Baxter, he assumed, had run amok and had done it with such uncompromising thoroughness that strong men ran panic-stricken before him.

Mild enough the ninth earl was by nature, a lover of rural peace and the quiet life, he had, like all Britain's aristocracy, the right stuff in him. It so chanced that during the years when he had held his commission in the Shropshire Yeomanry the motherland had not called to him to save her. But, had that call been made, Clarence, ninth Earl of Emsworth, would have answered it with as prompt a "Bless my Soul! Of course. Certainly!" as any of his Crusader ancestors. And in his sixtieth year the ancient fire still lingered. The Hon. Galahad, who had returned to watch the procession through the front door with a surprised monocle, turned back and found that he was alone. Lord Emsworth had disappeared. He now beheld him coming back again. On his amiable face was a look of determination. In his hand was a gun.

"Eh? What?" said the Hon Galahad, blinking.

The head of the family did not reply. He was moving toward the stairs. In just that same silent purposeful way had an Emsworth advanced on the foe at Agincourt.

A sound as of disturbed hens made the Hon. Galahad turn again.

"Galahad! What is all this? What is happening?"

The Hon. Galahad placed his sister in possession of the facts as known to himself.

"Clarence has just gone upstairs with a gun."

"With a gun!"

"Yes. Looked like mine, too. I hope he takes care of it." He perceived that Lady Constance had also been seized with the urge to climb. She was making excellent time up the broad staircase. So nimbly did she move that she was on the second landing before he came up with her.

And, as they stood there, a voice made itself heard from a room down the corridor.

"Baxter! Come out! Come out, Baxter, my dear fellow, immediately."

In the race for the room from which the words had appeared to proceed, Lady Constance, getting off to a good start, beat her brother by a matter of two lengths. She was thus the first to see a sight unusual even at Blandings Castle, though strange things had happened there from time to time.

Her young guest, Miss Schoonmaker, was standing by the window, looking excited and alarmed. Her brother Clarence, pointing a gun expertly from the hip, was staring fixedly at the bed. And from under the bed, a little like a tortoise protruding from its shell, there was coming into view the spectacled head of the Efficient Baxter.

18

A MAN who has been lying under a bed for a matter of some thirty minutes and, while there, has been compelled to listen to the sort of dialogue which accompanies a lovers' reconciliation seldom appears at his best or feels his brightest. There was fluff in Baxter's hair, dust on his clothes, and on Baxter's face a scowl of concentrated hatred of all humanity. Lord Emsworth, prepared for something pretty wild looking, found his expectations exceeded. He tightened his grasp on the gun and, to insure a more accurate aim, raised the butt of it to his shoulder, closing one eye and allowing the other to gleam along the barrel.

"I have you covered, my dear fellow," he said mildly.

Rupert Baxter had not yet begun to stick straws in his hair, but he seemed on the verge of that final piece of self-expression.

"Don't point that damned thing at me!"

"I shall point it at you," replied Lord Emsworth with spirit. He was not a man to be dictated to in his own house. "And at the slightest sign of violence—"

"Clarence!" It was Lady Constance who spoke. "Put that gun down."

"Certainly not."

"Clarence!"

"Oh, all right."

"And now, Mr. Baxter," said Lady Constance, proceeding to dominate the scene in her masterly way, "I am sure you can explain."

Her agitation had passed. It was not in this strong woman to remain agitated long. She had been badly shaken, but her faith

240

in her idols still held good. Remarkable as his behaviour might appear, she was sure that he could account for it in a perfectly satisfactory manner.

Baxter did not speak. His silence gave Lord Emsworth the opportunity of advancing his own views.

"Explain?" he spoke petulantly, for he resented the way in which his sister had thrust him from the centre of the stage. "What on earth is there to explain? The thing's obvious."

"Can't say I've quite got to the bottom of it," murmured the Hon. Galahad. "Fellow under bed. Why? Why under bed? Why here at all?"

Lord Emsworth hesitated. He was a kind-hearted man, and he felt that what he had to say would be better said in Baxter's absence. However, there seemed no way out of it, so he proceeded.

"My dear Galahad, think!"

"Eh!"

"That flower-pot affair. You remember?"

"Oh!" Understanding shone in the Hon. Galahad's monocle. "You mean . . . ?"

"Exactly."

"Yes, yes. Of course. Subject to these attacks, you mean?"

"Precisely."

This was not the first time Lady Constance Keeble had had the opportunity of hearing a theory ventilated by her brothers which she found detestable. She flushed brightly.

"Clarence!"

"My dear?"

"Kindly stop talking in that offensive way."

"God bless my soul!" Lord Emsworth was stung. "I like that. What have I said that is offensive?"

"You know perfectly well."

"If you mean that I was reminding Galahad in the most delicate way that poor Baxter here is not quite—"

"Clarence!"

"All very well to say 'Clarence!' like that. You know yourself he isn't right in the head. Didn't he throw flower pots at me? Didn't

241

he leap out of a window this very afternoon? Didn't he try to make me think that Beach—"

Baxter interrupted. There were certain matters on which he considered silence best, but this was one on which he could speak freely.

"Lord Emsworth!"

"Eh!"

"It has now come to my knowledge that Beach was not the prime mover in the theft of your pig. But I have ascertained that he was an accessory."

"A what?"

"He helped," said Baxter, grinding his teeth a little. "The man who committed the actual theft was your nephew, Ronald."

Lord Emsworth turned to his sister with a triumphant gesture, like one who has been vindicated.

"There! Now perhaps you'll say he's not potty? It won't do, Baxter, my dear fellow," he went on, waggling a reproachful gun at his late employee. "You really mustn't excite yourself by making up these stories."

"Bad for the blood pressure," agreed the Hon. Galahad.

"The Empress was found this evening in your caravan," said Lord Emsworth.

"What!"

"In your caravan. Where you put her when you stole her. And, bless my soul," said Lord Emsworth, with a start, "I must be going and seeing that she is put back in her sty. I must find Pirbright. I must—"

"In my caravan?" Baxter passed a feverish hand across his dust-stained forehead. Illumination came to him. "Then that's what that fellow Carmody did with the animal!"

Lord Emsworth had had enough of this. Empress of Blandings was waiting for him. Counting the minutes to that holy reunion, he chafed at having to stand here listening to these wild ravings.

"First Beach, then Ronald, then Carmody! You'll be saying I stole her next, or Galahad here, or my sister Constance. Baxter, my dear fellow, we aren't blaming you. Please don't think that.

242

We quite see how it is. You will overwork yourself, and of course nature demands the penalty. I wish you would go quietly to your room, my dear fellow, and lie down. All this must be very bad for you."

Lady Constance intervened. Her eye was aflame, and she spoke like Cleopatra telling an Ethiopian slave where he got off.

"Clarence, will you kindly use whatever slight intelligence you may possess? The theft of your pig is one of the most trivial and unimportant things that have ever happened in this world, and I consider the fuss that has been made about it quite revolting. But whoever stole the wretched animal—"

Lord Emsworth blanched. He stared as if wondering if he had heard aright.

"—and wherever it has been found, it was certainly not Mr. Baxter who stole it. It is, as Mr. Baxter says, much more likely to have been a young man like Mr. Carmody. There is a certain type of young man, I believe, to which Mr. Carmody belongs, which considers practical joking amusing. Do ask yourself, Clarence, and try to answer the question as reasonably as is possible for a man of your mental calibre: what earthly motive would Mr. Baxter have for coming to Blandings Castle and stealing pigs?"

It may have been the feel of the gun in his hand which awoke in Lord Emsworth old memories of dashing days with the Shropshire Yeomanry and lent him some of the hot spirit of his vanished youth. The fact remains that he did not wilt beneath his sister's dominating eye. He met it boldly, and boldly answered back.

"And ask yourself, Constance," he said, "what earthly motive Mr. Baxter has for anything he does?"

"Yes," said the Hon. Galahad loyally. "What motive has our friend Baxter for coming to Blandings Castle and scaring girls stiff by hiding under beds?"

Lady Constance gulped. They had found the weak spot in her defences. She turned to the man who she still hoped could deal efficiently with this attack.

"Mr. Baxter!" she said, as if she were calling on him for an after-dinner speech.

But Rupert Baxter had had no dinner. And it was perhaps this that turned the scale. Quite suddenly there descended on him a frenzied desire to be out of this, cost what it might. An hour before, half an hour before, even five minutes before, his tongue had been tied by a still lingering hope that he might yet find his way back to Blandings Castle in the capacity of private secretary to the Earl of Emsworth. Now he felt that he would not accept that post were it offered to him on bended knee.

A sudden overpowering hatred of Blandings Castle and all it contained gripped the Efficient Baxter. He marvelled that he had ever wanted to come back. He held at the present moment the well-paid and responsible position of secretary and adviser to J. Horace Jevons, the American millionaire, a man who not only treated him with an obsequiousness and respect which were balm to his soul, but also gave him such sound advice on the invest-ment of money that already he had trebled his savings. And it was this golden-hearted Chicagoan whom he had been think-ing of deserting, purely to satisfy some obscure sentiment which urged him to return to a house which, he saw now, he loathed as few houses have been loathed since human beings left off liv-ing in caves.

His eyes flashed through their lenses. His mouth tightened.

"I will explain!"

"I knew you would have an explanation," cried Lady Constance.

"I have. A very simple one."

"And short, I hope?" asked Lord Emsworth restlessly. He was aching to have done with all this talk and discussion and to be with his pig once more. To think of the Empress languishing in a beastly caravan was agony to him.

"Quite short," said Rupert Baxter.

The only person in the room who so far had remained entirely outside this rather painful scene was Sue. She had looked on from her place by the window, an innocent bystander. She now found herself drawn abruptly into the maelstrom of the debate. Baxter's

244

spectacles were raking her from head to foot, and he had pointed at her with an accusing forefinger.

"I came to this room," he said, "to try to recover a letter which I had written to this lady who calls herself Miss Schoonmaker."

"Of course she calls herself Miss Schoonmaker," said Lord Emsworth, reluctantly dragging his thoughts from the Empress. "It's her name, my dear fellow. That," he explained gently, "is why she calls herself Miss Schoonmaker. God bless my soul!" he said, unable to restrain a sudden spurt of irritability. "If a girl's name is Schoonmaker naturally she calls herself Miss Schoonmaker."

"Yes, if it is. But hers is not. It is Brown."

"Listen, my dear fellow," said Lord Emsworth soothingly. "You are only exciting yourself by going on like this. Probably doing yourself a great deal of harm. Now, what I suggest is that you go to your room and put a cool compress on your forehead and lie down and take a good rest. I will send Beach up to you with some nice bread-and-milk."

"Rum and milk," amended the Hon. Galahad. "It's the only thing. I knew a fellow in the year '97 who was subject to these spells—you probably remember him, Clarence—Bellamy—Barmy Bellamy we used to call him—and whenever—"

"Her name is Brown!" repeated Baxter, his voice soaring in a hysterical crescendo. "Sue Brown. She is a chorus girl at the Regal Theatre in London. And she is apparently engaged to be married to your nephew Ronald."

Lady Constance uttered a cry. Lord Emsworth expressed his feelings with a couple of tuts. The Hon. Galahad alone was silent. He caught Sue's eye, and there was concern in his gaze.

"I overheard Beach saying so in this very room. He said he had had the information from Mr. Pilbeam. I imagine it to be accurate. But, in any case, I can tell you this much. Whoever she is, she is an impostor who has come here under a false name. While I was in the smoking room some time back a telegram came through on the telephone from Market Blandings. It was signed Myra Schoonmaker, and it had been handed in in Paris this afternoon. That is all I have to say," concluded Baxter. "I will now leave you, and I sincerely hope I shall never set eyes on any of you again. Good-evening!"

His spectacles glinting coldly, he strode from the room and in the doorway collided with Ronnie, who was entering.

"Can't you look where you're going?" he asked.

"Eh?" said Ronnie.

"Clumsy idiot!" said the Efficient Baxter, and was gone.

In the room he had left, Lady Constance Keeble had become a stone figure of menace. She was not at ordinary times a particularly tall woman, but she seemed now to tower like something vast and awful, and Sue quailed before her.

"Ronnie!" cried Sue weakly.

It was the cry of the female in distress calling to her mate. Just so in prehistoric days must Sue's cave woman ancestress have cried to the man behind the club when suddenly cornered by the sabre-toothed tiger which Lady Constance Keeble so closely resembled.

"Ronnie!"

"What's all this?" asked the last of the Fishes.

He was breathing rather quickly, for the going had been fast. Pilbeam, once out in the open, had shown astonishing form at the short sprint. He had shaken off Ronnie's challenge twenty yards down the drive and plunged into a convenient shrubbery, and Ronnie, giving up the pursuit, had come back to Sue's room to report. It occasioned him some surprise to find that in his absence it had become the scene of some sort of public meeting.

"What's all this?" he said, addressing that meeting. Lady Constance wheeled round upon him.

"Ronald, who is this girl?"

"Eh?" Ronnie was conscious of a certain uneasiness, but he did his best. He did not like his aunt's looks, but then he never had. Something was evidently up, but it might be that airy nonchalance would save the day. "You know her, don't you? Miss Schoonmaker? Met her with me in London."

"Is her name Brown? And is she a chorus girl?"

246

"Why, yes," admitted Ronnie. It was a bombshell, but Eton and Cambridge stood it well. "Why, yes," he said, "as a matter of fact, that's right."

Words seem to fail Lady Constance. Judging from the expression on her face this was just as well.

"I'd been meaning to tell you about that," said Ronnie. "We're engaged."

Lady Constance recovered herself sufficiently to find one word. "Clarence!"

"Eh?" said Lord Emsworth. His thoughts had been wandering.

"You heard?"

"Heard what?"

Beyond the stage of turbulent emotion Lady Constance had become suddenly calm and icy.

"If you have not been sufficiently interested to listen," she said, "I may inform you that Ronald has just announced his intention of marrying a chorus girl."

"Oh, ah?" said Lord Emsworth. Would a man of Baxter's outstanding unbalanced intellect, he was wondering, have remembered to feed the Empress regularly? The thought was like a spear quivering in his heart. He edged in agitation toward the door and had reached it when he perceived that his sister had not yet finished talking to him.

"So that is all the comment you have to make, is it?"

"Eh? What about?"

"The point I have been endeavouring to make you understand," went on Lady Constance, with laborious politeness, "is that your nephew Ronald has announced his intention of marrying into the Regal Theatre chorus."

"Who?"

"Ronald. This is Ronald. He is anxious to marry Miss Brown, a chorus girl. This is Miss Brown."

"How do you do?" said Lord Emsworth. He might be vague but he had the manners of the old school.

Ronnie interposed. The time had come to play the ace of trumps.

"She isn't an ordinary chorus girl."

247

"From the fact of her coming to Blandings Castle under a false name," said Lady Constance, "I imagine not. It shows unusual enterprise."

"What I mean," continued Ronnie, "is, I know what a bally snob you are, Aunt Constance—no offence, but you know what I mean—keen on birth and family and all that sort of rot. Well, what I'm driving at is that Sue's father was in the Guards."

"A private? Or a corporal?"

"Captain. A fellow named—"

"Cotterleigh," said Sue in a small voice.

"Cotterleigh," said Ronnie.

"Cotterleigh!"

It was the Hon. Galahad who had spoken. He was staring at Sue open mouthed.

"Cotterleigh? Not Jack Cotterleigh?"

"I don't know whether it was Jack Cotterleigh," said Ronnie. "The point I'm making is that it was Cotterleigh and that he was in the Irish Guards."

The Hon. Galahad was still staring at Sue.

"My dear," he cried, and there was an odd sharpness in his voice, "was your mother Dolly Henderson, who used to be a serio at the old Oxford and the Tivoli?"

Not for the first time Ronald Fish was conscious of a feeling that his Uncle Galahad ought to be in some kind of a home. He would drag in Dolly Henderson! He would stress the Dolly Henderson note at just this point in the proceedings! He would spoil the whole thing by calling attention to the Dolly Henderson aspect of the matter, just when it was vital to stick to the Cotterleigh, the whole Cotterleigh, and nothing but the Cotterleigh. Ronnie sighed wearily. Padded cells, he felt, had been invented specially for the Uncle Galahads of this world, and the Uncle Galahads, he considered, ought never to be permitted to roam about outside them.

"Yes," said Sue, "she was."

The Hon. Galahad was advancing on her with outstretched hands. He looked like some father in melodrama welcoming the prodigal daughter.

"Well, I'm dashed!" he said. He repeated three times that he was in this condition. He seized Sue's limp paws and squeezed them fondly. "I've been trying to think all this while who it was that you reminded me of, my dear girl. Do you know that in the years '96, '97, and '98 I was madly in love with your mother myself? Do you know that if my infernal family hadn't shipped me off to South Africa I would certainly have married her? Fact, I assure you. But they got behind me and shoved me onto the boat, and when I came back I found that young Cotterleigh had cut me out. Well!"

It was a scene that some people would have considered touching. Lady Constance Keeble was not one of them.

"Never mind about that now, Galahad," she said. "The point is—"

"The point is," retorted the Hon. Galahad warmly, "that that young Fish there wants to marry Dolly Henderson's daughter, and I'm for it. And I hope, Clarence, that you'll have some sense for once in your life and back them up like a sportsman."

"Eh?" said the ninth earl. His thoughts had once more been wandering. Even assuming that Baxter had fed the Empress, would he have given her the right sort of food and enough of it?

"You see for yourself what a splendid girl she is."

"Who?"

"This girl."

"Charming," agreed Lord Emsworth courteously, and returned to his meditations.

"Clarence!" cried Lady Constance, jerking him out of them.

"Eh?"

"You are not to consent to this marriage!"

"Who says so?"

"I say so. And think what Julia will say."

She could not have advanced a more impressive argument. In this chronicle the Lady Julia Fish, relict of the late Major General Sir Miles Fish, C.B.O., of the Brigade of Guards, has made no appearance. We, therefore, know nothing of her compelling eye, her dominant chin, her determined mouth, and her voice, which at certain times—as, for example, when rebuking a brother

249

—could raise blisters on a sensitive skin. Lord Emsworth was aware of all these things. He had had experience of them from boyhood. His idea of happiness was to be where Lady Julia Fish was not. And the thought of her coming down to Blandings Castle and tackling him in his library about this business froze him to the marrow. It had been his amiable intention until this moment to do whatever the majority of those present wanted him to do. But now he hesitated.

"You think Julia wouldn't like it?"

"Of course Julia would not like it."

"Julia's an ass," said the Hon. Galahad.

Lord Emsworth considered this statement and was inclined to agree with it. But it did not alter the main point.

"You think she would make herself unpleasant about it?"

"I do."

"In that case—" Lord Emsworth paused. Then a strange, soft light came into his eyes. "Well, see you all later," he said. "I'm going down to look at my pig."

His departure was so abrupt that it took Lady Constance momentarily by surprise, and he was out of the room and well down the corridor before she could recover herself sufficiently to act. Then she too hurried out. They could hear her voice diminishing down the stairs. It was calling, "Clarence!"

The Hon. Galahad turned to Sue. His manner was brisk yet soothing.

"A shame to inflict these fine old English family rows on a visitor," he said, patting her shoulder as one who, if things had broken right and there had not been a regular service of boats to South Africa in the 'nineties, might have been her father. "What you need, my dear, is a little rest and quiet. Come along, Ronald, we'll leave you. The place to continue this discussion is somewhere outside this room. Cheer up, my dear. Everything may come out all right yet."

Sue shook her head.

"It's no good," she said hopelessly.

"Don't you be too sure," said the Hon. Galahad.

"I'll jolly well tell you one thing," said Ronnie. "I'm going to marry you whatever happens. And that's that. Good heavens! I can work, can't I?"

"What at?" asked the Hon. Galahad.

"What at? Why—er—why, at anything."

"The market value of any member of this family," said the Hon. Galahad, who harboured no illusions about his nearest and dearest, "is about threepence-ha'penny per annum. No! What we've got to do is get round old Clarence somehow, and that means talk and argument, which had better take place elsewhere. Come along, my boy. You never know your luck. I've seen stickier things than this come out right in my time."

19

SUE STOOD on the balcony, looking out into the night. Velvet darkness shrouded the world, and from the heart of it came the murmur of rustling trees and the clean, sweet smell of earth and flowers. A little breeze had sprung up, stirring the ivy at her side. Somewhere in it a bird was chirping drowsily, and in the distance sounded the tinkle of running water.

She sighed. It was a night made for happiness. And she was quite sure now that happiness was not for her.

A footstep sounded behind her, and she turned eagerly.

"Ronnie!"

It was the voice of the Hon. Galahad Threepwood that answered.

"Only me, I'm afraid, my dear. May I come onto your balcony? God bless my soul, as Clarence would say, what a wonderful night!"

"Yes!" said Sue doubtfully.

"You don't think so?"

"Oh yes."

"I bet you don't. I know I didn't that night when my old father put his foot down and told me I was leaving for South Africa on the next boat. Just such a night as this it was, I remember." He rested his arms on the parapet. "I never saw your mother after she was married," he said.

"No?"

"No. She left the stage and—oh, well, I was rather busy at the time—lot of heavy drinking to do, and so forth, and somehow we never met. The next thing I heard—two or three years ago—was that she was dead. You're very like her, my dear. Can't think why I didn't spot the resemblance right away."

He became silent. Sue did not speak. She slid her hand under his arm. It was all that there seemed to do. A corncrake began to call monotonously in the darkness.

"That means rain," said the Hon. Galahad. "Or not. I forget which. Did you ever hear your mother sing that song—No, you wouldn't. Before your time. About young Ronald," he said abruptly.

"What about him?"

"Fond of him?"

"Yes."

"I mean really fond?"

"Yes."

"How fond?"

She leaned out over the parapet. At the foot of the wall beneath her Percy Pilbeam, who had been peering out of a bush, popped his head back again. For a detective, possibly remembering with his subconscious mind stories heard in childhood of Bruce and the spider, had refused to admit defeat and returned by devious ways to the scene of his disaster. Five hundred pounds is a lot of money, and Percy Pilbeam was not going to be deterred from attempting to earn it by the fact that at his last essay he had only just succeeded in escaping with his life. The influence of his potations had worn off to some extent, and he was his calm, keen self again. It was his intention to lurk in these bushes till the small hours, if need be, and then to attack the waterspout again, and so to the Garden Room where the manuscript of the Hon. Galahad's Reminiscences lay. You cannot be a good detective if you are easily discouraged.

"I can't put it into words," said Sue.

"Try."

"No. Everything you say straight out about the way you feel about anybody always sounds silly. Besides, to you Ronnie isn't the sort of man you could understand anyone raving about. You look on him just as something quite ordinary."

"If that," said the Hon. Galahad critically.

"Yes, if that. Whereas to me he's something—rather special. In fact, if you really want to know how I feel about Ronnie, he's the whole world to me. There! I told you it would sound silly.

253

It's like something out of a song, isn't it? I've worked in the chorus of that sort of song a hundred times. Two steps left, two steps right, kick, smile, both hands on heart—because he's all the wo-orld to me-ee! You can laugh if you like."

There was a momentary pause.

"I'm not laughing," said the Hon. Galahad. "My dear, I only wanted to find out if you really cared for that young Fish."

"I wish you wouldn't call him 'that young Fish.'"

"I'm sorry, my dear. It seems to describe him so neatly. Well, I just wanted to be quite sure you really were fond of him be-cause—"

"Well?"

"Well, because I've just fixed it all up."

She clutched at the parapet.

"What!"

"Oh, yes," said the Hon. Galahad. "It's all settled. I don't say that you can actually count on an aunt-in-law's embrace from my sister Constance—in fact, if I were you, I wouldn't risk it—she might bite you—but apart from that, everything's all right. The wedding bells will ring out. Your young man's in the garden some-where. You had better go and find him and tell him the news. He'll be interested."

"But—but—"

Sue was clutching his arm. A wild impulse was upon her to shout and sob. She had no doubts now as to the beauty of the night.

"But—how? Why? What has happened?"

"Well—you'll admit I might have married your mother?"

"Yes."

"Which makes me a sort of honorary father to you."

"Yes."

"In which capacity, my dear, your interests are mine. More than mine, in fact. So what I did was to make your happiness the Price of the Papers. Ever see that play? No, before your time. It ran at the Adelphi before you were born. There was a scene where—"

"What do you mean?"

The Hon. Galahad hesitated a moment.

"Well, the fact of the matter is, my dear, knowing how strongly my sister Constance has always felt on the subject of those Reminiscences of mine, I went to her and put it to her squarely. 'Clarence,' I said to her, 'is not the sort of man to make any objection to anyone marrying anybody so long as he isn't expected to attend the wedding. You're the real obstacle,' I said. 'You and Julia. And if you come round, you can talk Julia over in five minutes. You know how she relies on your judgment. And then I said that, if she gave up acting like a barbed-wire entanglement in the path of true love I would undertake not to publish the Reminiscences."

Sue clung to his arm. She could find no words.

Percy Pilbeam, who, for the night was very still, had heard all, could have found many. Nothing but the delicate nature of his present situation kept him from uttering them, and that only just. To Percy Pilbeam it was as if he had seen five hundred pounds flutter from his grasp like a vanishing blue bird. He raged dumbly. In all London and the Home Counties there were few men who liked five hundred pounds better than P. Frobisher Pilbeam.

"Oh!" said Sue. Nothing more. Her feelings were too deep. She hugged his arm. "Oh!" she said, and again, "Oh!"

She found herself crying and was not ashamed.

"Now, come!" said the Hon. Galahad protestingly. "Nothing so very extraordinary in that, was there? Nothing so exceedingly remarkable in one pal helping another?"

"I don't know what to say."

"Then don't say it," said the Hon. Galahad, much relieved. "Why, bless you, I don't care whether the damned things are published or not. At least—no, certainly I don't. . . . Only cause a lot of unpleasantness. Besides, I'll leave the dashed book to the nation and have it published in a hundred years and become the Pepys of the future, what? Best thing that could have happened. Homage of Posterity and all that."

"Oh!" said Sue.

The Hon. Galahad chuckled.

"It is a shame, though, that the world will have to wait a hundred years before it hears the story of young Gregory Parsloe and the prawns. Did you get to that when you were reading the thing this evening?"

"I'm afraid I didn't read very much," said Sue. "I was thinking of Ronnie rather a lot."

"Oh? Well, I can tell you. You needn't wait a hundred years. It was at Ascot, the year Martingale won the Gold Cup. . . . "

Down below, Percy Pilbeam rose from his bush. He did not care now if he were seen. He was still a guest at this hole of a castle, and if a guest cannot pop in and out of bushes if he likes, where does British hospitality come in? It was his intention to shake the dust of Blandings off his feet, to pass the night at the Emsworth Arms, and on the morrow to return to London, where he was appreciated.

"Well, my dear, it was like this. Young Parsloe . . ."

Percy Pilbeam did not linger. The story of the prawns meant nothing to him. He turned away, and the summer night swallowed him. Somewhere in the darkness an owl hooted. It seemed to Pilbeam that there was derision in the sound. He frowned. His teeth came together with a little click.

If he could have found it he would have had a word with that owl.

THE END